THE JUNKET MAN

Christopher Matthew's first job after Oxford was teaching in a girl's finishing school in Switzerland. Following a short stint as an advertising copywriter, he took up full-time writing in 1970.

His previously published books include three immensely popular accounts of the life and times of his accident-prone hero, Simon Crisp: DIARY OF A SOMEBODY, LOOSELY ENGAGED and THE CRISP REPORT (all available in Arrow), and HOW TO SURVIVE MIDDLE AGE. With Benny Green, he has recently annotated Jerome K. Jerome's comic classic THREE MEN IN A BOAT.

Christopher Matthew is a frequent broadcaster on Radio 4 and writes a weekly column on property in *Punch*.

He is married with three children and lives in London and Suffolk.

Also in Arrow by Christopher Matthew

Diary of a Somebody
Loosely Engaged
The Crisp Report

The Junket Man

CHRISTOPHER MATTHEW

ARROW BOOKS

© Arrow Books Limited
17-21 Conway Street, London W1P 6JD

An imprint of the Hutchinson Publishing Group

London Melbourne Sydney Auckland
Johannesburg and agencies throughout
the world

First published 1983

© Christopher Matthew 1983

Set in Baskerville by Photobooks (Bristol) Ltd.

Made and printed in Great Britain
by The Anchor Press Ltd
Tiptree, Essex

ISBN 0 09 932050 9

TO WILLIAM, WITH LOVE

1

'A glass of champagne, sir?'

The voice was surprisingly small for one so large. From her shoulders hung a full-length, ermine-trimmed robe of the sort that peeresses wear on Coronation Day. A tiny coronet with six shiny gold balls was perched precariously on stiffly-lacquered blonde curls, like a cherry on top of a meringue. Her face was completely round, her eyes were very large and her little white teeth sparkled inside a smiling, rosy mouth. She looked as though she had just won the House of Lords beauty contest.

'What?' said Roger. Large women had always excited him.

'Champagne. Would you like one?'

She pointed towards a tray of glasses on the table beside her. As she did so her robe fell open revealing that she was wearing nothing underneath except a two-piece bathing costume. A feeling of overwhelming euphoria passed through Roger as though he had just had a couple of stiff drinks on top of an empty stomach.

'Ah,' he said and gave her a lop-sided, faintly lascivious grin. He stretched an arm carelessly in the direction of the tray. At that moment she leaned forward to help, with the result that Roger's hand clamped itself firmly round her right breast.

The girl smiled at him conspiratorially.

'Pip pip,' she said.

'I beg your pardon?' said Roger, transferring his hand to one of the glasses.

'I said, "Pip pip." It's the company motto,' she explained.

'Gracious.'

'Yes. We were told to say it whenever we say goodbye to someone. That way we keep the company fresh in people's minds.'

'In that case, you'd surely do better to say "B.B." than "Pip pip".'

'What?'

'B.B.' said Roger. 'Initials for Blue Blood. That is the name of the company, isn't it? Blue Blood Tours?'

The girl giggled.

'I hadn't thought of that,' she said.

'Besides,' said Roger, 'do we really want to say goodbye to each other when we have only just said hallo?'

She giggled. 'Well, that rather depends, doesn't it?'

'Does it?' said Roger, who was by now only too aware of the silly smirk that had somehow become permanently attached to his face like a totally independent piece of matter over which he had no control.

'Well,' she riposted, 'doesn't it?'

A less fanciful man would have noted from the tone of her voice that she was beginning to flag from the suspense.

'What is your name?' Roger heard himself asking her.

Quite what he was hoping to achieve by this daring ploy was not altogether clear to him at this stage, and the discovery that her name was Jackie did little towards crystallizing his intentions.

However, the arrival of the travel editor of the *Daily Mail* relieved him of the need to ponder the matter further, and he turned his attention instead to the drama that was being played out in the rest of the room.

In the five years since he had forsaken the gritty world of detergents for the cleaner, more respectable life of freelance travel journalism, Roger had attended many bizarre functions in a variety of strange and often unlikely locations. He had been to couscous parties in the basements of North African restaurants in South Kensington, and rum parties on barges in the Pool of London. He had sipped hot spiced wine in full skiing kit and pouring rain at ten o'clock at night on an artificial ski slope in north London, and pulled a muscle attempting to win a Balkan dance contest in the ballroom of a spanking new hotel near King's Cross. He had flown to a featureless town with an unpronounceable name fifty miles inside the Arctic Circle in order to play golf at midnight in midsummer, and had juddered across a choppy Channel on a day trip to Boulogne to eat *belons*, dance in the streets to an accordion and spend a week in a Boulogne hospital recovering from food poisoning. Once he had attended a party in a circus tent in a field in Hertfordshire at which everyone had worn circus costume and been called upon to perform some daring stunt, and George Maxwell had been badly mauled by a llama. There were, it seemed to him sometimes, no ends to which the public relations departments of air lines, national tourist offices, package holiday operators, motoring organisations, national railways, and manufacturers of anything from ski wear to sun-tan oil were not prepared to go in their efforts to bring their products to the attention of the press. However, for sheer incongruity and downright silliness, Roger was not at all sure that the party thrown at the Windsor Castle public house to celebrate the launch of Blue Blood Tours Limited did not go a long way towards taking the biscuit.

If it hadn't been for Jean Hollingsworth he wouldn't have known of the existence of Blue Blood Tours until it was too late.

She had rung shortly after six. Maitland, with whom he shared a two-bedroomed flat in a mansion block in Maida Vale, was home early from the office and making preparations for the imminent arrival of his latest conquest, a pneumatic part-time waitress called Gloria. In other words he was slumped on the sofa in front of the television set with a large vodka and tonic in one hand and the *Radio Times* in the other. 'It's for you,' he had called out to Roger, who was in his bedroom when the phone rang. 'Jean somebody.'

'What ho,' Roger called cheerily down the phone.

'Oh Roger!' She had a habit when greeting a friend on the telephone of lowering her voice in a dramatic way as though she were about to announce the outbreak of war in Serbia but suspected a crossed line.

'What news on the Rialto?' enquired Roger.

'Not much. What are you up to *ce soir*?'

'Not a lot. Why?'

'I've just discovered this invitation on my desk from a company called Blue Blood Tours, to an Aristocratic Evening at the Windsor Castle, Ganser Road, S.E.27, if you can believe it. I wondered if you were going. It sounds rather your sort of thing.'

'My invitation must have gone astray,' he said. 'Who are these people anyway?'

'I haven't had a chance to read through all the blurb yet but basically I gather they arrange for social climbers with more money than sense to be entertained for varying lengths of time in country houses and stately homes by members of the aristocracy with more sense than money. But why not come along and find out for yourself? There might be rather a good story in it. They say six to eight-thirty, but I doubt if I'll make it much before seven.'

'Right then,' said Roger loudly, looking hard at Maitland. 'Windsor Castle. Seven-fifteen for seven-thirty.'

'Right then,' he repeated, replacing the receiver.

Maitland said nothing. Roger went into his room where he changed into a pair of dark blue trousers, an open-necked shirt and a sort of bush jacket which he had recently acquired in a summer sale. He brushed his hair, slipped a couple of pound notes into his pocket, just in case, and returned to the sitting room.

'Right then,'' he said. 'I'm off.'

'To Windsor Castle?'' said Maitland.

'Yes.'

'Dressed like that?'

'Oh, they're very informal up at the castle these days, you know,' said Roger, and walked out of the room closing the door firmly behind him.

As a venue for darts matches, youth club hops, Buffalo's Balls and the showing of blue movies, the upstairs rooms of the Windsor Castle public house could hardly have been bettered anywhere in South London. As a setting for the press launch of a company anxious to present itself as the arbiter and purveyor of elegant English upper class life, it fell short by several hundred miles. In an effort to impose a little style on the high, square, featureless room, gilt-framed portraits of someone's ancestors had been hung on two of the walls. At the far end of the room, above a pair of theatrical, throne-like chairs, a coat of arms of doubtful authenticity had been painted on to a piece of board which was attached to the wall by a length of string. From the centre of the ceiling an elaborate chandelier dangled threateningly above the guests like the sword of Damocles. Any atmosphere of elegance and quiet dignity that the organisers of the event might have hoped to achieve with these haphazard touches of decor was, however, lost in the stale cigarette smoke, the stench of alcohol and the familiar din of Fleet Street journalists getting stuck into free drink.

Roger recognised many of the faces from many a similar event. Vic Bartlett was there, of course, with his alopecia, talking in his usual intense way to Barbara Black.

God, he looks awful, thought Roger. No doubt Barbara Black thought otherwise, despite the fact that, even as he talked to her, her eyes were constantly on the move searching for yet stronger meat – a travel editor perhaps or someone with a bit of a name to whom she could attach herself for a spot of profitable ear bending. Rumour had it that in eight years of freelance travel writing Barbara had never once left a party of this sort without at least one firm commission safely under her girdle, sometimes more. Acknowledged by everyone in the industry to be the worst writer in the business, she never stopped working and her by-line was forever cropping up in the unlikeliest places. No one had been spared her split infinitives and her main clauses without main verbs. Yet she was reputed to earn as much as £20,000 in a good year and her villa in the Algarve had recently been featured in *Homes and Gardens*. It was also reported on the very best authority that she had had a thing with someone on every press trip she had ever been on. Even supposing she had slept with the same man on more than one occasion, that still meant she must have been known biblically to practically every man employed in the travel industry – except, oddly enough, Roger. He often wondered about that.

Standing next to Barbara was the man with the funny eye, who presented travel programmes on television. He was looking around him, eager for attention, only half-listening to the little man from British Rail whose wife was supposed to be having a thing with George Maxwell – though how George Maxwell was capable of having anything with anyone, the amount he drank, let alone with the wife of the little man from British Rail, was a mystery that few had so far fathomed.

Roger looked about anxiously for Jean. He thought he could spot her on the far side of the room, with her back to him, talking to the oldest, drunkest Fleet Street hand of them all, Reg Henshawe, who was leering in a happy, out-of-focus at the girls dressed in bikinis, black lace stockings, wing collars, bow ties and morning coats, who were trotting round the room on shiny black high heels carrying trays of drinks and little dried-up things on soggy toast. Roger had begun to move in their direction when he was brought up short by a heavy hand on the shoulder. He turned to find himself facing a tall man with black crinkly hair, matching moustache and skin the colour of Cadbury's Dairy Milk.

'Hi,' said the man, 'Ngogo.'

Roger stared at him blankly for several seconds, and then deep in the sludge of his memory something stirred, shook itself free and sprang quite effortlessly to the forefront of his mind and thence to his tongue.

'Djambo,' he replied politely.

'No,' said the man. 'Ngogo. Nigel Ngogo. Marketing Manager for Blue Blood Tours Limited. We haven't met.'

'I'm Noakes,' said Roger. 'Roger Noakes.'

'Ah yes. Are you a journalist or . . .?'

There was no real reason why the Marketing Manager for Blue Blood Tours should have heard of Roger. He was not a very well-known person outside the world of travel writing, or inside it, for that matter. Not yet. Even so, he didn't care to have it rubbed in.

'Forgive me,' said Ngogo. 'The thing is, I'm rather new to all this and . . ."

'I *am* a journalist,' said Roger, 'though actually I prefer to think of myself more as a travel writer who just happens to publish his stuff in the newspapers.'

'I always thought that was what the word journalist meant,' said Ngogo.

'There is a difference,' said Roger.

'Aha,' said Ngogo, solemnly nodding his head. 'Tell me, what exactly *is* a travel writer?'

Roger stared at him.

'Someone who travels,' he said, 'and then writes about it, of course.'

'Ah yes. And who exactly do you . . .?'

'I'm a freelance,' Roger interrupted him impatiently. 'You do know what a freelance is? Yes. I've written for all of them at one time or another. You name it, I've written for it.'

'The *Sunday Times*?'

'Well, I haven't actually had anything published by them yet. I was going to do something for them earlier this year, and I'm sure it's still on; but funnily enough you've chosen the one major newspaper I haven't actually . . .'

'*Telegraph*?'

'And I was just going to say the *Telegraph*.'

'Good, good,' Ngogo exclaimed, as though he had

13

suddenly discovered the solution to some problem that had been puzzling him. 'Well, anyway, it's super to see you. So glad you could spare the time to come along. I feel sure our managing director, Mr Casablancas, would like to have a word with you before you dash away. I'm not quite sure. . . He was here a moment ago.' He peered anxiously round the room.

'Really, it doesn't matter,' said Roger. 'Another time perhaps.'

'Well, all right then,' said Ngogo, his anxiety lifting like a cloud off the upper slopes of Ben Nevis. 'Look, why don't we get one of those pretty little girls over there to bring you another drink and I'll try and catch up with you later.'

He gesticulated in the direction of one of the girls in butler's outfits who was carrying a tray upon which were several glasses filled with orange-coloured liquid.

'Do you like Buck's Fizzer?' Ngogo said, seizing a glass from the tray and thrusting it into his hand.

'Fizz,' said Roger.

'We've decided to adopt it as the company's drink. I hope you like it.'

'Fizz,' repeated Roger. 'It's called Buck's Fizz. I know it very well. As a matter of fact I once met the chap after whom it was named.'

'Really? So did I,' said Ngogo. 'Limbo dancer from Trinidad. Runs his own bar now in Montego Bay, you know. Nice fellow. Don't rush away now. Pip pip.' And he plunged into the crowd like a Labrador after a winged partridge.

Roger sipped at his drink. The orange juice was tinned, and if he was not very much mistaken, the champagne was not champagne at all; it was too sweet. Probably some sparkling white wine. He went back to the table by the door.

'Excuse me,' he said to Jackie, 'but do you have any

14

literature about the company? Brochures, hand-outs, bumph, anything?'

'We did have some,' she said brightly, 'but they've all gone now. They were very nice. Like scrolls of parchment. All hand-done. Most unusual. Very nice.'

'But they've all gone,' said Roger.

''fraid so.'

'Pity,' said Roger.

'Yes,' said Jackie. 'They were ever so nice, too.'

Henshawe was standing alone, propped against the wall, about to lift yet another glass in the direction of his face. The girl whose back had borne such a striking resemblance to Jean's had decided she had better things to do than stand around being propositioned by a heavily-veined assistant sports editor – even if he had once been in line for great things at *Reynolds News*.

Henshawe raised the glass very slowly, peering into the liquid, his eyes bulging with suspicion, as though expecting that at any moment something extraordinary would come leaping out at him. A blue marlin perhaps. Then, opening his mouth very wide, he gave a sudden upward movement with his arm and threw the entire contents of the glass straight past his face and on to the wall behind him where they mingled tastefully with the greasy finger marks and beer stains from countless club socials and football club get-togethers.

Henshawe closed his mouth with a snap, like a turtle catching a piece of squid. He worked his jaws about for a while, smacked his lips in a puzzled sort of way, glared accusingly into the empty glass and finally shrugged his shoulders and lurched off in the direction of a passing butler.

Seven-fifteen and still there was no sign of Jean.

A brown hand, as big as an armchair, settled on his

15

shoulder. Standing beside Ngogo was quite one of the smallest, thinnest men Roger had ever seen. Had it not been for his exuberant hair-style that sprang skyward like a great hunk of wire wool above which someone was holding a powerful magnet, he would almost certainly have passed entirely unnoticed throughout the whole evening. He puffed quickly and without evident pleasure at a very long cigarette which he held limply between the middle two fingers of his left hand.

'Mr Casablancas,' said Roger genially, suddenly feeling slightly bulkier than Raymond Burr. 'Thank you for letting me come. Jean Hollingsworth said it would be all right. I was just looking for her as a matter of fact . . .'

He extended a giant paw, at which the dwarfish creature pushed out a delicate right hand, discovered he was holding a glass in it, transferred the glass to his left hand, found he was holding his cigarette in a way that prevented him getting a good hold on the glass, went very red in the face, placed the glass between his knees and, with his body now in a crouching position as though avoiding sniper fire, pointed a limp hand in the general direction of Roger's groin. Roger took it gingerly like a man accepting an under-the-counter gift of pork sausages during the dark days of the war, and gave it a slight squeeze at which it disintegrated into a damp, shapeless piece of Funny Putty. As he did so its owner uttered a series of squeaking sounds that might have been a stab at words or possibly an expression of pain.

'May I,' said Ngogo, 'introduce Prince Claus of Schloss-Gluckstein who has very kindly consented to join the company in a freelance advisory capacity.'

'Advising on what?'

'Oh, you know,' said Ngogo, 'etiquette, dress, behaviour, how to address people – that sort of thing.'

'How to make a deep, lasting impression on people when you first meet them?'

'That sort of thing,' said Ngogo.

The little chap stood there between the two of them,

looking up at each in turn like a nervous mountain goat trying to decide which of two crags to leap on to next. Then he gave off a small, high-pitched braying sound and relapsed into a twitching silence.

Roger said, 'Er. . . the thing is, I came rather late and I'm not entirely sure yet what Blue Blood Tours do.'

'But surely I sent you all our literature along with your invitation?' said Ngogo.

'I came uninvited,' said Roger. 'With Jean Hollingsworth. Or rather, without her. But she did say it would be all right.'

'We have copies by the door.' Ngogo showed a mouthful of very large, very white teeth.

'They've all gone. I gather they were very nice.'

Ngogo reeled back and clapped his hand theatrically against his perspiring forehead.

'I knew this would happen,' he cried, and disappeared once again into the crowd.

Roger looked down to find that Prince Claus was still standing next to him.

'Awfully good party,' squeaked the prince.

'Awfully.'

'Are you in on this junket too?'

'Junket?' said Roger. 'What junket would that be then?'

'The Inaugural Weekend, of course,' said the prince. 'Hatching Park.'

'Hatching Park?'

'The Fox-Bronzings' place. At Toughingham. In Norfolk. Blue Blood Tours are having a trial run there, I understand. Under exam conditions, so to speak.'

He pronounced the place as though it were spelt T-o-m-b-.

'Is that the place one always thinks ought to be pronounced Tuffingham?' said Roger.

'If one does not know any better,' said the prince.

Roger did not care greatly for foreigners who were over-familiar with arcane examples of English eccentricity, particularly when they spoke with exaggerated English accents.

'It's possible,' said Roger carelessly. 'Why? Are you?'

'I would' the prince sighed. 'Fiona Fox-B. did ask me, and she is rather a sweety. But I promised Daphne Steeple-Morden I'd spend a few days with them at Whitney Priory. She's such a dear. Eighty-five and still cubbing.'

'I'm glad,' said Roger. 'I suppose you wouldn't have any idea who *is* going?'

The prince shrugged and waved an airy hand.

'I was told but none of the names meant anything to me. They're all journalists, I believe. From what I can gather it's not so much a house party as a publicity stunt. To think of the Fox-Bronzings of all people going commercial. The Rothschilds yes, but not the Fox-Bronzings. I can't stick the Rothschilds at any price – can you?'

Roger said that he had never cared for them a great deal.

'In 1893,' continued the prince, 'they married into my family, and they are the only black mark on our pedigree in over five hundred years.'

'I wonder you can even bear to mention their name,' said Roger.

'Indeed. . .'

Roger felt like saying that if he was representative of his family, then the unfortunate bankers had far more cause for regret than the obscure Germanic brood to whom they had been unwise enough to ally themselves in those heady, blameless days before the turn of the century, but at that moment Ngogo re-appeared with an urgent enquiry about the correct procedure when meeting a bishop for the first time.

As Roger stared after the puny figure as it was swallowed up in the throng, he realised that for the first time in five years – perhaps for the first time in his life – he knew exactly what he wanted to do next.

2

To say that Hernando Casablancas, Managing Director of Blue Blood Tours Limited, was a conceited man would be like saying that Robert Sangster was quite well off. But, even Roger had to admit, he had something to be conceited about. True, the well-proportioned figure beneath the dark grey pin-striped, double-breasted suit was held in that uncomfortably over-stiff posture that implied the aid of whalebone and elastic, and the hair was just that little bit too dark to be true. Nevertheless, there were few men under the age of thirty in the upstairs room of the Windsor Castle public house that evening who, if pressed, would not have admitted that if by the age of fifty-five they still looked anything like Hernando Casablancas, they'd count themselves very lucky men indeed.

The accent was as smooth and dark as the skin on his face and its origins equally hard to place. Greece perhaps? Lebanon? Mexico possibly? Or Malta? In any event, certainly not those of a fellow who is invited into the drawing rooms of English country houses unless for a specified purpose. A less suitable and at the same time a better qualified type to be introducing the foreigners and the under-privileged to the mysteries of English upper class life it would be hard to imagine.

Aware of the deep mistrust in which he was held by most of the men in the room and of his attractiveness to most of the women, Hernando Casablancas was enjoying himself hugely as he stood on the dais beneath the spurious coat of arms, and as he warmed to his subject, he seemed to glow in the light of his own self-confidence.

'We believe,' he was telling the hushed assembly,

19

moving his head through a one hundred and eighty degree arc so that not one member of his audience should miss the benefit of his complete range of profiles, 'that we are performing not only an important social and recreational function in enabling those with the means to do so to experience for a while a way of life that normally is reserved for a privileged minority, but at the same time an essential historical and sociological one in prolonging a way of life which otherwise might soon disappear once and for all. We are not, let me hasten to confess, the first to have spotted the potential in keeping English country house life alive in this way. Several others have tried it: lunch with the Duke and Duchess of So and So; a night in Such and Such a stately home; tea and a tour round the gardens with the Marquis of Somebody or Other. Yet none of them has really caught on in a big way, and for one very simple reason. The owners of the houses in question have tolerated their visitors' being there only because of the amount of money involved. I'm not saying they did not like their faces or their conversation, but those were minor considerations. As far as Blue Blood Tours are concerned quite the opposite is the case. I was talking with someone earlier this evening and at one point he was saying that there was bound to be a certain element of make-believe in the proceedings, but that was neither here nor there. Ladies and gentlemen, it is very much here and, to an even greater extent, there. The whole point of our operation is that nothing that we offer our clients is make-believe: neither the Country House Weekends, nor the Goodwood and Cowes Weeks, nor the Fishing and Shooting Fortnights in Scotland. Firstly, all guests will receive a personally written invitation from their hostess exactly as they would if they were going to stay with friends. Secondly, the whole time they are there they will be treated in precisely the same way as they would if they were personal friends: neighbours may very well drop in for drinks with them, members of the family could easily arrive to stay while they are there. Family life will go on in the house in just the same way as it would if they were not there. And thirdly, and most importantly, instead of being sent a bill, they will be asked to make a generous contribution towards the Blue Blood Historic Homes Appeal Fund which we have set up. In this way we shall not only avoid any unnecessary feeling on the part of the client that he is a paying guest, but we shall be making a genuine contribution towards the upkeep and preservation of these wonderful and historic houses which are so much part of our great heritage.'

Casablancas paused and bowed his head. One or two people began to clap. He lifted his head abruptly and at the same time raised his hand to quell any untimely demonstrations of approval.

'As you may or may not have heard, we are planning an Inaugural Weekend, not this weekend but next, to which we have invited what we believe to be an excellent cross-section of press representatives, to take a look at our little venture through fresh and unbiased eyes. The venue chosen for this vital launch is one of the most outstanding houses in the country, and the family who owns it is one of the oldest and most distinguished in Europe. I am only sorry I was not able to include every one of you in this invitation but, as you can imagine, this would have been impossible. Apart from anything else, one of the aims of our weekends is that they should be small, intimate affairs rather than giant bear fights. Those of you who will be joining us will experience exactly what our clients will experience: no more and certainly no less. To you, may I say that your comments and criticisms will be as welcome as your hymns of praise. In the meantime, all that matters is that you should come along with us, eat, relax and thoroughly enjoy yourselves in whatever way pleases you best. To the rest of you, I say: let us hope you may join us on another occasion. Thank you all for coming. Pip pip.'

As the applause died away, a man on the far side of the room said quite clearly: 'Silly sod.'

*

Later, Roger was on the point of leaving when he was confronted by a small girl with long, dark hair framing a tiny face which was largely obscured by a pair of enormous, round, heavily rimmed spectacles, through the smoked lenses of which two big, bright eyes shone enthusiastically.

'Hi,' she said.

'Hallo,' said Roger, delightedly. He was never normally approached at parties by people he did not know and rarely by women.

'I've wanted to meet you for years,' she said.

'Really?'

'I read you every day.'

'Every day?'

'Well, not every day exactly, but pretty well.'

'Are you sure . . .?'

'I'm a journalist myself.'

'Well done.'

She fiddled about in the Balkan peasant bag that hung from her shoulder and produced a packet of very small cigarettes.

'Smoke?'

Roger shook his head.

'The thing I've been wanting to ask you for years,' she said, lighting up, 'is how you manage to get all those amazing stories? I mean, do people ring you up and tell you things, or do you really know all those people, or what?'

Roger straightened his shoulders and pulled in his stomach slightly.

'Well,' he said, 'it all depends really.'

'Angie?'

The man who had suddenly appeared at the girl's side and wrapped an arm round her tiny waist was the sort of person who, if he were to break into your house one night, assault your wife, strangle your cat, rip up the carpet, set fire to the curtains, tie you to a chair and sit with a knife at your throat staring you in the face till dawn, and afterwards the police were to ask you to give them a description of what he looked like, you would be hard pressed to remember a thing about him. He was of medium height, and wore a grey suit, brown leather lace-up shoes, and a blue tie with a light pattern in it. He had medium coloured hair, cut to a medium length, and a longish sort of face with medium brown eyes. Set in the context of such overwhelming anonymity, the fierce red spot just to the right of his chin shone out like Beachy Head lighthouse on a grey morning in November. Deep in the sludge of Roger's memory something stirred, thought better of it and settled back into the mire.

'Oh hallo, darling,' the girl said, 'have you met Johnny Knode?'

'Who?' said the medium man.

'Johnny Knode, the gossip columnist.'

'No, why?'

'Well, you have now.'

'Have I? Where?'

'Here, right in front of you.'

'That? That's not Johnny Knode. That's an exceedingly unpleasant man I was at school with called Roger Noakes.'

'No, it isn't, darling,' the girl persisted. 'It's Johnny Knode. We've just been talking about gossip.'

'Just because you talk to a man at a party about the Waura tribe of the Upper Xingu it doesn't automatically follow that the man in question is David Attenborough. I'm telling you, this man is not Johnny Knode. He is an occasional freelance journalist called Roger Noakes. I was in the same house as him at school.'

In his house at school? Who could he possibly be? Ralston? No. Elton-Bouverie? Surely not.

'Dick,' Roger said out loud. 'Cyril Dick.'

'You remembered then?'

'No, but I've remembered now. Spotty Dick. Well, well; fancy seeing you here.'

'Actually,' said Dick, 'it was Clever. Clever Dick.'

'Not to eighty per cent of Middle Hall it wasn't,' said

Roger. 'Spotty by name, spotty by nature. And by the look of things, not a lot has changed over the years.'

'My God, Noakes,' said Dick. flushing furiously, 'you always were a foul swine, you and your clever friends in Middle Hall. God, how I hated you. I hated you then and I hate you now.'

'You wouldn't by any chance be referring to the pyjamas incident in Lower-Middle Dorm, would you? That was over twenty years ago. We're all grown men now.'

'If you remember, *I* was the one who was gated and had to miss the Australian Test,' said Dick.

'Do you know,' the girl told Roger, 'I suspected you were a low type the moment I set eyes on you.'

'And I'd say,' countered Roger, 'that you know nothing about it.'

'Rude, too.'

'How dare you speak to my fiancée like that,' said Dick.

'Oh really, this is the silliest conversation I've ever had in my life,' said Roger. 'Why *are* you here as a matter of interest?'

Dick sulked a little longer and finally admitted to being a feature writer on the *Norwich Mercury*. Roger said he was rather far from home, to which Dick replied that he had been invited to go on the Inaugural Weekend, and, come to that, what was Noakes's particular interest in Blue Blood Tours?

Roger looked at him for a moment; then he said. 'You always were a devious little worm, Dick. You were also a very bad fag.'

The party ground on. There seemed no reason why it should ever end. When the champagne ran out, which it did at about half past eight, people went on to gin and whisky. Those who had already been drinking gin and whisky merely continued to do so.

Shortly before nine, there was a brief moment of

excitement when a little man from British Rail struck George Maxwell sharply across the head with an empty champagne bottle. However, George Maxwell by that stage was too drunk to notice, so nothing came of it.

Roger seriously considered asking Jackie out to dinner, but nothing came of that either.

He also tried to find out from Ngogo who had been asked on the Inaugural Weekend and was cheered to learn that one or two people had dropped out and that as a result there was still some doubt about the composition of the final party.

At ten past eight, Barbara Black left with a firm commission from the *News of the World* for a piece on night-life in Copenhagen and the man with the funny eye who did travel programmes on television.

Five minutes later, Roger, who had finally given up all hope of Jean coming at all, went across to the drinks table to deposit his empty glass. The white cloth was covered with evil-looking stains, all the bottles and glasses were either empty or half-empty and someone had stubbed out a cigar in a bowl of olives. Behind the table one of the girls wearing a butler's outfit and a surly expression was packing dirty glasses into an empty cardboard box, apparently quite deaf to the repeated entreaties of Reg Henshawe on the other side of the table that it would be no skin off her nose if she could see her way to just one more teensy-weensy gin and tonic.

'Nine p.m. we was hired till,' she told him finally, 'and it's nearly that now. If I let you have another drink, I'll have to let everyone else have another one, and at that rate I'll never get away. I've got to draw the line somewhere.'

But Reg Henshawe had not spent thirty-two years in Fleet Street to be told by some flibbertygibbet of a girl that he could not have another gin and tonic at a party to which he had been invited in all good faith, even if she did have big knockers, and frankly, unless she was prepared to come across with a glass of the requisite funny water and that eftsoons, he would be obliged to refer the matter to his host

25

for the evening who, he felt certain, would not be all happy at the prospect of reading about the meanness of his company in the columns of a newspaper with a circulation of over six million . . .

'Piss off,' said the girl.

Henshawe's eyes wavered uncertainly in Roger's direction and then back again to the girl's left breast.

'Oh hallo, young Noakes,' he roared. 'I say, here's a go. This young lady here won't let me have another drink. Bit much, don't you think? I mean, I thought this was supposed to be a party, didn't you? Well, as my poor old father always used to say, you can't launch a battleship in a bathtub, and by the same token you can't hope to launch a company with the name of Blue Blood Tours on a couple of measly gin and tonics. Don't you agree, old man?'

His eyes swivelled round, as though floating in warm oil, and settled unsteadily on an area slightly to the left of Roger's chin.

'Have you by any chance been invited on this weekend junket, Reg?' Roger asked him.

'I should just say I have, my dear old chap. Drinkies on the terrace with the neighbours, dinner in the Great Dining Room, mah-jong and dancing to a gramophone afterwards, church on Sunday morning. Lovely. Just up my street.'

'In that case,' said Roger solemnly, 'I imagine you will be afforded ample opportunity to relieve your host of all the drink you can get down you from Friday week onwards, so why not call it a day now and give it all you've got the weekend after next?'

'By God, you know, you're absolutely right, old boy. Hit the greasy sod for all he's worth the weekend after next!'

Then as suddenly as he had sprung into life, he assumed an air of deepest gloom.

'Only one drawback as I see it,' he said.

'What's that, Reg?'

'Fat chance of a bit of grumble.'

'What makes you say that, Reg?'

'Plenty of the old funny water, give you that. Cellars full to the ceiling with it, likely as not. Give you that. But all that stuff about rolling around in the attics with seventeen-year-old housemaids in tight black dresses with their whatsits falling out all over the place – all that stuff went out with Ramsay MacDonald's pipe. Take my word for it, old boy. I've made a special study of this sort of thing.'

'I don't doubt it, Reg.'

'Fact is, all the ones that are any good these days are off in Knightsbridge and Chelsea working as so called bloody models. The only menials you'll come across these days are bloody university graduates and doctors of philosophy with bloody fantastic brains and thick legs – when really it should be the other way round. Unless of course they've laid on something special. Wouldn't put it past them. Dirty bugger, that Casablancas. Like all wogs. Did you see that secretary of his – Jackie?'

'I did speak to her briefly, Reg.'

'Secretary, my Aunt Fanny! Mark my word, he's a dirty sod, that Casablancas. Crying shame really. To think of that beautiful superstructure going to waste like that.'

'Reg . . .' said Roger. 'What do you think the chances are of my getting in on this junket?'

Henshawe squinted at him and lifted both hands in an expansive gesture of welcome.

'Chap with your qualifications?' he said with a knowing grin.

'But that's the trouble. I don't have any qualifications,' said Roger.

'What's that got to do with it?' said Reg.

3

'Albert, you swine!'

The voice came from the sitting room. Roger leapt to his feet, catching his knee against the edge of the scrubbed-wood kitchen table.

'What is it? What is it?' he yelled, skidding dangerously on one of the many pieces of newspaper that had been spread across the hall floor, and coming to rest finally against the door-frame. "Where are you?'

'Here.'

From behind the sofa emerged a well-rounded bottom in bottle green velvet, followed by a broad back in a cream silk shirt, a mass of long dark wavy hair and finally a pair of outstretched arms culminating in two hands that were clutching a medium-sized tortoise.

'You little beast,' said Jean, giving him a shake.

The clear-cut Home Counties accents, which in their time had had many a Fleet Street editor trembling at the knees, rang round the room, rebounded off the rubber plant, ricocheted off the lithograph of a charging elephant, on to the Edwardian reading lamp and finally homed in on Roger's inner ear.

'Why? What has it done?'

'He. Albert's a he. He's gone and done big potties on the carpet behind the sofa, that's what he's done. Why there? That's what I don't understand. He's got all the rest of the room at his disposal.'

'Perhaps you should send him away to be house trained?'

'What do you think all this paper's for?'

'Perhaps he doesn't care for newsprint,' suggested

Roger. 'Why not try lavatory paper? More suggestive. Like the doctor running a cold tap when he wants a sample.'

'I don't see how you could ever hope to housetrain an animal who comes from a long line of Sumatran jungle folk,' said Jean, holding Albert up and peering at the hole where his head had gone in. 'You can't even give them a good smack.'

'You could bang his shell with a hammer,' said Roger. 'Give him a nasty headache.'

'On the other hand it might drive him completely mad.' She gave the shell a shake.

'Naughty Albert. You'll have to be off carrot tomorrow.'

'I can't think why you bother to keep a tortoise anyway.'

'Company,' she said. 'It's jolly comforting having someone to say "Hallo, I'm home" to of an evening, especially if it's like this one was.'

'What did happen exactly?'

'I had every intention of coming to the Blue Blood thing, but then the Galloping Major rang to say that he was in town for the evening unexpectedly and did I fancy doing a show and gnawing on a chop somewhere afterwards. Well, you know how utterly incapable I am of saying no to anything, and before I knew it I was in the stalls of the Savoy Theatre watching "Murder at the Vicarage" – and I simply can't bear detective plays. And then afterwards we went to the Ivy, and he made a scene about the wine. And the editor was sitting at the next table. I didn't know it was possible to be so embarrassed.'

'I thought you were so keen on him that weekend of the Regimental Ball.'

Jean groaned. 'I was. He was absolutely wonderful, especially the following morning, striding across the Yorkshire moors with a sixteen-bore under his arm and brisk nor'easter ruffling his golden hair. He was like Peter Fleming and Chinese Gordon rolled into one. A bit taller, of course.'

'Taller than whom? Peter Fleming or Chinese Gordon?'

'Both. People always picture Gordon as a giant of a man, which he was of course in many respects, but in fact he was only five-foot-five.'

'I never knew that,' said Roger.

'Peter Fleming was short, too.'

'Really?'

'But heroic.'

'Quite.'

'It's an unfortunate fact of life that certain people in this world are non-transferable. I suppose I should have learnt my lesson from that ski instructor in Wengen who pursued me to London. Whizzing about the slopes he was wonderful, but sitting in the stalls at Covent Garden with his little brown face sticking out of the top of that ill-fitting brown suit, he looked like Albert on a bad day. Same with the major.'

'Did he wear a brown suit?'

'No, dark grey with a thin pin stripe. Expensive, of course. But from seeming like a colossus bestriding, if not the world, then at least the Yorkshire moors, he had been reduced to the proportions of a stockbroking pigmy. It's always the same: water ski instructors, Spanish fishermen, army officers – they should at all costs avoid moving out of their natural surroundings.'

'Talking about natural surroundings, you're definitely going on this Inaugural Weekend then?'

Jean placed Albert on the Weekend Review section of the *Sunday Times*, returned to the kitchen table and picked up her mug of coffee.

'So my secretary told me just before I left the office. I really hadn't bothered to go through all the stuff they'd sent me, otherwise I'd have said something to you on the telephone. Anyway, there was this personal letter from Lady Fox-Bronzing saying how much she was looking forward to seeing me and so on, and describing some of the things that have been laid on. It sounds rather jolly.'

'Yes, I know. Reg Henshawe was telling me. Drinks on the terrace, dinner, dancing and mah-jong. It sounds the sort of life I've always believed I am best suited for, but have never quite been able to achieve.'

'Darling, which of us has?' said Jean. 'I'm surprised they didn't ask you. It's just your sort of story.'

'I know,' said Roger. 'I spoke to the PR man but apparently my name meant nothing to him at all. I know I'm not exactly James Cameron, but my by-line is surely not completely unknown in the trade.'

'In some circles, you are just as well known as James Cameron, if not more so,' said Jean, who came from a theatrical family and suffered from a tendency to exaggerate.

'The thing is, I know that one or two of the people they originally asked have dropped out, and I was seriously thinking of giving them a ring tomorrow and proposing myself as a suitable substitute.'

'Oh, do,' said Jean. 'It would be divine if you came.'

'The thing is,' said Roger, 'I was just wondering if perhaps it might help if you were to give them a call too. Tell them who I am and so on. There's nothing like a personal recommendation, as it were, to get people interested.'

'Absolutely,' said Jean.

'The thing is, I'm pretty sure I could write it up for someone.'

'Oh easily.'

'I mean, I wouldn't have to specify who at this stage, would I? Just as long as Blue Blood felt sure they were going to get value for their money.'

'Quite.'

'So what time will you call them then?'

'When I've got a moment.'

'Morning or afternoon?'

'I said. . .'

'Sorry. Good, well that's that then.' He yawned and

looked at his watch. 'Good heavens, is that the time? I must be off to the land of Nod.'

'Nod will have to wait a little longer,' Jean said briskly. 'We haven't even begun to sort out my problems with the Galloping Major yet.'

4

In the days when he worked for the soap company, it had been Roger's habit to appear in the office on Friday mornings wearing a three-piece suit and a soft brown hat as if he were planning to leave after work for some smart weekend house party in the country.

In fact, apart from an occasional visit to his aunt in Surrey, he rarely left London at weekends, and after work on Friday evening, he would almost always return to his flat where he would take off the suit and hang it up carefully in the wardrobe in a polythene bag where it would remain until the following Friday morning.

Nevertheless it gave him great satisfaction to think that he was, if only symbolically, helping to keep alive the English tradition of the country house weekend.

He was not at all certain that such things still existed, but if they did, he felt confident that he would make a perfect house guest. Although not possessing all the required qualifications (he doubted for example if he could ever bring himself to kill anything) he was a confident and, on occasions, an extremely witty conversationalist, a keen walker, a talented carver of roast beef and an enthusiastic, if clumsy, competitor at croquet. He was a graceful ballroom dancer, an adroit flatterer of older women, and he knew how to mix a dry martini.

The Inaugural Weekend of Blue Blood Tours at Hatching Park might not be quite up to Cliveden in its heyday, but if there was a journalist in London better qualified than he to report on the event, he had yet to meet him.

When Ngogo rang him later that morning, he would tell him so.

'Blue Blood Tours eh?' said Maitland at breakfast, lighting a small cigar and scratching at his chest-hairs between the open folds of his bath robe.

He puffed at his cheroot, filling the room with the aroma of burnt nail clippings. His hair, the mere sight of which was enough to set Roger's teeth on edge, received further ministrations from his smooth white fingers. His voice had assumed a drawl that was quite out of keeping with his background and education, but which he had a tendency to assume at moments like this one.

Roger said nothing.

Maitland leant back with his arms behind his head. 'I have this vision,' he said, 'of a coachload of peers of the realm being shunted round the country in a charabanc with occasional stops to visit typical working-class homes. "Our next stop will be 43 Khartoum Road where Mr and Mrs Smith will take us on a personally conducted tour of their front room, and afterwards entertain us to tea and marmite sandwiches in their charming late 1930s kitchen-dinette." '

'I expected you'd make fun of this enterprise,' Roger said. 'Not only is it a way of maintaining beautiful houses that might otherwise fall into disrepair and have to be demolished, but it also, and I'm surprised at a City man like you for not grasping this straight away, it also earns money for the country at a time when every dollar and every yen and every penny count.'

'Bollocks,' said Maitland. 'It's a cheap, shoddy and, from everything you have told me about it so far, badly-run little outfit whose only aim is to squeeze as much money out of well-meaning, bumbling, woolly-brained aristocrats and under-privileged idiots with ideas above their station as it possibly can before everyone concerned recognises it for the second-rate con it really is. What on earth makes you think it is going to make a penny for this country? Did they tell you last night where they pay their taxes? Or where the company is registered? Or what their present assets are? The whole thing is obviously thoroughly suspect, and, if you ask me, you'd be wise to stay as far away from it as you possibly can. Naturally, being a romantic and a snob, you will not take my advice. Well, that's your decision. All I can tell you is that I wouldn't go near any of them with a barge-pole. And as for making money for the country, as you so naïvely put it, I prefer to stick to invisible exports.'

'Ah yes,' said Roger. 'Invisible exports. Tell me, Maitland, I've always meant to ask you. What exactly *are* invisible exports?'

Maitland drew on his cigar which he held cupped between the thumb and forefinger of his right hand.

'With someone like you, I wouldn't know where to begin,' he said.

'Just as I said: narrow-minded and bigoted,' said Roger. 'And incidentally, while we are on the subject of money, I don't mind Gloria making long-distance calls on our phone. I don't even mind if she forgets to reverse the charges. But I do think she might ask first. The telephone is, after all, very much a lifeline as far as a journalist is concerned, and I do happen to be expecting a pretty important call that could be worth a lot of money.'

'Would you consider that to be more or less important than the fact that Gloria's mother is at this very moment recovering from open-heart surgery?'

'Open-heart . . .? Well naturally I had no idea . . . I mean, had I known . . . of course . . . how awful . . .'

At that moment the door opened and Gloria issued into the room brandishing the telephone on the end of its long cord, like the huntress Diana after a good day's sport among the rabbits.

'Any good?' said Maitland.

'No reply,' she said.

'Out?'

'Round at the betting shop, I expect.'

'Your mother?' said Roger.

'Yes, why?'

Roger stared at Maitland.

'But I thought you said. . .'

'Just keeping you on your toes, old lad,' said Maitland, standing up and putting on his coat. 'Like a boy scout, a journalist should always be prepared. And adaptable. Besides, I'm sure five minutes one way or another will not make all that much difference to your story. It's not as though they're sitting down there in Fleet Street crouched over the hot metal waiting for the phone to ring so that they can start making up the front page, is it? I mean, we're not exactly in Hildy Johnson country, are we?'

And on that note, the two of them strode out of the room and out of the flat like the Ugly Sisters, leaving him with the washing up.

5

Lunchtime came and went that day and still Roger had heard nothing from Blue Blood Tours. He had rung Jean's office at eleven but nobody knew where she was nor at what hour she was expected. So then he rang her home number, but there was no reply. At two-thirty, Roger decided to call Ngogo himself. He tried on numerous occasions in the next hour. Finally, at a quarter to four, he set out to call upon Blue Blood Tours in person.

The address on Ngogo's visiting card was a terrace of Regency houses off Knightsbridge. Behind some pretty black railings was a tiny garden consisting of a patch of crazy paving, an unkempt rose bush and a hole with some steps leading down to a basement flat. In the middle of the white panelled front door was a heavy brass knocker.

Roger pressed the bell beside the door, which was soon opened by a familiar figure whose substitution of a crisp white blouse and black skirt for ermine-trimmed robe and coronet merely had the effect of making her seem even more alluring and even more stupid.

'What ho,' said Roger. 'Is Nigel in by any chance?'

'Mr Ngogo's no longer with the company,' said Jackie, looking rather embarrassed.

'Oh?'

'No. He left us. At lunchtime today actually.'

'Gracious,' said Roger. 'How unexpected.'

'I suppose so,' said Jackie. 'If you weren't expecting it.'

'Indeed,' said Roger. 'What happened exactly?'

'I think Mr Casablancas felt he was not projecting the right image for the company, but it's not really for me to say.'

'Aha! Who's taken over in his place then?'

'Mr Hahned. He's very nice. He went to Oxford.'

'Perhaps I could have a word with him?'

'He doesn't start till Monday.'

'Is there anyone I can speak to apart from yourself who is remotely connected with the company?'

'Mr Casablancas is in.'

'A word with him perhaps?'

'He's in conference at present.'

'Ah.'

'With our Transport Director, Mr Legge. But he won't be long.'

'Perhaps I could wait?'

'If you'd like to come in, I'll tell him you're here.'

She spoke very slowly and precisely, as though programmed. It had the effect of making everything she said of enormous importance and deep interest. Roger, in turn, found himself responding with all the politeness and deliberation of a Linguaphone record.

'Thank you very much,' he mouthed, giving an odd little bow. 'If you would.'

'If I would what?'

'Tell him I'm here. It is quite important.'

'If you would care to follow me.'

'Thank you,' said Roger gravely, and waded behind her through the deep brown carpet that ran the length of the thin, narrow hall. There were Redouté flower prints in thin gold imitation antique frames on the walls.

'I tried to ring you earlier,' said Roger conversationally. 'Several times. But the number was always engaged.'

'I expect that was Mr Casablancas,' she said, 'talking with his accountant. He's been talking with him quite a lot in the last few days. Something to do with money, I expect,'

'Very possibly,' said Roger.

The room into which she led him was arranged in the form of a sitting room. In the middle was a smoked-glass table on short chrome legs on which were two red plastic ash-trays, a white plastic object in the shape of an elongated pyramid, and some copies of *Vogue*, *Penthouse* and the *New Statesman*. Ranged round the table were two mauve armless armchairs and a cane-bottomed rocking chair. Beneath it, a skimpy white woolly rug covered a small portion of the varnished wooden floor, like a meagre scrap of sheep-skin round the shoulders of a Mongolian shepherd.

Above a stripped-pine fireplace hung a large, gilt-framed mirror, and the ceiling had sprouted the usual heavy crop of chrome lamps from which beams of light criss-crossed haphazardly, like searchlights above London during a heavy bombing raid, until they found their targets in potted palms, shapeless lumps of stone statuary and expensively-framed daubs of colour hanging from the hessian-covered walls.

Accepting Jackie's offer of a cup of coffee, Roger sat down on one of the mauve chairs, was immediately blinded by the reflected light from the glass of the picture opposite, moved to the rocking chair and picked up a *Penthouse*.

After a while, Jackie emerged from the small kitchen at the back of the room with a mug of coffee and a bowl of sugar. Roger quickly put down the *Penthouse* and picked up the *New Statesman*.

Jackie sat down at a smoked-glass table in front of an electric typewriter and settled to some solid work on her fingernails.

Roger asked her if she would be going on the Inaugural Weekend.

She said that she hoped so, at which a feeling of enormous excitement swept over Roger.

Those lovely breasts; that little flat stomach glimpsed tantalisingly beneath the ermine and red; that eager smile above; that sense of youthful eagerness, concealed for the time being, and understandably so, beneath the cool veneer of professional good manners; that downright dumbness. . . .

'I'm glad that Reg Henshawe's going,' she said.

'What?'

'He doesn't half make me laugh.'

'Reg? Makes you laugh?'

'I think a sense of humour's very sexy, don't you?'

'Hardly sexy.'

'I think so.'

'Wit, possibly.'

'I love men with lined faces,' she said thoughtfully. 'The scars of experience.'

'Or alcohol.'

Jackie looked up sharply.

'I think that's a horrible thing to say.'

'I only meant. . .' began Roger.

'I know what you meant all right. Just because he's older than you and doesn't speak with a posh accent and all that, doesn't mean. . .'

'I like Reg very much as a man. . . .'

'Sounds like it. He's one of the nicest men I've ever met. He reminds me of my father who died last year.'

'Please don't misunderstand me,' Roger persisted, in a desperate attempt to make up lost ground.

'He also happens to be,' Jackie continued, 'extremely interesting about his travels round the world. Do you know, he was once on Stavros Niarchos's yacht and he walked into the wrong cabin by mistake, and who do you think was sitting up there in bed?'

'Brigitte Bardot, I expect.'

'How did you guess?'

'I've known Reg for a long time,' said Roger.

Before Jackie had a chance to reply to this conversational body-blow, the door at the side of the room opened and in walked Casablancas, accompanied by a very small, stocky man of about forty, with Germanically short, dark hair, mutton-chop whiskers and a connecting moustache. The overall effect was of an elaborately designed lavatory brush.

Casablancas bared his huge teeth and strode forward with one hand outstretched in an exaggerated gesture of welcome. Roger struggled from the rocking-chair barely in

40

time to encounter Casablancas's olive paw in a not very firm grip.

'My dear fellow.' The voice seemed even darker and browner than it had in the Windsor Castle, the accent even more marked, the 'o' sound even smaller. 'It's Mr . . .?'

'Noakes.'

'Noakes, of course. May I introduce our Transport Director, Mr Legge?'

The Lavatory Brush moved forward in a rolling gait and seized Roger's hand so firmly that the joints at the bottom of his fingers were crushed together, causing him extreme pain.

'Call me Buster,' he said. He had a habit when talking of ducking and weaving with his head, at the same time easing his shoulders about as though he were warming up in a boxing ring.

'Buster is responsible for our fleet of luxury Rolls Royces in which our guests travel down to the country,' said Casablancas.

'Ah,' said Roger.

Casablancas said he would be with him in just a moment and accompanied Buster Legge into the hall where they held a low muttered conversation. Then the front door closed and Casablancas came back into the room.

'Now then Mr. . . er. . .'

'Noakes.'

'Noakes. What can I do for you, my dear fellow?'

'Perhaps if we could discuss this in your office. . .?' Roger looked anxiously in the direction of Jackie who was now on her penultimate fingernail.

'Miss Ericson is privy to everything that goes on in the company,' said Casablancas. 'She is my right hand.'

He waved a hand in the direction of one of the chairs. Roger sat down and Casablancas took the sofa.

'I am really very interested in your operation,' said Roger. 'Really very interested indeed.'

'Good, good,' said Casablancas with a medium show of teeth.

'I understand Mr Ngogo has left since I last spoke with him?'

Casablancas examined his immaculately manicured fingernails for a moment or two, then looked up, his face suddenly hard and serious.

'I really do not feel that I am in a position to comment upon the matter at this moment in time,' he said.

'The reason I mention it—'

'No comment,' shrugged Casablancas. He smiled. 'Now could we move on to another question?'

'Yes, of course,' said Roger, rather confused. 'I understand two members of your original press party have dropped out.'

Casablancas frowned. 'I should prefer, if you do not mind, to concentrate on the more positive aspects of our enterprise rather than to harp on the inevitable, and I should have thought, extremely unimportant little setbacks that occur when anyone sets sail on a voyage of discovery across unchartered seas.'

Roger stared at him.

'Do you never take notes?' Casablancas asked him.

'Occasionally,' said Roger, 'Why?'

'Just so long as you do not miss the salient points.'

'I think you can rely on me to give a pretty good account of the proceedings,' said Roger, relieved that the matter has been resolved so quickly and easily.

'Very well,' said Casablancas. 'In that case, let us proceed. What else would you like to know?'

'Well, let me see now . . . the arrangements, I suppose. When exactly do you leave and from where?'

'We leave from the Centurion Hotel in Duke's Street at three p.m. on Friday next, the sixteenth of June, in our fleet of luxury Rolls-Royces and drive to Hatching Park, Toughingham, in Norfolk, the home of Sir George and Lady Fox-Bronzing. Our estimated time of arrival is seven p.m., in time for cocktails on the terrace followed by dinner and a moderately early bed.'

'How lovely,' said Roger. 'And the following morning I

suppose it's down to breakfast at nine, kedgeree and kidneys under silver covers on the sideboard, and away we go.'

'Well, away *we* go certainly,' said Casablancas smiling. 'Your weekend arrangements are your own affair.'

Roger wondered. Perhaps Reg Henshawe had been right all the time and Casablancas *had* laid on something special.

Roger gave him a knowing grin.

'And to a certain extent our newspapers',' he said slyly.

'I of course have no idea what form of contract you have with the *Daily Mirror*,' said Casablancas, 'However . . .'

'Oh I'm not with the *Mirror*,' said Roger.

'Not with the *Mirror*?'

'No, no. I'm a freelance. Of course, I do have certain connections, for instance with the *Sunday*—'

'There must be some misunderstanding,' said Casablancas. 'I understood that you had been sent by the *Daily Mirror* to do an interview with me.'

He turned with a puzzled expression towards Jackie.

'Jackie dear, didn't you tell me that a man was coming from the *Mirror* to do an interview with me?'

Jackie nodded.

'But this gentleman is from one of the Sunday newspapers.'

'One of the Sunday newspapers,' she said. 'Fancy that!'

'Not from the *Daily Mirror*.'

Jackie looked up rather crossly.

'Well, I could hardly be expected to tell that just by looking at him, now could I? The *Mirror* rang to say they was sending someone round to interview you, then this bloke turns up, so naturally . . .'

'But you know me,' said Roger. 'We spoke at the Windsor Castle reception.'

'Darling, I met thousands of fellows at the Windsor Castle reception,' she said.

43

She smiled at Casablancas.

'Never mind,' she said. 'Perhaps he'd like to interview you too. Would you like to interview him?'

'A profile would be more interesting,' said Roger.

'And more profitable. For you, I mean.'

'And what is the difference between an interview and a profile?' said Casablancas.

'Well,' said Roger, 'an interview would be me sitting here talking to you and asking you questions and so on and then writing down what you said. A profile would be far more in depth than that. I mean, I would have to spend a bit of time with you, follow you around, observe you in action and so on and then write it all down. A profile gives a far more rounded portrait of someone than a straightforward interview.'

'In other words,' said Casablancas, 'you want to come on the Inaugural Weekend.'

'Well, no, not exactly,' Roger said with a little laugh. 'I mean, that would be very nice of course, but by no means necessary.'

'Of course not,' said Casablancas. 'Which newspaper did you say you were from? The *Sunday Times*, was it?'

'Well, actually I'm not exactly *with* any newspaper,' said Roger. 'By that I mean I'm not on the staff of any newspaper, which of course doesn't mean I do not have very strong ties with certain Fleet Street editors. . . .'

'I see,' said Casablancas, not very convincingly. 'Do you by any chance happen to know Ed Branigan of *World* magazine?'

'I know the name, of course,' Roger lied helpfully.

'No-one I've spoken to has ever heard of him,' said Casablancas. 'You're the first person I've come across who has. And yet when I rang *World*'s office in London, to ask if there was anyone they could send to cover our weekend, they immediately suggested him. Said he was the best in the business at that sort of thing.'

'So is he coming?'

'No one knows. No one knows where he is. They think he

44

is either in the Danakil Country of Ethiopia or else in Bucharest.'

'How romantic,' said Jackie.

'He certainly sounds very much the man for the job,' said Roger.

'And you say you've heard of him?' Casablancas asked him again.

'Definitely,' said Roger.

'I see,' said Casablancas. 'Jackie, could you get on to *World* again and find out if they've had any more news about Mr Branigan?'

'Er, about this profile you wanted done . . .' began Roger.

'What?' said Casablancas distractedly. 'Oh, the weekend. If it's an invitation you're after, why didn't you say so in the first place?'

6

The Centurion turned out to be one of those new large red hotels which a few years ago seemed to pop up once a week or so, like giant toadstools, all over London, from King's Cross to the Cromwell Road. Its large ground-floor windows were hung on the inside with red gauze curtains, and its name, tacked to the wall beside the revolving front door in an imitation Ancient Roman typeface, was as irrelevant and charmless as the architecture of the building and the street in which it had been constructed.

Roger and Jean found the party in the Forum Bar, throwing back champagne and laughing rather too loudly. They lurked behind a large potted plant and watched them. Casablancas seemed to be doing most of the talking. Henshawe, already looking the worse for wear, was having his glass filled by Jackie. Cyril Dick was standing slightly apart from the crowd, his fingers straying constantly, as though of their own volition, in the direction of a new spot on the side of his nose, and Barbara Black's eyes strayed constantly in the direction of Dick. Roger could also descry the elegant, firm-jawed, crinkly-eyed, slightly aloof figure of Jeremy Powell-Brett, who was reputed to be the only travel writer whose private income allowed him to go in for travel writing purely for fun, and the stout shape of Audrey Veal, the Wine and Food Editor of *Host and Guest* magazine, dressed in a white linen frock several sizes too small and a large, sloping hat several sizes too large.

A small, olive-skinned man whom Roger took to be Ngogo's successor, Mr Hahned, was standing next to Casablancas, his hands clasped behind his back, looking helpful and occasionally directing a waiter towards an empty glass.

Roger uttered a small groan. He always did at this point of a junket, no matter how exciting the destination or how glamorous the company. Generally speaking he was happy enough once the thing got under way, but he hated the beginning of a trip – particularly at moments like this, when organisers and junketers alike tended to behave in an inordinately jolly manner, and tossed back alcohol when what they really wanted was tea, and felt headaches coming on, and one way and another wished they were at home with their bossy wives and noisy children in Tooting, or indeed anywhere other than *en route* for Barbados or Baden-Baden or any of the other stamping grounds of the complimentary jet set.

Roger looked at Jean and she looked at him. Simultaneously they pulled faces at each other.

'Do you think we can get a cup of tea anywhere here?' she said.

They crept away from the doorway of the Forum Bar and waded through thick green carpeting in the direction of the Colosseum Coffee Shop which was separated from the rest of the lobby by a series of glass partitions supported by fluted Roman columns.

A waitress in a toga brought them two teas in heavy pottery beakers with embossed seals on the sides.

'I'm not entirely sure that I'm going to be able to go through with this after all,' said Jean.

'Would you prefer coffee?'

'I meant the weekend.'

'It's only three days out of our lives and it might turn out to be quite funny.'

'I can't see any reason why it should.'

They drank their tea in gloomy silence.

After a while Jean said:

'What time is it?'

'Ten past three, why?'

'It's just that I'm wondering if they're waiting for us in there.'

'Oh Lord, do you think we ought to . . .?'

47

'I think we should.'

'Oh Lord.'

They had been waiting for them.

'We were beginning to think you had had a better invitation,' said Casablancas, and laughed loudly. But it was clear he wasn't pleased.

'The funny thing is,' said Roger, 'that we were outside in the lobby waiting for you.'

'Yes, well, these little mistakes can happen,' said Casablancas. 'Would you care for a drink? I think there's some left. Jackie . . .?'

Jackie poured them half a glass of champagne each which they sipped at politely.

'Do you know everyone?' he said.

'Well . . .'

But he went through the names anyway. The party broke up into small groups and Roger found himself face to face with Cyril Dick.

'Hullo, Dick,' he said.

'Afternoon, Noakes,' said Dick, his finger wavering towards his nose. 'Well, I must say this is quite a surprise seeing you. I had no idea you were in on the thing. How did you manage to wangle it?'

'I was invited, not that it's any business of yours.'

'You didn't say anything about it at the party.'

'The conversation, if I remember rightly, centred largely on our schooldays. The subject of this weekend was barely touched upon.'

'I was talking to the editor of *East Anglian Life* at a function in Norwich last night and I gather you're quite a regular contributor,' said Dick. 'Who are you writing for on this occasion?'

'The *New Yorker*,' said Roger, and walked quickly away.

At the bar he encountered Reg Henshawe, having his glass filled by the barman.

'Not an unpromising start by any means, old lad,' he said. 'Not at all unpromising. If they have begun as they intend to carry on, I have a feeling a jolly time might very well be had all round.' He wobbled his eyebrows up and down suggestively, lowered his head towards the glass and drank as deeply as if it had been his first. 'Ah, that's better,' he said, smacking his lips enthusiastically. Then he lowered his voice and looked about him conspiratorially. 'Tell you one thing though. Not what you might call a lot of talent amongst this lot is there? I mean, normally speaking, by this stage of the proceedings one has sorted the wheat from the chaff, one knows who is likely to be with whom and what is likely to be what. But there's nothing much here I see myself getting the old leg over. I don't know what your feelings are on the matter, my dear old chap?'

'The secretary's not bad,' said Roger.

'Who?'

'Jackie, the secretary.'

'Oh her,' said Reg without a lot of enthusiasm. ''ere's me tits, me arse is coming. I rather fancied the look of her myself at first. Then a few moments ago she engaged me in light badinage during the course of which she announced that I reminded her of her old dad. Put me right off, that did.'

'Perhaps they've laid something on specially, Reg.'

'Wouldn't put it past them,' said Reg, tapping the side of his nose. 'Dirty sod that Casablancas.'

Roger was introduced to Audrey Veal with whom he had once been on a gastronomic trip to Avignon. As the Food and Wine Editor of *Host and Guest*, her pronouncements on the various wines that had been drunk and dishes that had been laid before them were awaited by everyone, their French hosts included, with keen anticipation. Unfortunately, she had failed to impress on that occasion and had, among other things, deeply wounded the owner of Le Bison d' Or in Toussaint by describing his Château la Bosse 1945 as possessing 'a porty little nose'. Nevertheless, she was still Food and Wine Editor of *Host and Guest*, and as long as she remained in the job, people would presumably continue to invite her hither and thither to sample their wines and taste their food and afterwards reveal her findings in the glossy pages of her pretentious little publication. After all, when it came down to it, what earthly difference did it make whether or not she could tell Bordeaux from Burgundy or beef from lamb, just as long as she mentioned the establishment in question and, where possible, got the telephone number right.

'We met in Provence,' said Roger.

'Did we?'

The voice immediately brought back memories of warm summer nights, scented with lavender and thyme and asphodel, of baby lamb roasting on a spit, of 'dance, and Provençal song, and sunburnt mirth', not to mention the odd 'beaker full of the warm South! Full of the true, the blushful Hippocrene, With beaded bubbles winking at the brim, And purple-stainèd mouth' – which surprised Roger, since such remembered delights were strangely at odds with the high-pitched, nasal accents, the heavily-painted bovine features, and the grotesquely swollen figure that confronted him.

'I'm sure we did,' she said with a gracious smile. 'My problem is that I travel so much these days and meet so many people, that often I cannot remember where I was and who I met the week before last let alone eighteen months ago.'

'It's not really important,' muttered Roger, inwardly cursing the upbringing that had taught him the paramount necessity of good manners at all times and in the face of the greatest impoliteness. Luckily he was spared added insult by the intervention of Casablancas, wanting to know whether either of them would care for anything else, since the cars had arrived and he expected them to be leaving at any moment.

Roger, more out of politeness than of genuine interest, asked his host if he had had any news of Ed Branigan. Casablancas thanked him for asking and said that he was believed now to be somewhere in France but that he was

50

still extremely confident that he would be joining them at some stage during the weekend.

'Whenever you are ready, perhaps if you would like to point out your luggage to the porter, he will take it out to the front door.'

A uniformed hotel employee now appeared in their midst with a request for Mr Hernando Casablancas to come to the telephone. Casablancas frowned, looked hard at Jackie, raised an eyebrow at Hahned and hurried away.

'News of your American star journalist perhaps,' Roger said to Hahned.

'I don't think so somehow,' he replied darkly and began to shepherd everyone in the direction of the front door. Unfortunately, the party did not seem anxious to abandon the cosy familiarity of the bar for the relative insecurity of the Great North Road and the bleak expanses of north Norfolk, nor even of the fleet of luxury Rolls-Royces. All that could and would be faced in due course. In the meantime, there were more important matters to see to, namely, in the words of Reg Henshawe, the sorting of the wheat from the chaff – the preliminary sifting out of who, over the next couple of days, was likely to be with whom and what was likely to be what.

Jean, Roger was interested to notice, was getting on extremely well with Jeremy Powell-Brett. Knowing her predilection for clean young Englishmen with firm jaws, blue eyes, wavy fair hair, and private incomes, this did not surprise him. To judge from the expression on her face, he was doubtless at that very moment holding her enthralled with beautifully worded – and carefully rehearsed – descriptions of his fifteenth-century manor house in Somerset, his 1938 drop-head Delage with the Amherst supercharger and his grand friends. Jean was slightly flushed and giggled a lot; Jeremy wrinkled his eyes and smiled in a cool, detached way. Mentally they were both half way to the altar already.

Cyril Dick was also in the process of being enthralled by

Barbara Black – although perhaps hypnotised might be a better description, like a rabbit out on an evening stroll who suddenly comes face to face with a stoat. Roger might have been astonished that any woman could have such poor taste in men were he not so convinced that Barbara was incapable, utterly incapable, of looking at a man without wanting to get into bed with him. For a moment Roger felt quite sorry for the fellow.

'Only one problem about this sort of junket, old boy,' Reg Henshawe said mournfully to Roger as they stood outside the front door of the hotel watching the luggage being loaded.

'What would that be, Reg?'

'You really can't make very much on your expenses.'

'Really? Why's that, Reg?'

'Stands to reason,' said Reg. 'Always the same, junketing in England. I suppose I could always pretend that it was up to each of us to make his own way to Hatching Park: three hundred miles there and back in my own car at eighteen p a mile – that'd be fifty-four quid, plus *en route* refreshments, telephone calls, assorted research costs – eighty quid the lot at best. The trouble is, the Rolls-Royces are all part of the set-up, and as for spending money while we're in Norfolk, well, I'd be very hard put to it to make up more than half a pony at the most – if that.'

The two motor cars, although undeniably large and unquestionably both Rolls-Royces, proved to be something of a disappointment as far as Roger was concerned. The phrase 'fleet of luxury Rolls-Royces' had somehow summoned up in his mind a vision of a long line of spanking new vehicles, gleaming from many hours' ministration of wax and duster, from the bodywork of which aerials sprouted in all directions like points on the antlers of a handsome stag in Richmond Park; of heavy doors being swung open on soundless hinges by silent chauffeurs in dark suits and caps and sunglasses, and cream carpets that tickled your ankles, and deep, expensively-upholstered seats, and polished-walnut cupboards which opened to reveal heavy tumblers, and whisky in cut-glass decanters.

Thirty years before, twenty even, such might well have been the case. But not even the best car in the world can escape the corruption of common-or-garden moth and rust, not to mention the overturned coffee cup and the carelessly placed shoe, and the two members of the Blue Blood Tours fleet had, like a pair of aged courtesans, suffered more than their fair share of knocks and humiliations.

Supervising the loading of the first car, his shoulders working beneath the dark blue jacket, his bare head constantly on the move as he called out instructions to the hotel porters, was the company's Transport Director, Buster Legge.

The driver of the second car, a man by the name of Eddie Fowler, was dressed in a similar way to Legge except that he was wearing a peaked cap with a badge attached to the front in the shape of a pair of B's placed back to back. He had a long nose that turned sharply upwards at the end and rather protruding eyes that gave him the look of a surprised and superior duck. His manner was that of a department store supervisor who, owing to an unfortunate misunderstanding, has been asked to leave and, in order to make ends meet, has been compelled to take on work that would normally be very much beneath him; so that while Buster Legge bustled hither and thither shouting, bullying, coaxing, cursing as the luggage was loaded, found not to fit, unloaded and loaded again with precisely the same result, Eddie Fowler remained by the boot of his car, his hands behind his back, barely moving and never once raising his voice, as he supervised the arrangement of the bags and cases of his passengers. Buster was clearly far from pleased.

He had even less to be pleased about when, in the midst of the confusion, Casablancas marched out through the front door and shouted to him, 'Where is your cap, Legge? Put it on this instant. This is Blue Blood Tours, not a day trip to Southend.'

Roger had never seen anyone quite so angry and upset as Casablancas was at that moment. His normally tanned features had assumed the complexion of a marble-topped table and he was quivering like a jelly in a British Rail dining car. Whatever had been the import of the telephone call, it had obviously shaken him profoundly.

Buster scowled at his managing director, opened his mouth to say something, thought better of the idea and reached into the front seat of the car for the missing item of apparel.

Casablancas beckoned Hahned to his side with a short, sharp gesture and the two walked back into the lobby of the hotel where they stood deep in conversation.

After a while Casablancas re-emerged from the hotel, clapped his hands together, coughed and said:

'Ladies and gentlemen. Owing to unfortunate and unforeseen circumstances, I shall not be joining you this afternoon. . . .'

He paused dramatically. If he was hoping for an outburst of protest and dismay from the assembled company he was in for a disappointment, for his announcement was greeted with blank indifference. He gave a nervous little laugh.

'Something rather unexpected has occurred which requires my immediate attention, and so I must return to my office. I will follow on later and join you all in time for dinner.'

He gave his hands a final wring, ran one of them across his scalp, adjusted his tie, brought them together again, then extended them in a gesture of apology, like a hotel manager who has been called up to a room to explain the presence of tadpoles in the lavatory pan.

'Mr Hahned will of course still be accompanying you to Hatching, as will Jackie my secretary. I have the utmost confidence in both of them. In the meantime, please do sit back, relax, enjoy the journey just as you would if I were with you. *A bientôt, mes amis*. Pip pip.'

His huge teeth gave a final curtain call, he turned crisply on his Gucci heel and walked quickly back into the hotel.

'What do you think that was all about?' Roger asked Reg.

'Been taken over by the Mafia, I shouldn't wonder,' said Reg.

Everyone laughed at Reg's little joke – more out of relief than appreciation. Then they piled into the cars and set off for Norfolk. They tried very hard for a while to make conversation, but it had been a very tiring afternoon, and by the time they reached Hendon, they were all fast asleep.

7

'Nestling amidst rolling parkland, ready to strike all who descend the hill between East Witteringham and Toughingham St Peter with surprise and delight, is Hatching Park. At Hatching can be seen the architecture of two distinct periods: the age of Wren and the age of Adam. The main body of the house, three storeys high and constructed of red brick with stone dressings, was built in 1702 for Sir Charles Fox-Bronzing whose son, immediately upon inheriting the house from his father in 1758, commissioned Robert Adam to re-arrange and redecorate all the ground floor rooms and to add two wings to the north side of the house to embrace the entrance forecourt. The drawing room, formerly the library, contains many notable examples of eighteenth-century French furniture, nineteenth-century English landscape paintings and a number of valuable medieval curiosities. The dining room, formerly the drawing room, has an original carpet by Moore, and the ceiling, although perhaps not an example of Adam at his best, nevertheless displays much of his early exuberance, and the charming foliage scrolls remind one more of Roman stuccos than of the then fashionable French rococo ornamentation. The gardens, running down to the River Ulph, were created in the mid-nineteenth century, and contain one of the finest topiaries in the south of England.'

Henshawe looked up from the *County Guide Book* which lay open on his knee – or to be more accurate, upon Jackie's knee which was in turn upon his.

'I never realised,' he said, solemnly, 'that they had wild animals there.'

Roger sighed deeply, closed his eyes and let his head bump up and down painfully on the soft upholstery.

Contrary to what the breathless author of the *County Guide Book* had promised, there was at least one car-load that descended the hill between East Wittingham and Toughingham St Peter that day that was not struck with surprise or delight by the sight of Hatching Park nestling amidst rolling parkland. The main reason for this was that by the time they had taken a wrong turning on the outskirts of Swaffham and driven halfway to King's Lynn, been misdirected twice and developed carburettor problems near Fakenham, dusk had begun to descend and with it a clammy sea fog, so that it was not easy to see ten yards in any direction, let alone be struck with surprise and delight by an obscure English country house nestling amidst anything.

'Well, that's drinks on the terrace we can strike off our list for a start,' said Roger whose headache and concern for the working man had over the last hour or so taken a distinct turn for the worse.

'And dinner, too, if we go on at this rate,' said Jackie.

'Won't be long now, any minute now,' Eddie muttered over and over again in a low, monotonous voice like a Tibetan monk at prayer.

'Just so long as we get something to drink,' said Reg.

'Won't be long now, any minute now.'

Audrey Veal leaned forward until her chubby features were very close to the back of the driver's head.

'You are a complete bloody fool,' she said slowly and deliberately as though to someone very old and very deaf, 'A complete and utter bloody fool. Do you understand? A bloody, bloody fool.'

'Any moment now,' said Eddie, 'Won't be long now.'

They had closed the main gate and they had to sit outside hooting for almost a minute before a wrinkled retainer emerged, fumbling with the buttons of his cardigan and squinting into the headlights.

57

'Blast, you're late,' he grumbled in sing-song East Anglian accents that were strangely at odds with the content of his message.

The drive of Hatching Park was very wide, and, so it seemed to Roger with his thumping head, interminable. For what seemed like hours they rolled and jogged past vast wastelands of grass only slightly less extensive than the Canadian prairies, with only the occasional overhanging oak or delicate sapling in a wire cage to remind them that they were in England and not lost in some ghastly rural limbo.

Their eventual arrival in front of the house produced in Eddie a psychological reaction of such severity that he drove straight though a bed of wallflowers, across the bottom of a huge flight of steps and into a heavy stone urn before bringing himself to apply foot to brake. He then reversed slowly and carefully into the urn's twin brother that guarded the other side of the bottom of the steps. Cursing gently he went forward again, mounted the next step up, and reversed again, this time with even more force, into the urn.

Observing this automobilic derring-do from the vantage point of the top step, was a tall, exceedingly frosty-looking butler. Standing there motionless in his black morning coat and striped trousers, his long, pointed nose held high, his eyes unblinking, he looked like an eagle biding its time over a particularly stupid rabbit. And then he stooped. Raising his hand imperiously in the air, he quickly descended the steps, circled the car, and drew up beside Eddie's open window. The engine abruptly stalled.

'If you would care to leave the vehicle where it is for the moment and allow the passengers and luggage to be disembarked, I will arrange to have it moved to the garage in due course,' he said in a voice like double Devon cream being poured over a *crème caramel*.

Eddie, tired and defeated, took the *coup de grâce* without a murmur.

The butler moved swiftly to the rear door and opened it.

Audrey Veal was the first to disembark. She was followed in slow succession by Jackie, Henshawe and Hahned, who had scarcely uttered a word since leaving the Centurion Hotel and appeared to have no intention of doing so now. Roger waited for the butler to open the door and, when the man failed to do so, made an unnecessary fuss performing the task himself.

The group stood huddled together on the steps while the fog swirled round them and Eddie fiddled with the lock of the Rolls's boot. The butler viewed him for a while in a detached sort of way, then raised his eyebrows very slightly and intoned gloomily: 'If you would all care to step this way.'

'Why?' said Reg fatuously. 'What's wrong with the way we step already?'

But not even Jackie laughed this time.

The butler led the way up the steps and into a vaulted entrance hall that was brightly lit by all manner of lamps and lights: wall lamps of elaborate design, table lamps with large blue and gold porcelain bases, standard lamps in the form of lightly draped women, and, the centrepiece of the illuminations, a huge gilt chandelier. Directly in front of them, across the black and white chequered stone floor, was a grand staircase that swept upwards past a number of large oil paintings of eighteenth-century figures in splendid costumes and improbable poses before peeling off left and right and disappearing into the bedroom area. To either side of the hall was a pair of double doors, large enough to accommodate a Greenline bus. Above and around them were hung more portraits of men and women in elaborate wigs and finery, amongst which the study of a dark, haired man with aquiline features dressed in white tie and tails and smoking a cigarette seemed oddly out of place.

To the left of the staircase, there was a baby grand piano with its lid open. Quite apart from the grandiose and exotic pediments above the two double doors, the walls and ceiling of the hall were lavishly decorated with stucco work consisting largely of big-busted, though curiously sexless,

women and round-bummed young boys, disporting themselves in an exuberant and irresponsible fashion in vaguely
sylvan settings. This abundance of decoration being, as
the *County Guide Book* had rightly pointed out, an example
of Adam's less mature work, was not of a particularly high
quality, any more than were the majority of the paintings,
or the light fittings. However, the overall effect was, Roger
had to admit, quite striking in a rather superficial sort of
way. Reg Henshawe was the first to express his sense of
wonder and appreciation.

'Fuck my old boots,' he said quietly.

'How very charming,' said Audrey Veal in loud and
exaggerated tones, as though in an effort to make up in
charm and genuine appreciation for Reg's crude and
obviously unrepresentative reaction.

'It's lovely,' said Jackie in the hushed tones of a tourist
who has just set foot for the first time in St Peter's, Rome.

'Very nice,' said Roger, determined to make it clear
from the start to everyone, host and guests alike, that as one
who had stayed in a few country houses in his time, he
knew what bad form it was even to remark on the manner
in which one's host had furnished or decorated his house,
let alone make a production number out of it.

'Typically Wren, those doors,' said Audrey.

'How very clever of you to have noticed. Actually, they
are a little later. Robert Adam to be precise. But it is true
that much of the house shows distinct signs of Wren's
influence.'

The voice was very nearly that of the late Ronald
Colman, though a little deeper and with a touch more
drawl to it. Its owner was a tall, stooping figure in heavy,
fawn corduroy trousers, an ancient, well-cut tweed jacket,
boldly patterned in reds, browns and blues, and a heavy
silk scarf, the ends of which flowed out over the front of his
open-neck shirt. His head was very thin, his nose long and
pointed, his eyes behind round horn-rimmed spectacles
rather small and his white hair brushed straight back
across the narrow crown of his head. He reminded Roger of

one of those aristocratic wading birds one never bothers to stop to look at in zoos but which one would instinctively miss if they weren't there. This ornithological effect was further heightened by the fact that, as he walked, he held his head slightly at a tilt and his hands rather stiffly at his side. In the fingers of one of them he was holding half of a large, expensive-smelling cigar; the other he extended in welcome as he bore down on Mrs Veal who had assumed one of the silliest expressions Roger thought he had ever seen on a human being. Presumably it was meant to be a smile, but the effect was of someone about to be violently sick.

'How do you do,' said the man with the Ronald Colman voice. 'My name's George Fox-Bronzing. I'm so sorry you had such trouble getting here. Norfolk roads are never easy at the best of times, but when these beastly sea fogs decide to blow up for no reason whatsoever, even I sometimes experience difficulty in finding my way home, and I've lived here nearly seventy years.'

He took Audrey's outstretched paw and held it while he talked, shaking it up and down slightly as he talked as if to emphasise further the depth of his sympathy. If the elegant, silver-haired figure actually had been Ronald Colman, Mrs Veal could not have behaved worse. Her bulky frame had suddenly shrunk to half its normal size, and what there was left of it she had begun to wriggle about awkwardly like a twelve-year-old schoolgirl. Her eyelids fluttered coyly and her face contorted itself with unconcealed delight.

'Oh, Sir George . . .' she finally managed to squeak out.

'Good, good. Well anyway you're all here, that's the main thing. I understand Mr Casablanca has been detained in London on urgent business, but he hopes to be joining us in the morning. Which of you is Mr Hahned? Ah yes, of course. How do you do? Well, anyway, come along and join the others in the Music Salon. What a pity you missed drinks on the terrace. The view down the Long Walk to the river was particularly charming this evening.

Never mind. You'll be able to see all that tomorrow. Everyone else has changed but you've got time for a quick drink while your luggage is being taken up. Come along, come along.'

He held his right hand up in a languid, shepherding movement, and the tired party shuffled forward towards the passage that began behind where the piano stood and disappeared into the inner recesses of the house.

'I thought you'd never ask,' said Henshawe.

'What a charming frock,' Sir George said to Audrey Veal. 'That's it, straight through, first on the left. You'll find everyone in there.'

Roger, bringing up the rear of the party, was about to follow the rest when Sir George suddenly seized him by the arm and drew him to one side.

'I say,' he muttered, 'I suppose you haven't the foggiest idea when I'm likely to get paid for all this, have you? It has cost me quite a lot of money, you know, one way and another, what with all the food and wine and extra staff and so on. This fellow Casablanca—'

'Casablancas,' Roger corrected him.

'—promised me an advance to cover my initial expenditure over two weeks ago, and I still haven't seen a penny of it. And now the man has just telephoned to say he won't be here till tomorrow morning. To tell you the truth, it's a bit of a worry.'

Roger goggled at him.

'Well, as a matter of fact, sir, I'm not really very . . .'

'No, no, I didn't suppose you were,' said Sir George wearily. 'It's just that you looked a sensible sort of chap and I thought to myself . . . Well, it doesn't really matter. I daresay it'll all be sorted out eventually.'

His voice tailed away sadly. He put the remains of his cigar in his mouth, found it had gone out, took it out again, looked at it gloomily, placed it in a large marble ash-tray on a side table and ushered Roger through after the others.

If Reg Henshawe had been impressed by the entrance hall, Roger did not like to think what expressions of admiration had dropped from his parched lips as he walked into the Long Library. Apart from the three tall windows, the whole of the facing wall was taken up with books. The principal feature of the room, which extended for most of the length of the east front, was a magnificent ceiling, decorated in the most exquisite, formal stucco work, in the centre of which was a large medallion of the Three Graces in a pastoral setting. Supporting the ceiling at either end of the room were two pairs of elegant fluted columns behind which were large curved recesses containing more bookshelves and a pair of writing tables. On the near wall there were two long, low bookshelves flanking a fireplace, above which hung a not very well-known Titian. Arranged in a square in front of the fire were three large, comfortable-looking sofas, in and around which were arranged in turn, Jean Hollingsworth, Jeremy Powell-Brett, Barbara Black, Cyril Dick, a big jolly-looking lady in her late forties who was introduced as Sir George's sister, Mrs Venables, and an exceedingly pretty girl of about twenty-five with huge eyes, a round face, a mass of long, fair hair which tumbled down on to her shoulders and a small, soft mouth of the sort you normally encounter only in the paintings of Burne-Jones or the pages of *Vogue*.

The two parties quickly mingled and the butler was beginning to move among them with a tray of drinks by the time Roger entered. As he did so, the girl floated forward, smiling brightly, both hands clasping a half empty glass of champagne to her bosom like a stricken animal.

'My dear,' said Sir George, 'this is Mr. . .er. . .'

'Noakes.'

'. . . Noakes.'

'How do you do?' said Roger softly, unable to take his eyes from her face.

Her mouth opened to reveal perfect teeth, but Roger did not hear what she said. His head was filled with the sound of church bells, cannon fire and martial music. His stomach had suddenly assumed the consistency of milk jelly, his legs had begun to vibrate, and his heart was pumping wildly like Arkwright's Mule on a bad day, as he realised that, for the first time in thirty-four years, he was utterly and hopelessly in love.

'My wife, Fiona,' said Sir George.

If Roger had suddenly woken from a deep sleep to find himself going over Niagara Falls in a barrel, he could hardly have come to with a greater shock. Some appropriately charming phrase was clearly called for and the result after a moment or two of desperate mental research was, 'Really?' It didn't seem quite enough under the circumstances.

'Yes,' said her husband, slowly and clearly, 'really. What is it, Hedges?'

The butler, moving swiftly and silently as though on castors, had suddenly materialised in a discreet cough at Sir George's elbow.

'Excuse me, sir, but the driver of the second car reports that, owing to a technical fault beyond his control, the luggage of the second party will not be available for at least another hour.'

'Technical fault? Not available? Why not? What's happened?'

'It would seem, sir, that the lock securing the boot in which the luggage belonging to the second party is stored is jammed. I have suggested to the driver that he take the car down to Bedwell's Garage in Toughingham St Peter where they will no doubt be able to put the matter right in due course.'

'Quite right, Hedges, quite right. Oh dear, that means that the people who arrived first will be dressed for dinner, while our latest arrivals will have to dine in their day clothes. How very awkward and embarrassing for everyone concerned.'

Lady Fox-Bronzing looked at Roger and smiled.

'Would it embarrass you, Mr Nudds?'

'What?' Roger, still stunned, had not been really following this latest twist in the drama.

'There you are, you see, darling,' she said brightly,

turning to her husband. 'I'm sure nobody will mind in the least if everyone is dressed differently.'

'I agree,' interpolated Reg Henshawe. 'Good grub is good grub whether you're in your soup and fish or your birthday suit.'

Sir George took even less notice of Reg's comments than he had earlier in the hall.

'Perhaps the best thing would be if those who have already changed would possibly be very kind and change back into suits and day clothes while the others merely wash and brush up as best they can under the circumstances. That way no one can possibly feel the slightest bit under- or over-dressed. Hedges, if you would be so good as to show our newest arrivals to various rooms and inform Mrs Eames that dinner will now be at nine?'

'Very good, sir.'

As they were all leaving the room, Lady Fox-Bronzing went across to her husband and took him fondly and reassuringly by the arm. Roger thought that if the man had suddenly taken it into his head to seize one of the heavy pairs of fire tongs from out of the grate and start beating him savagely about the head and neck, he could not have felt more anguish than he did at the sight of that simple show of marital affection.

He wondered vaguely whether Maitland experienced similar feelings every time he saw Gloria's bottom being squeezed by one of the coarser customers in the Kit Kat Coffee Bar, but decided it was unlikely. There are people in this world who, if they have any feelings at all, certainly never allow them to show or in any way disturb the steady, self-centred progress of their lives, and one of them was Maitland.

Suddenly Roger actually found himself envying his flatmate.

8

During the course of his travels, Roger had slept in many different bedrooms, some very small, a few very large and most neither large nor small.

On the whole, the majority of the bedrooms to which he had been shown during his short career as a professional traveller had been comfortable without being luxurious, spacious without being palatial, and pleasantly decorated without being gaudy or ostentatious. There had been one or two occasions, however, when he had found himself in bedrooms in which the ceiling had been so high, the bed so large, the decorations so rich, and the proportions so overwhelming, that he had finally been forced to confess that he really was not up to it. One notable occasion was the night he had spent in the Honeymoon Suite of the Beverly Wilshire Hotel, in Beverly Hills; another was in a suite in the Waldorf Towers in New York; a third was in a beach cottage at a hotel in Montego Bay in Jamaica.

However, all of them, magnificent though they undoubtedly had been, seemed in retrospect like so many spare rooms in semis in Cricklewood compared with the Green State Bedroom of Hatching Park into which Roger was shown by the frosty Hedges.

'I trust everything will be to your satisfaction, sir,' he said in tones that dared Roger to express anything but wild delight with his accommodation. 'If there is anything you require, Edward will be only too delighted to comply.'

'Edward?'

'Edward is your valet, sir.'

'Aha, yes, of course. Silly of me.'

'Not at all, sir. How could you possibly have known?'

'Aha, no, of course not.'

'You will find a bell beside the fireplace there, sir, and another beside the bed, and a third in the bathroom.'

'That should see me through tonight anyway.'

'Sir?'

'Oh, nothing.'

Hedges moved very slowly in the direction of the doorway where he hovered expectantly. Roger was rather nonplussed. He had never been shown to a room by a butler before and was not entirely clear about the correct procedure. Was he expected to tip him? Or engage him in light conversation? Roger began to fumble in his pocket where he knew he had some loose change, then changed his mind, threw the man a half smile, followed it up with a muttered, 'Thanks awfully,' and turned his attention to the room. A discreet thud and a click behind him told him that the man had taken the *congé*, and Roger could begin to breathe again.

He stood for a moment looking about him at the tapestry-covered walls, at the Poussin hanging above the great marble fireplace, at the broad armchairs and couches, footstools and ottomans upholstered in heavy green damask, and at the vast bed over which loomed a massive canopy, also in green damask and topped with a gilt crown. He had a sudden vision of Fiona Fox-Bronzing lying naked across the bed, soft and pale and terribly vulnerable, her limbs heavy and languorous, her honey-coloured hair cascading over her shoulders and childish breasts, her mouth parted slightly and . . .

Suddenly, in a series of swift and almost violent movements he stripped off his jacket, his trousers and his shirt, threw them across the ottoman at the foot of the bed and marched into the bathroom. He was busy washing his armpits when there was a knock on the door. 'Hang on a tick,' he called out, but to no avail; someone was already in the room. Drying himself as best he could, he tiptoed to the bathroom door and peered round it to see a figure bending over the ottoman and doing something with his clothes.

'What are you doing?' he demanded.

The figure straightened and turned.

'Folding your clothes. Why?'

'Aha.'

'I am your valet. My name is Edward.'

The face, sharp and rather foxy, seemed familiar; so too did the voice.

'Have we met before?' Roger asked him.

'I can't tell,' said the valet. 'It's possible. People always look quite different when they're dressed only in under-pants and socks. Did you want anything?'

'Er, no . . . nothing, thank you. I suppose you have no idea what time my luggage will be here? There are one or two things in it that might get creased if they are not unpacked very soon.'

'I wouldn't know anything about that,' said the valet, and headed for the door. For some time after he had gone, Roger stood there with his towel clutched firmly beneath his left arm. He felt sure he had seen him before somewhere. Then he walked across to the door, turned the key firmly in the lock and returned to the business in hand, or, more precisely, in armpit.

He was still in his underpants, dabbing at his forehead with a towel dipped in cold water in a desperate effort to suppress the hammer blows that his headache was inflicting against his skull, when a voice said, 'You're putting on weight.'

Roger straightened, struck his head sharply against the glass shelf above the wash-basin, cursed, seized the top of his skull and turned to find Jean Hollingsworth standing in the doorway. She looked cool and elegant in a flowery shift, her dark hair was piled on top of her head in a way that Roger had never seen before, and she had accentuated the size of her eyes with rather more make-up than usual. Roger instinctively hauled in his stomach.

'Too late for that now,' she said briskly.

'How did you get in?' he said. 'I locked the door.'

'But not *all* the doors,' she said.

'What do you mean?'

'I'll show you.'

Jean opened one of the splendidly carved cupboard doors to reveal that at the back was another door which opened into the bedroom next door.

'This is where I am sleeping,' she said.

'How very ingenious,' said Roger.

'Like everything else in the world, it all boils down to sex.'

'How do you mean?' he said nervously.

'In Edwardian times, it was always understood that married couples arrived at country house parties as respectable twosomes but, once inside, hopped about from room to room and bed to bed like bugs. It must have been like the Hammersmith flyover out on the landing. In less liberated times, however, it was the connecting walls that seethed with traffic.'

'Unfortunately, tonight Mrs Fitz Herbert came squeezing through to the royal quarters to be confronted with good old Prinny and not, as she had hoped, with Beau Brummell.'

'Oh, Roger,' said Jean, 'you guessed.'

'About Powell-Brett?'

She nodded like a small child who has just eaten a whole bag of Smarties and been found out.

'I think it was possibly the way you seized his hand and pressed it to your bosom when you were first introduced that gave me the clue.'

'Oh, I didn't. I didn't press his hand anywhere near my bosom, did I? Oh Lord, are you trying to tell me that I was so smitten that I completely lost control of myself and now can't remember a thing about it? Tell me I didn't. I didn't really, did I, Roger? Oh crikey!'

Jean slumped with a deep sigh into one of the big armchairs beside the fireplace.

'No, no,' said Roger solemnly, 'of course you didn't.

Still, I was rather surprised at the way you clung to the tails of his coat when he announced he was just popping out to get something out of his bag before the journey. Anyone would have thought he was referring to an old girl friend who owed him money.'

'Oh, my God,' muttered Jean. She reached into her bag for a cigarette which she lit with shaking fingers. 'Now I come to think of it, I did stick rather close to him in the hotel. The thing was, I was terrified we might be put into different cars, and I thought, well, if that Barbara Black once decides to get her teeth into him . . .'

'Don't worry, she already has, or rather hasn't. In Alicante, if my sources are correct. Apparently, it was all a bit of a flop – in every sense.'

'My God, Roger. You don't mean . . .?'

'Apparently. Still, speaking as one who has woken at three in the morning to find the very woman clambering into his bed, I believe him. He has nothing to be ashamed of, and you have nothing to fear. She's far too occupied at the moment with netting the wretched, pock-marked Cyril Dick.'

'I wish I had your faith,' said Jean, stubbing out one cigarette and immediately lighting another. 'Oh but seriously, Roger, don't you think Jeremy Powell-Brett is quite the most beautiful thing that has ever walked this earth? I mean, he really *is* Peter Fleming *and* Chinese Gordon *and* Philip Roth *and* Dr Donoghue all rolled into one.'

'Who's Dr Donoghue?'

'He's my doctor.'

'Ah.'

'Well, don't you agree?'

'To women who like that sort of man he is, I suppose, that sort of man.'

'My God, but you're meaner of spirit than I ever gave you credit for.'

'Well, what do you want me to say? That he's the man you've been looking for all your life and that without any shadow of doubt, strike me dead if I don't tell the truth, he will be faithful and good and honest and true to you until death, as well as a kind, understanding, faultless father to the eight beautiful children you are planning to have by him – possibly this evening? Is that what you want to hear?'

'Yes,' said Jean.

'Then that,' said Roger, 'is what he is.'

'I knew I was right,' said Jean.

'What about me now?'

'Why? What about you?'

'I'm not a little smitten myself.'

'Yes, you told me. With Jackie.'

'No no. I mean, yes, I did tell you that. But that was nothing. That was a mere flea-bite. This one is more like a black mamba's – fast, totally effective, and quite incurable.'

'Good heavens. It sounds very painful.'

'It is. She belongs to another, and can never be mine.'

'Oh don't be so defeatist,' said Jean impatiently. 'Who is she anyway?'

'Fiona Fox-Bronzing.'

'I might have known it.'

'But you must admit, she is quite the loveliest thing ever to have walked the earth – or at any rate, north Norfolk.'

'She's very pretty, I agree . . .'

'Beautiful, I should have said.'

'All right then, beautiful. But she's almost young enough to be your daughter. She's certainly young enough to be Sir George's. Still, if she's really the one you've got between your sights, then who am I to gainsay you? Still, look at it this way. Half an hour ago, you weren't even aware of her existence. Just think; for the whole of your life, less thirty minutes, you have managed to jog along without her. By applying a little mental discipline, I see no earthly reason why you should not succeed in making it down the home straight in a similar state of blissful ignorance.'

'I suppose so,' said Roger glumly. 'I might say the same about you and Powell-Brett.'

'You might,' said Jean. 'But, of course, he's not married.'

'No.'

'Good, well that's settled then. Time for nosebags. Love usually puts most people off their food, but it's quite the opposite with me. Of course, it might be just the country air.'

On the dot of nine, the entire party staggered across to the Small Dining Room, where they sat down to smoked salmon mousse, consommé, veal in a wine sauce, oranges in brandy, a cheese soufflé, *petits fours* and coffee. They drank ice cold vodka flavoured with lemon peel with the mousse, amontillado with the soup, a Château Léoville-Barton with the veal, a Château Yquem with the oranges, and port with the coffee.

Sadly, the quality of the cuisine, to which the Food and Wine Editor of *Host and Guest* made frequent and lengthy reference, and the excellence of the wines, which also came in for their share of pretentious comment, were almost entirely lost on Roger who very quickly became exceedingly drunk, and could as easily have been consuming plate after plate of coloured blotting paper for all the effect it had on his taste buds. He remembered leaning across the table towards his host every time a new wine was poured and saying 'Superb, superb,' a word that normally never crossed his lips, but apart from that, his energies were devoted entirely to staring at Lady Fox-Bronzing.

After the coffee, Sir George made a speech.

'Now I know how tired you must all be after your long, and for some of you not altogether easy, journey, so I won't keep you long. However, I should just like to say how very happy we both are to welcome you all to Hatching for what I trust will be the first of many such weekends. This house has been in our family for over four hundred years, and has played host to many great public figures of the past, including Lord North, Wellington, Sir Robert Peel, Disraeli, Asquith and John Logie Baird. In 1735, George II spent the night here as the guest of my ancestor, Sir Samuel Fox-Bronzing, and the Green State Room is very much the same today as it was when he slept in it. In fact it was George II who was responsible for the curious pronunciation of the name of our village. Until then, it had been pronounced, as you would expect it to be pronounced, Tuffingham. However, it seems that the king, who could barely speak English at the best of times, experienced great difficulty with the word, and finally gave up the unequal struggle with the words: 'I call it Tomb. Tomb by name; Tomb by nature.'

He paused briefly to allow for the laughter that invariably greeted this regal anecdote.

'Silly bugger,' muttered Reg Henshawe.

If the comment reached Sir George's ears, he showed no sign of it. Even so, his face assumed a melancholic expression.

'Up till now,' he continued, 'I have been extremely fortunate in that I have been able to keep the whole thing going without having to call upon outside assistance or to resort to any ventures or gimmicks of a purely commercial nature. This is a private house, not a museum or a place of public entertainment. However, it has become more and more clear to me over the last two or three years that unless I could think of some way of boosting funds to meet the crippling costs of maintaining it all, I should be in serious trouble.

'Last summer I decided, with great reluctance, to open the house and gardens to visitors three times a week. So far, the experiment has been reasonably successful. I lost a rather good box of cigars one afternoon, but the silver is still intact.' 'Obviously one of my relations,' Reg whispered to Jackie.

'However,' continued Sir George, 'it soon became clear that even that would not produce enough income by itself to meet the needs. And then your Mr Casablanca wrote to me, outlining his plan. I gave the matter a great deal of thought and finally replied that, provided he could guarantee to provide me with the sort of guests who can mix easily with our friends and neighbours, who appreciate good food and wine, who know how to behave with servants, who do not mind joining in some simple country pursuits, who enjoy good conversation, and who, one way and another, understand and sympathise with our way of life—'

'And who are sufficiently free and easy with the spondooliks,' said Reg.

'—then I should be delighted to participate in his scheme. He then suggested that we should undertake what he described as a "dry run" and invite a group of distinguished writers and journalists with a particular knowledge and interest in this kind of thing to come along for a weekend to see how it goes and hopefully write something about their experiences afterwards in their respective journals, and . . . well . . . here you all are, and very happy we are to see you.

'I hope you will enjoy your stay here and that you will feel as happy and comfortable here as you would in your own homes. I hope to dispense with formality as much as possible. However, as you know, there is to be a special dinner tomorrow night in the Great Dining Room next door here, and we would very much like it if you would all dress for that. Tomorrow we have asked a few people in for drinks before lunch. This will be followed by a picnic lunch by the river with punts available for those who fancy exploring the wilder reaches of the river Ulph. There are one or two house guests still to come: Mr Casablanca, who has been detained in London over some financial matter, but who assures me will be with us by lunchtime tomorrow at the latest; Mr Ed Branigan of *World Magazine*, who I gather is either in Baghdad – or is it Bonn? – but who also hopes to be with us soon; and my brother, Claud, the Bishop of Kananga, who is home on leave from West Africa and tells me he hopes to get down in time to give the sermon at Matins in Toughingham St Peter church on Sunday morning.'

'Now, I daresay you are all looking forward to an early night tonight, so I won't keep you any longer. Perhaps, my dear, if you would like to take the ladies with you into the drawing room, we'll join you very shortly.'

'Such a gentleman,' Audrey murmured to Roger as, to the accompaniment of much chair-scraping and throat-clearing, the party rose from the table.

After the port bottle had been round a couple of times, and Reg Henshawe had told his story about Niarchos's yacht and Brigitte Bardot, which, owing to the fact that Sir George had never heard of either of them, was received with considerably less enthusiasm than Reg had become used to over the years in the hostelries of E.C.4, the elderly aristocrat suggested that they join the ladies.

'I don't know if anyone would like to go in the garden first,' he added, indicating the door.

Encouraged by the sounds of general approval, he unbarred and unlocked the door and, in a wave of alcohol and cigar smoke, his male guests issued forth onto the gravel, and thence on to the smooth, velvety surface of the circular piece of grass in the centre of the drive, where they stood breathing in mouthfuls of fresh air and staring up at the sky. The fog had lifted during dinner, and the heavens were alight with stars.

'Well,' Reg's slurred tones came winging out of the darkness, 'I must say, this is very nice. Very nice indeed. Yes, I must say, I could get very used to this sort of thing. Very used indeed.'

'I'm so glad,' said Sir George politely.

'Yes, I must say,' boomed Powell-Brett, 'that Léoville-Barton was really extremely drinkable.'

'Do I take it that you are something of a wine connoisseur?' Sir George asked him pleasantly.

'Connoisseur is perhaps stretching it a bit far,' Powell-Brett told him, 'but I know a good wine when I taste one.'

'It's very kind of you to say so,' said Sir George. 'As a matter of fact that particular Bordeaux is one that I have been keeping for a special occasion such as this for several years now. It is nice to know that it has been appreciated.'

'Very much so, Sir George, very much so,' said Reg and belched lightly.

Roger screwed up his face in an expression of disgust. What upset him was not so much the crudeness of their behaviour as the thought that Sir George, and thus his wife, might suppose that he, Roger, knew as little about how to behave in polite society as they did. Anyone, for instance, with the slightest experience of staying in country houses knew that it was customary for the male members of the party to relieve themselves in the garden after dinner, as Sir George had suggested, before joining the ladies in the drawing room.

He unzipped his flies and began to urinate unostentatiously on the grass.

As the party walked back up the steps, Sir George took him by the arm. 'By the way,' he murmured. 'We do have plenty of places for that in the house, you know. You only have to ask.'

Over coffee and more drinks in the Small Drawing Room, Sir George pointed out some of the more obvious treasures.

'That ormolu clock on the mantelpiece came from Versailles. The vases are Chinese – eighteenth-century. The desk by the window is Louis Quinze. The gold writing case on it was a gift from Madame de Pompadour to an ancestor of mine. My butler came across it by chance one day while clearing out a cupboard in the attic. The carpet is Aubusson, but not particularly remarkable. Most of the pictures are English. That's a Constable over there. The portrait of my ancestor, Sir Roderick Fox-Bronzing, is almost certainly by Gainsborough, though no one seems entirely sure. The little foot-stool belonged to Marie Antoinette. Unfortunately, it has lost some of its value since one of the dogs got in here one day and lifted its leg on it. The card table and the matching chairs come from

Beauvais and are rather rare. That clock is Empire . . .'

He rambled on. Roger's eyelids drooped. The effect of the drink at dinner had begun to wear off and the general feeling of euphoria was rapidly being replaced by a headache that was even more uncomfortable than the earlier one. Even Fiona Fox-Bronzing had begun to lose some of her initial allure.

However, she made up a certain amount of ground in his book by announcing eventually, 'Darling, if you go on at this rate, there won't be anything left to show our guests in the morning.'

Sir George said he was very sorry and hoped he hadn't been boring them, after which everyone began to stand up and stretch and look at their watches and express astonishment at the lateness of the hour.

Breakfast was set for nine o'clock, Hedges arrived to announce that the luggage had at last arrived and been placed in various rooms and, shortly afterwards, the party retired to their rooms for the night.

Roger arrived in his bedroom to find a coal fire burning in the grate, a bottle of Malvern Water and a box of Petit Beurre biscuits on his bedside table, his pyjamas laid out and the sheets of his bed turned back. The valet had not only hung up his suit and trousers in the wardrobe and placed his shirts and handkerchiefs in a lavender-scented drawer, but he had also laid out the entire contents of his spongebag on the glass shelf in the bathroom, including a small bar of soap on which were clearly stamped the words: Centurion Hotel, London.

Roger lay in bed for a while, trying to devise sentences to explain to the valet that in his profession hotels and similar organisations were forever pressing small gifts upon those whom they believed might do them a good turn. None of them sounded terribly convincing.

Soon afterwards he fell asleep and dreamed that he was standing on the lawn at Windsor Castle, completely nude, urinating on a bed of geraniums, at the same time attempting to explain to the Duke of Edinburgh that he was deeply in love with Princess Anne, even though she was married to Cyril Dick, and that he was not, nor ever had been, in the habit of accepting a meal from the Royal Family without paying for it.

9

Roger was woken at six the following morning by the sound of someone being murdered, or more precisely strangled, on the lawn beneath his window.

He lay there for a while, staring blindly across the room at the drawn curtains, his heart racing like a motor-mower engine. If it happens again, he promised himself, I will definitely get up and investigate.

Half a minute later the cry came again, harsh, desperate and this time even nearer.

'I meant the third time,' he told himself.

He pulled the sheet up over his sweating forehead and fell fast asleep.

'I hope the peacocks didn't disturb you,' said the valet, Edward, when shortly after eight he appeared beside the bed with a small tray of tea and Marie biscuits.

'Not in the slightest,' Roger told him.

'It's a wonder they didn't. They woke me, and I can usually sleep through anything. Bloody birds. For two pins I'd wring their wretched necks.'

'Now I come to think of it,' said Roger airily, 'I believe I did hear something round about six.'

'I knew you would have,' said Edward.

'I didn't take a lot of notice though. I suppose it's because I'm fairly used to that sort of thing.'

'Oh yes?' said Edward .

'Yes,' said Roger firmly.

'Shall I run a bath for you?' Edward asked.

'I am quite capable of running my own bath, thank you all the same,' said Roger stiffly.

'As you wish,' said Edward. He walked, rather affectedly Roger thought, towards the door. He opened it, turned, and said, 'Oh by the way, the bar of soap from the Centurion Hotel in the bathroom. I put it there myself. The hotel very kindly sent us a small supply as a gesture of goodwill for our little venture. The one you picked up from the hotel yourself is still in your jacket pocket.'

He closed the door silently behind him.

Roger helped himself to a cup of tea and a Marie biscuit, leaned back against the pillows and reflected upon the state of play so far for that day. Despite the valet's last-minute late cut through the slips for four, there was little doubt in his mind that in overall terms the honours thus far that morning had been his. On the other hand, he thought, it might be just as well if he took care to avoid coming into contact with the fellow any more than was absolutely necessary in the next couple of days. There was no point in rubbing salt into the wound.

He drank another cup of tea and ate another Marie biscuit. Then, with a quick, decisive movement, he threw back the sheets, raised his feet high in the air, paused momentarily, then hurled his legs down and forward and landed upright about four feet from the bed.

He strode across to the window to be confronted with all the makings of a perfect May morning. Sunshine gilded the grounds of Hatching Park, birds twittered in the ivy and bees murmured contentedly as they pottered among the banks of rhododendrons and azaleas that lined the smooth green strip of lawn that sloped away towards the distant river.

Roger threw open the window and took in several mouthfuls of crisp morning air, thus dispelling the last lingering traces of the previous day's headache.

'Ah,' he said loudly, 'that's more like it.'

A solitary peacock on the terrace below looked up, and, ever hopeful, puffed out his chest and spread his tail feathers.

'Don't push your luck,' Roger told the bird, whereupon

his tail collapsed into a dull point, and he stumped off disconsolately round the corner and out of sight.

Crossing the hall on the way to the breakfast room half an hour later, he paused to give a large barometer a sharp tap. As he did so, the whole thing fell off the wall and would have crashed on to the stone floor had Roger not sprung forward and seized it in both hands. He stood there for a while holding it awkwardly like a man suddenly landed with a particularly large and ungainly girl in a Paul Jones. He peered at the small ragged hole in the wall then turned the object round to find that the hook had come away attached to the top of the barometer. He examined it for a while, then turned the whole thing round again and looked at the face. The arrow was pointing at *Changeable*.

'Eighteenth-century, German, rather rare.'

Roger spun round guiltily. Standing halfway down the staircase was Sir George, a number of rolled-up newspapers under his arm. Behind him was the supercilious Edward, wearing a knowing smile. Above, leaning over the banisters, was Mrs Venables.

'What's happening?' she boomed out.

'Nothing, Vera,' her brother-in-law told her. 'It's only Mr Nudds having some trouble with the barometer.'

'Noakes,' murmured Roger.

'What sort of trouble?'

'I gather the barometer just fell,' Sir George told her.

'They said on the eight o'clock news that it might rain,' said Mrs Venables and withdrew.

Roger was suddenly aware that Edward had also disappeared and that his place had been taken by Cyril Dick.

'Actually,' said Dick, 'it didn't just fall. Noakes was fiddling with it.'

'I don't know what you mean,' said Roger.

'I saw you,' said Dick, his eyes glinting evilly like a rat that has just seen a way out of the trap.

'Obviously the hook badly needed replacing,' Roger said to his host. 'It was a lucky thing I happened to be passing when it fell, otherwise you would now be the proud possessor of a rare eighteenth-century German heap of matchwood and broken glass.'

'It certainly was an extraordinary coincidence,' said Sir George. 'Well, let's not tempt Providence too far. May I suggest you place the barometer carefully on the floor against the wall, and then let's all go and have breakfast. All this unexpected excitement first thing in the morning has given me quite an appetite.'

Roger placed the heavy ornate object carefully on the floor as instructed and followed his host along the passage towards the breakfast room.

'My God, Noakes,' Cyril Dick hissed in Roger's ear as they were going in, 'you were a liar at school and you're still a liar. I've said it before and I'll say it again. A leopard never changes its spots.'

Roger stopped and turned.

'Cyril,' he murmured confidentially, drawing him close by the arm, 'I want to tell you something.'

'Well?' said Dick.

'My spots may have remained unchanged since my schooldays, but at least they haven't grown in size and quantity.'

'Do please help yourself to whatever you want,' Sir George said, waving a vague hand at a long sideboard that ran the length of one side of the little Breakfast Room and upon which stood an array of cold and hot dishes, the like of which Roger had hitherto believed to have existed only in the fanciful imaginations of writers like Dornford Yates and Angela Thirkell.

There were fried eggs, scrambled eggs and boiled eggs, crisp bacon and cold ham, fried tomatoes, sausages, kidneys and lamb cutlets, kippers, smoked haddock and kedgeree.

'If anyone would care for some waffles with maple syrup, there are plenty downstairs in the deep freeze. My sister has had a passion for them ever since she visited the Montreal World Fair in 1968, and I keep a supply for her.'

Roger was standing, fork poised over the sausage dish, when a voice by his side murmured,

'Fifteen-love.'

He turned to find Reg with a plate in his hand and a facetious expression on his face, peering at the dish of kedgeree.

'I beg your pardon?'

'I said fifteen-love,' muttered Reg.

'I heard what you said, Reg. But what does it mean?'

Reg tapped the side of his nose with the forefinger of his spare hand.

'Told you he was a dirty sod, that Casablancas. What's this stuff then?'

'Kedgeree.'

'Never could fancy foreign food. Quickest way to a gippy tummy. And the way things are going right now, that would never do.'

'The way *what* things are going, Reg?'

'How are you two getting on?' said Sir George, appearing suddenly between them.

'Very well, thank you, my dear old chap,' said Reg. 'Very well indeed.'

'Good, good, that's the way. Help yourself to some kedgeree. It's Hedges' speciality. He'll be very disappointed if you don't do it real justice.'

'Tell you the truth, I've always been more of an egg and bacon man myself.'

'It looks delicious,' said Roger enthusiastically, in an effort to make up for his colleague's charmless behaviour and at the same time to restore such ground as he may have lost over the barometer incident. 'I'm certainly going to have some. There's nothing like a good kedgeree, I always say.'

'Oh really, do you?' said Sir George vaguely. 'I can't stick the stuff at any price. Always gives me a tummy upset.'

As Roger ploughed his way through the enormous plateful of dry, stodgy mixture which Sir George had insisted on ladling out, he looked enviously across at Reg who was tucking in with obvious pleasure to a generous helping of bacon, egg, sausage, kidney and scrambled eggs. What on earth could he have meant by fifteen-love? And where did Casablancas come into it? Had he arrived late last night bringing with him a supply of large-breasted, wide-hipped girls in housemaids' outfits specially for Reg's benefit? Was that perhaps why he had had to stay behind in London? Had he laid on something special after all?

'Any word from Mr Casablancas?' Roger said to no one in particular.

Jeremy Powell-Brett looked up briefly from his porridge and shook his head. Dick shrugged his shoulders. Reg had just forced half a sausage into his mouth and was unable to speak. Sir George put down his coffee cup and peered across the table.

'Not a word so far,' he said. 'I imagine he'll be here as soon as he has sorted out whatever it was that needed sorting out. More coffee anyone? Mr Henshawe? No? Aha, here come the papers, at last. If you'd just like to leave them there on that chair, Hedges, we'll sort them out in a moment. Any message from Mr Casablanca yet?'

'No, sir.'

'Or the American journalist, Mr Branigan?'

'No, sir. However, her ladyship did receive a telephone call a few minutes ago from Bishop Fox-Bronzing to say that he fully expected to be here in time to give the sermon at Matins tomorrow morning.'

'Did he say what time we could expect him?'

'Her ladyship did not acquaint me of the precise time of his arrival, sir. Will there be anything else, sir?'

'No, thank you, Hedges.'

The butler slid out of the room, various newspapers were distributed, more coffee was poured and toast spread, and the sun continued to pour in through the French windows along with the sound of small birds doing their warming-up exercises in preparation for a full day's singing ahead.

Roger looked round the room – at the elephants and

dromedaries and palm trees and Red Indians, an eight-eenth-century artist's impression of the four continents, with which the four walls were covered; at the silver covers gleaming on the sideboard and the collection of snuff boxes in the glass-fronted cabinet beside the door and the vista of lawns and herbaceous borders stretching away from the French windows – and thought what a pity it was that once again his chances of total enjoyment were being spoiled by having to share it with people who were not really up to it.

Jeremy Powell-Brett seemed to be under the impression that he was in the Bahamas, with his flowery open-necked shirt, his mustard-coloured trousers and his espadrilles. Reg, looking as though he were about to set out on a cut-price tour of Kenya, was sporting a pale blue Terylene safari suit and white Dralon crew-necked pullover. Cyril Dick's double-breasted blue blazer had a large badge on the breast pocket declaring him to be a member of some yachting club near Great Yarmouth.

The thought that Sir George, his wife and their staff might take him for a cheap hack like the rest of them, or even worse, a potential stealer of rare eighteenth-century German barometers, worried Roger deeply. It was high time he established himself.

'I expect you know the Cox-Moores,' he said to Sir George. 'They live near Norwich.'

'No,' said Sir George.

At that moment the telephone rang in a small recess at the far end of the room.

'Hallo,' said Sir George. 'Yes. Yes, this is George Fox-Bronzing speaking. Who? The son? Whose son? Oh the *Sun*. Am I doing what? Helping to launch a new travel company? I think you must be mistaken. I simply have a few friends staying for the weekend. Goodbye.'

Roger made a mental note to treat Casablancas with a little more respect in future.

'Excuse me, sir.'

'Yes, what is it, Hedges?'

'The Managing Director of Blue Blood Tours has just arrived.'

'Excellent news,' cried Sir George. 'Show him in at once.'

'Very good, sir.'

Hedges turned, but had scarcely taken two steps before a voice called out, 'That's all right. I'll show myself in.' And into the room walked Harold Maitland.

10

It was the dark suit that Roger found more offensive then anything else.

'This is supposed to be a *country* house party, you know, Maitland,' he told his flat-mate.

'I have better things to worry about than the colour and texture of my suit,' said Maitland.

They were seated alone over the remains of breakfast. The three journalists had disappeared to look at the garden; Sir George to speak with his wife.

'Now look here,' said Roger. 'I know I may be a bit dim about the workings of the City and so on, but I do happen to know a thing or two about the travel industry—'

'But not apparently about Blue Blood Tours,' Maitland interrupted him.

'What?'

'Blue Blood Tours had gone bust even before they threw the party at the Windsor Castle. Fortunately the landlord there is the sort of person who has his own way of collecting overdue debts, so at least that's one less problem we have to worry about.'

'Who exactly are *we*?'

'Da Silva Kleinman of course.'

'Who on earth are they?'

'I've only been working for them for the last five years.'

'I never knew you were in a foreign firm. I always thought you worked for some English insurance people in Finsbury Circus.'

'I've never worked in insurance or in Finsbury Circus in my life. Da Silva's is one of the largest and most respected groups of financial consultants in the City of London. What's more, every single partner is as English as you and me.'

'I always thought you were Scottish, Maitland,' Roger said. 'Anyway, so they ran out of money. In that case, why on earth did they go ahead, and where do you come into it?'

'Apparently the man who put the money up in the first place was an African by the name of Ngogo . . .'

'Nigel Ngogo?' exclaimed Roger. 'The PR man?'

'Merely a cover,' said Maitland. 'In fact, the whole operation was the brainchild of Ngogo's uncle, Nelson Mintole, who was, you will recall, Prime Minister of Kananga until a couple of weeks ago when he was assassinated by some anti-OAU fanatic in Burungi. Mintole had already had dealings with Casablancas over some foreign exchange fiddle and was so impressed that, when he sent his nephew Nigel off to London to set up Blue Blood Tours, he instructed him to rope in Casablancas and set him up as a front man while he pulled the strings from behind. It was merely a device for getting money out of the country. A nest-egg for his old age.

'All went well until Mintole was bumped off whereupon the supply of money dried up instantly. The cost of mounting the operation had been enormous. The promotional budget for Dallas alone came to over 45,000 dollars, and by that stage they still hadn't had a single booking. And so there they were, stuck with astronomic bills in America which they couldn't pay, an elaborate journalistic junket to Hatching Park in England all set up and ready to go, and not a bean in the bank.'

'A no Ngogo situation, one might almost say,' said Roger. 'He certainly got out in time.'

'What do you mean?' said Maitland.

'I was told Nigel had left the company for good.'

'Not for good,' said Maitland. 'For Switzerland. In a last minute bid to relieve the gnomes of some of his uncle's numbered millions. So far unsuccessfully, it would seem.

Still, he somehow managed to persuade Casablancas that it was worthwhile going ahead with the weekend, and, well, here we all are.'

'More to the point, so are you,' said Roger. 'Why are you the new Managing Director of Blue Blood Tours?'

'We had been acting as financial advisers to Mintole for five years before the idea of Blue Blood Tours ever entered his head.'

'So, when things went wrong, Da Silva Kleinman took over the company and made you Managing Director.'

'Merely a temporary arrangement,' Maitland said, lighting a cheroot. 'Until Blue Blood Tours gets off the ground anyway.'

'And will it?'

'It will,' said Maitland grimly, 'if I have anything to do with it. First things first, though, we've got to get through this weekend without any of these ace newshound colleagues of yours getting the faintest sniff of the true state of play. Naturally, as a friend, I rely on your discretion.'

'Just so long as Sir George can rely on you for the money. He hasn't had a penny yet.'

'I know,' said Maitland impatiently. 'All that will be seen to as soon as possible. I am due to meet him and his wife in five minutes in the Robert Adam Saloon. They tell me she's a real corker.'

'I don't think you're quite her type.'

'What's that got to do with it?' Maitland flashed him a familiar leer. 'No, seriously. The problem, as I see it, is this: the bulk of Blue Blood's business is going to come from America, from Australia, from Japan, from the Middle East and from West Germany. Yet all the journalists on this junket write only for English publications, and some of them pretty second-rate ones at that.'

'What about this American from *World* magazine we hear so much about?'

'The famous Ed Branigan, you mean? The one who might have been in Bulgaria? Or was it Ethiopia? I spent most of yesterday evening trying to track him down. I found him at last at one o'clock in the morning.'

'Where was he? In Bulgaria or Ethiopia?'

'Neither. He was in the Centurion Hotel. The Julius Caesar Suite. He'd been there for the last week. Researching, or so the girl who answered the phone informed me. Anyway, he should be here shortly before lunch, and his story will be running in *World* sometime in the next three weeks.'

'How can you be so sure?'

'Look, laddie,' said Maitland, drawing on his cigar and blowing the smoke out noisily, 'I may not know a lot about journalism, but I do know something about money. So why don't you just potter about here for the next couple of days, pretend you're a real guest at a real country house party if you must, dabble in your usual undergraduate way with a little flirtation, then go away and write a nice, funny, romantic piece about it all for the *Sunday Times* . . .'

'*Observer*, more likely.'

'*Observer. Sunday Times.* Who cares? I doubt that either of them will attract the sort of paying customers we want anyway. Just write the piece. Your friends and relations will ring you up and tell you, as usual, how much they enjoyed reading it. And one day, after a lot of telephone calls and memos and general grumbling, a nice little cheque for a hundred pounds will drop through the letter box, which will just about cover your share of the rent for a month, and your career will have taken one more tiny, hesitant step forward. I, in the meantime, will devote as much time and attention as I can to taking hold of this half-baked project, turning it upside down, knocking it about the head, and one way and another shaking it until its teeth rattle, until I finally begin to knock some sense into it. The methods I employ will be unscrupulous, vulgar and crude, and your sensitive soul will no doubt be deeply wounded. My presence here will doubtless embarrass and irritate you, but at least by the time we all go home, the Fox-Bronzings will have been woken from their dream world and made to understand what going into business is all about; you and your friends from Fleet Street will have ceased to treat this weekend as an excuse to eat and drink and laze about and get something for nothing; and Blue Blood Tours will be well and truly launched.'

'By a strange coincidence,' said Roger, 'my thinking has been very much along the same lines . . .'

'He's planning to do what?' said Jean.

'Make a film of the whole weekend,' Roger said. 'A documentary. You know.'

'I know what a documentary is. What I want to know is, what for?'

'For publicity, I suppose. He thinks he's going to be able to sell it to television companies all over the world. I think it's rather a good idea myself.'

They were in Jean's bedroom. Roger was in an armchair by the window; Jean was on the floor painting her toe nails. The remnants of breakfast were scattered over a tray on the unmade bed.

'It's certainly enterprising,' Jean admitted.

'It can't do us any harm to appear on American television. It might lead to something. You never know.'

'Like what, for instance?'

'I don't know. Something.'

'Has Sir George been informed of this latest development yet?'

Roger looked out of the window. On the round lawn in the middle of the drive, Sir George, Fiona and Maitland were deep in conversation.

'I rather think he's being told of it now,' he said.

'I wonder if he has any idea of the havoc even the smallest film crew can wreak within seconds of setting foot inside someone's house?'

Sir George was smiling and rubbing his hands together. Maitland was making wild, film-directorish gestures with his hands. Fiona was looking at him impassively.

'I doubt it,' said Roger.

'Should someone tell him, do you suppose?'

'Oh, I don't think so,' said Roger.

11

Half an hour later the film crew arrived. There were two of them: a cameraman called Brian and a sound engineer called Keith, or possibly vice versa. It was difficult to tell. They were more or less the same person – short and plump with heavy sideboards, balding crowns and Mexican moustaches. When they spoke, which they did rarely and never at great length, they had identically flat, south London accents. They were dressed in identical denim suits and open-necked shirts, gold-bullion nestled in their greying chest hairs and small cigars smouldered permanently between their fingers. There seemed to be a certain amount of doubt in their own minds which one was which, since often both answered to either name. They were the Rosencrantz and Guildenstern of the film documentary world.

They were unfailingly polite and listened carefully to Maitland's briefing, but showed little anxiety to get started.

'As I see it,' Maitland explained to them as they stood on the South Terrace sipping at glasses of Pimms Number One, 'this film should be a story.' The pair nodded solemnly and buried their noses among the mint and apple slices. 'In other words, it should have a beginning, a middle and an end.'

'Got you,' said Brian.

'We begin by showing the guests arriving by car at Hatching Park. We go on to show them meeting their hosts, settling in, laughing and talking over drinks in the Long Library and so on. Then we show them retiring for bed, getting up next morning, having breakfast, enjoying the picnic by the river, punting and so on. Then we show them having tea. . . .'

'I think we get the picture,' said Keith.

'Just as long as we do, that's all that matters,' said Maitland.

'No sweat,' said Brian.

'Only one problem, the way I see it,' said Keith.

'Whassat?' said Brian.

'We can't show them arriving and all that early stuff, seeing as how they're here already.'

'Mock it up.'

'Why not?'

'This is really most interesting,' Sir George interrupted them with a little cough. 'One has heard so much about the trickery and so on that goes into film-making, and here one is, actually in a position to see for oneself how it is really done – behind the screen, as it were. When you say mock it up, for instance, what precisely are you planning to do?'

'Simple. Get everyone back into the cars, load up the luggage and film the arrival just as it happened last night.'

'What, now?' said Sir George.

'Why not?' said Brian.

'For one thing, it was dark when everyone arrived.'

Brian looked at Keith.

'Day for night?' he said.

'Why not?' said Keith.

'What does that mean exactly?' asked Sir George.

'It means,' explained Brian patiently, 'that we put on a special filter so that although we are filming in broad daylight, it comes out looking like night-time.'

'Oh, I think I've seen that, haven't I?' said Sir George. 'In "The Dark Lady", with Margaret Lockwood. I'm very fond of Margaret Lockwood, aren't you?'

'Can't say I've ever seen her in anything,' said Keith.

'Not *seen* her in anything?' exclaimed Sir George, with a little frown. 'But I don't understand. How can you possibly be in the film industry and never have seen Margaret Lockwood?

She was the greatest star this country has ever known – after Anna Neagle, of course. Why, the British film industry was founded on those two ladies. I'm shocked at the pair of you. However, we'll let that pass. When you say you wish to film the arrival now, do you mean now? This minute?'

'Well . . . er . . .'

'Excellent, excellent. I'm certainly keen to get ahead with it straight away. In a way, of course, what you are asking us all to do is to *act* the arrival. How exciting. I haven't acted in anything since . . . let me see . . . when was it I played Servant to Antony at school? 1923, was it, or '24? I forget now. I suppose you would like us to improvise the dialogue rather than prepare a script? Yes, of course you would. So much more natural. Shall you want us to wear make-up? What sort of clothes should one wear? I have a feeling that the jacket I was wearing last night went off to the cleaners this morning, didn't it, my darling?' He turned towards his wife who, smiling indulgently, stepped forward and took the old man by the arm. 'I hope,' he continued, 'that you will give my wife plenty to do in your film. She is a professional actress, you know.'

'Was,' she said softly. 'For about three months. Now before we all get carried away too far with all this, let us get one thing straight. How long do you suppose this arrival scene will take?'

Brian and Keith looked at each other in silence for several seconds, as though in telepathic communication, then turned back to Fiona.

'About a couple of hours should see us through,' said Brian.

'Oh, I'm afraid in that case it's quite out of the question,' said Sir George. 'Luncheon is at one thirty down by the river, and it is midday already. We shall have to postpone it until this afternoon.'

'But, Sir George,' said Maitland, 'this afternoon we have the punting and so on. We shall certainly want to film that in progress. Unless of course you were thinking of mocking

95

that up tomorrow. At that rate we shall all be here for weeks.'

'We might lose the sun, too,' said Brian.

'Put paid to our day-for-night idea,' said Keith.

Sir George said, 'In that case, let's film the arrival this evening.'

He was clearly becoming rather confused, not to say irritated, by this obstructive attitude which everyone suddenly seemed to have assumed towards what appeared to him to be a perfectly simple and straightforward plan of campaign.

'Impossible,' said Fiona. 'Drinks with the Dishforths.'

'Put them off until tomorrow,' said Maitland.

'The Dishforths happen to be my oldest and dearest friends,' said Sir George with a frown. 'Francis and I were at school together. They have very kindly, and at considerable inconvenience, agreed to look in before dinner tonight for a drink by way of a personal favour to me. It may be customary in your line of work, Mr Martin, to alter arrangements at the last moment. If so, then the City of London has changed a great deal since I was a young man. Nevertheless, this is not the way we do things in the country, and I have no intention of putting off Sir Francis and Lady Dishforth for you or anybody else. And if these two chaps here are incapable of polishing off what I should have thought was a comparatively simple scene within the next hour, then I suggest we leave it out altogether. We've wasted ten minutes talking about it, as it is '

'I would remind you, Sir George,' said Maitland coolly, 'that the film will benefit you every bit as much as it will benefit us. We're not all here for fun, you know. This is business, and in the commercial world there's no place for sentimentality if you want to make money.'

Sir George nodded glumly.

'So I am beginning to understand.'

Maitland turned to the film crew.

'Can you film this scene between now and quarter-past one?'

They pulled faces.

'Well . . . you know how it is . . .'

'Yes or no?' snapped Maitland. 'If not I'll hire someone else.'

'In that case . . .'

'Right,' said Maitland. 'Let's get on with it then.'

Apart from a couple of technical hitches, and an unfortunate tendency on the part of Sir George to overact, the filming could not have gone better.

At twelve forty-five, Buster Legge and Eddie, looking rather self-conscious in their caps and uniforms, drove the Rollses up to the front door. Empty suitcases were stowed away in the boots and guests, dressed in a variety of outfits ranging from Jeremy Powell-Brett's Jamaican night-club wear to Audrey Veal's Ascot outfit, complete with hat and ostrich feathers, clambered inside. Sir George in a loud tweed suit and plus-fours and his wife in a flowing floral shift stood nervously on the top step outside the front door, flanked by as many servants as could be rustled up at short notice: Hedges, more aquiline than ever; Mrs Eames in her apron and mob cap, who, despite her protestations that she had work to do, was clearly enjoying every moment of it; Edward, the valet; three girls from the village; two kitchen maids; Mudd the head gardener and his dopey, red-headed boy, William; and Mr Hahned, who had been persuaded against his better judgement to swell the domestic group and was barely concealing his irritation beneath a thin smile.

The cars trundled away down the drive, turned and waited for Maitland to wave his white handkerchief – the signal for filming to begin.

'Reg,' said Roger, who was jammed between Henshawe and Jackie in the back seat of the second car.

'Roger,' said Reg.

'I've been thinking about what you said to me at breakfast this morning. What did you mean exactly – fifteen-love?'

'It was a joke,' muttered Reg.

97

'I don't get it,' persisted Roger. 'Fifteen-love. Something to do with a game?'

'Sort of,' said Reg, grimacing in the direction of Jackie who was squinting into one of the small illuminated mirrors at the back of the car, as she made last minute adjustments to her eye make-up.

'You mean . . .?'

Reg raised his eyes heavenward in an attitude of despair. Now it was Roger's turn to be embarrassed.

'Ha ha, yes, of course. Sorry. Not thinking. Ha ha.'

Although Roger's interest in the girl next to him had virtually evaporated the moment he had clapped eyes on Fiona Fox-Bronzing, and although the vision of Reg Henshawe romping naked around a four-poster bed was not one upon which he cared to linger, that of Jackie Ericson most definitely was. The mere thought that in such respectable surroundings things like that were not only being contemplated but actually taking place excited him no end. How many other secret couplings had taken place in the last twelve hours? he wondered. Jean and Jeremy? Possible but unlikely. Barbara and Cyril Dick? Knowing Barbara, some sort of assault would undoubtedly have been carried out upon that wretched, pock-marked body, but probably to very little purpose.

And what of Fiona and her husband? A picture flashed through Roger's mind of her naked form stretched out on the bed, her hair tumbling about her breasts like caramel sauce over blancmange, and, leaning over it, the bony figure of Sir George, demanding and perpetrating all manner of sexual atrocities. A dull pain shot through his stomach and into his thighs, as if he had been eating too many Brussels sprouts.

'I don't get it either,' said Jackie.

'What?' said Roger.

'The joke.'

'Joke?'

'About the tennis.'

'Oh?'

'Fifteen-love?'

'No,' said Roger, 'neither do I really.'

'Here we go,' said Eddie. And the two cars began to move in slow and stately procession through the trees towards the waiting cameras.

'I must say,' Audrey Veal said to Sir George as they made their way between the rhododendrons towards the river, 'that valet of yours was very good in the close-up with the suitcases.'

Obviously much taken by the ageing aristocrat, she had barely left his side all morning, hanging on his every word, applauding his every suggestion, choosing every possible opportunity to murmur something into his ear, implying an intimacy between them that certainly did not exist, but which Roger himself would have been only too happy to foster. Now she took his arm as easily as if she had known him for years.

'I agree,' said Roger who was walking on Sir George's other side, dressed now in a striped blazer and white flannels.

'I can't think why you should be so surprised,' said Sir George. 'It is his job, after all.'

'Being a valet?'

'No, film work.'

'What do you mean?' said Roger.

'Edward is an actor. Or, more precisely, an out-of-work actor. He's only doing this to fill in time and make a little money before joining some repertory company on the East Anglian coast. You may have seen him in that television series about Lily Langtry, playing a valet. That's what gave me the idea.'

'I knew I'd seen him before,' said Audrey.

So had Roger, he now realised. He was normally very good at recognizing people – not just actors, but people he had met during his life and who had made some sort of impression on him, chaps he had been at school with, girls he had met at dances, sometimes people he had not seen for twenty years or more and whose physical appearances had changed totally. There was still something in their eyes, or the tilt of their head, or the way they pulled at their nose – something that struck a chord deep in his subconscious – and a name would spring, often instantaneously, to his lips. Once, travelling on a number 88 bus along Oxford Street at the height of the rush hour, he had glanced casually down at the seething mass of humanity on the pavement outside Debenham and Freebody and recognised Ernest Kippax with whom he had been at prep school. His failure to recognise the actor Edward Holt beneath the superior façade of the valet Edward was made doubly irritating by the thought that, had he known from the start he was only an actor, he would never have been forced into the position of making such a fool of himself over the tablet of soap.

'The sooner he returns to the stage the better,' he told Sir George. 'As a valet he leaves something to be desired. As a matter of interest, where did you find him?'

'He's my godson,' said Sir George.

'An actor,' twittered Audrey. 'Fancy that. Next you will be telling us Hedges isn't a real butler.'

'He isn't,' said Sir George. 'He's an architect.'

12

It was no use pretending Roger was not disappointed in Sir George Fox-Bronzing, because he was. The discovery that two of his servants were not servants at all but members of a quite different profession was not so earth-shattering that it was going to undermine Roger's faith in the human race, but it had certainly given him cause to rethink one or two basic principles of life that he had hitherto taken very much for granted. It was as though he had suddenly been told that Harold Macmillan wore clip-on bow ties.

The party arrived at the end of the Long Walk and turned on to the broad stretch of lawn that ran down to the water's edge, where a pair of swans and some unusual looking ducks pottered about among the water plants and bullrushes. To the left was a small boathouse and a landing stage to which four punts with gaily striped cushions were attached by chains. Nearby, several large white linen tablecloths had been spread over the grass upon which, shaded by two enormous striped umbrellas, was laid the most sumptuous picnic Roger had ever seen.

There was smoked salmon and smoked trout, cold chicken and duck and pheasant, a whole York ham, a huge fresh salmon garnished with parsley and caviare, pork pies and pâtés, terrines and mousses, bowls of lettuce and tomatoes and spring onions and beetroots, of Russian salad and potato salad and tomato salad and cucumber salad, of mayonnaises and dressings, and small, speckled plovers' eggs. There were French *baguettes* and crisp rolls and crusty farmhouse loaves, and dishes of butter on ice, and enough cheese to supply the entire population of

Toughingham St Peter for a month or more: a whole Stilton, a whole Brie, Cheddar and Cheshire, Wensleydale and Double Gloucester, Danish Blue and Camembert, Petits Suisses and Carrés de l'Est.

To one side, there was a long table on which were several dozen glasses, a large jug of Pimms, another of sangria, and six bottles of hock in ice buckets. Beneath it was a crate of Château Batailley 1966, a crate of bottled beer and a crate of cider. Behind it stood Hedges, Edward, Hahned and three girls from the village in black dresses with white frilly aprons.

Scattered around the gargantuan feast were a number of chairs – deck chairs with awnings, long cane chairs on wheels and upright canvas chairs – and small tables over which smaller umbrellas had been erected.

The sun shone from a cornflower blue sky, the glasses and the cutlery winked and shone, the ducks croaked contentedly among the bulrushes, the bees hummed happily in the herbaceous border, and beside the long table, waving gently in the soft breeze, Reg Henshawe helped himself to another pint of Pimms.

'Hallo, lads,' he called out cheerily as the party hove into sight. 'Thought for a while I was going to have to deal with all this by myself.' He waved an arm vaguely across the drinks table.

'Good afternoon,' said Sir George politely. 'I'm so sorry we're late. We've just been having a little tour of the house.'

Audrey Veal gave Sir George's arm a knowing squeeze.

'Speaking for myself, I wouldn't have missed it for anything,' she cooed. 'That French furniture and those ormolu vases. And as for that painting on a cobweb, I don't think I've ever seen anything like it.'

'It is unique,' said Sir George quietly.

'I'm not at all surprised. You certainly missed something, Reg.'

'Oh, I wouldn't know about that, love,' said Reg, slurring his words slightly. 'I too have been sampling the delights of country house life in my own little way.'

'Evidently,' she said primly, looking towards Sir George for moral support.

'Quite right too,' said Sir George. 'The whole essence of a weekend party is that everyone should be allowed to do exactly what they want.'

'I couldn't agree more, my dear fellow,' said Reg amiably. 'What are you having?'

He waved his hand in the general direction of the Pimms jug.

'A glass of white wine, I think, would be very pleasant. How about you, my dear?'

'Wine would be fine,' said Audrey in a state of some confusion.

'Two glasses of vino coming up,' Reg called out in a mock publican voice. 'If you would be so good,' he added, turning to Hedges.

'Hitting the greasy sod for all he's worth?' Roger muttered to the assistant sports editor, as the party began to spread itself about in the chairs and on the grass.

'I don't know what you mean, old man,' said Reg in an offended tone of voice, his eyes beginning to do their imitation of two fried eggs swimming in oil.

Roger reminded him of their conversation at the party at the Windsor Castle.

'Ah yes,' said Reg, 'but that was when that dago fellow was running the show. Different thing altogether now. This chappie's a gentleman.' He pointed towards Sir George, who was busy helping Audrey Veale to a plate of smoked salmon.

'Comes from a long line of people, you know. Family fought at Agincourt, that sort of thing. Beautiful house, beautiful wife. Backbone of the country. What the Hitler war was all about; but of course you're far too young to remember that. Nice drop of wine, this.'

Reg drained the remains of his glass and held it out in the direction of Hedges who obligingly refurbished it with cold hock. Reg took another faceful.

'Cost you a few bob in El Vino's that. Ah well, vive le freeloading, that's what I always say.'

'What's happened to this American, then?' Roger asked Maitland.

'Should be here any minute now,' Maitland said confidently. 'Probably got caught up in the Saturday morning traffic.'

'Probably.'

Roger was peeling a plover's egg when Fiona Fox-Bronzing appeared by his side.

'Do you know how to punt?' she said.

'Yes,' he said. 'As a matter of fact I do. I'm a bit rusty mind you, but . . .'

'Good,' she said. 'I rather thought you might. In that case, you can punt me after lunch.'

'But what about your husband?'

'What about him?'

'Won't you want to . . . I mean, I rather assumed you'd be going with him.'

'I do see him all day and every day,' she replied. 'If I want to go punting with him, I can do so anytime I choose. Besides, he always disappears into his study after lunch.'

'Really. Why?'

'He always claims it's to go over the farm accounts. I know it's to watch the Test Match on television.'

'Well, in that case, if you really mean it. But what about the others? I mean, will there be enough punts to go round? I mean . . .'

'Do you want to come or not?'

'Well, yes . . .'

'Right then. We'll be leaving in half an hour.'

*

Roger decided that one way and another it was one of the better days of his life, and peeled another plover's egg.

Brian and Keith were enjoying themselves, too, as they wandered among the picnickers, capturing little gems of *cinema verité*.

There was nothing that anybody said or did during the two hours or so that the picnic lasted that Brian and Keith did not see in terms of a great shot, or a terrific contrast, or a very useful cutting point. The moment anyone poured a glass of wine, Brian and Keith would be at their side like a pair of faithful Labradors, asking them to 'Hold it just there, love. Up a bit, so the sunlight filters through. Lovely. Towards me a bit, that way I can just get the corner of the boathouse in as well. Terrific. Now hold it just there.' If anyone so much as leant forward to seize a tomato or help himself to some raspberries, they would as like as not have their gesture halted in mid-air with: 'Could we just do that again, love? Only this time, I want you to reach out very, very slowly, as though you were in a dream. Know what I mean?'

It was Audrey Veal who was the first to give vent to her irritation.

'Oh, for God's sake,' she snapped at the two of them, 'I'm bored with this game. And full up. I don't want to show delight at another spoonful of ice-cream. Get someone else to do it. Get Fiona. She's supposed to be an actress.'

'I rather agree with Mrs Veal,' Sir George said before either of the two men could reply. 'I think we have covered the picnic pretty thoroughly now. Why don't we just relax and enjoy our coffee and liqueurs and do some more filming in the punts in about an hour or so? I don't know about everyone else, but I'm quite tired.'

Everyone laughed sympathetically and murmured their agreement.

Maitland said: 'I really do think we should do as much as we can while we've got the sun, Sir George.'

'We've been filming practically non-stop for the last three hours,' Sir George pointed out politely. 'My guests are not professional performers. They are here to enjoy themselves and to get some idea of what our future guests can expect when they come. Now let's leave it for an hour, shall we?'

It was clear from his tone of voice that he meant what he said to be final. Not, however, to Maitland.

'Your guests are not here to enjoy themselves, and neither are you. In point of fact, they are not your guests anyway, they are mine. We are all of us here to work, and I must insist . . .'

'You must do nothing of the sort,' snapped Sir George. 'This is my house and if I say there shall be no more filming for an hour, then there shall be no more filming for an hour. I do not wish to hear another word about it. Now, please, all relax and enjoy the rest of the meal. I fear you must excuse me for a while. I have some estate business to attend to up at the house. I'm only sorry I shall not be able to join you for the punting. However, I shall see you again in time for drinks at six-thirty.'

He turned and had begun to walk away towards the house when Maitland stopped him in his tracks. 'You haven't forgotten that the local radio people are coming at four to interview you, have you, Sir George?'

'Radio people?' said Sir George. 'What radio people? I know nothing of any radio people.'

'Oh, I only fixed it just before lunch,' said Maitland calmly. 'I was going to tell you, but what with the filming and everything, it must have slipped my mind.'

For a moment it looked as though Sir George might lose his temper at last. Instead he turned on his heel and strode away towards the house. Maitland ran after him and walked up beside him. Roger heard him say: 'It could be very useful if we can manage to sell the tape to radio stations in America. . . .'

And then the pair of them had turned into the Long Walk and out of hearing.

*

'I'm impressed with your flatmate,' said Jean, handing Roger a cup of coffee. 'He's far more positive and effective than you had led me to believe.'

'Impressed?' exclaimed Roger. 'With Maitland? The man's a gorilla.'

'He's a business man. He knows what he wants and he knows how to get it.'

'You admire that sort of thing?'

'In a way yes. Probably because I am not really determined and single-minded enough myself. It's your trouble, too.'

"You're either made that way or you're not,' said Roger stiffly. 'It is not something to be admired.'

'Perhaps admire is the wrong word,' said Jean. 'It certainly interests me.'

'You mean, you fancy Maitland?' Roger was genuinely horrified.

'Power is always attractive.'

'What about looks, charm, manners, decency?' said Roger scornfully. 'What about a man like Sir George, for instance?'

'Of course I think all those things are splendid in a man, and Sir George is a thoroughly admirable fellow. But that's all.'

Apart from a week or so when they had first met and gone to a couple of cinemas, eaten some meals and kissed goodnight with moderate enthusiasm, there had never been anything more than simple friendship between Jean and Roger. And yet suddenly Roger felt more jealous than he had ever felt in his life before – not just of Maitland but of all those hard-edged, unsentimental and uncompromising men who, over the years, had taken away from under his nose so many beautiful girls that he had almost lost count.

He wanted to continue with the conversation with Jean, to try to diminish Maitland in her eyes by scorning his bad behaviour, his lack of sensitivity, his lack of humour, his downright bad manners. He wanted her to agree that his sudden appearance at breakfast had completely altered the whole atmosphere of the weekend, and turned it from fun into a chore and an embarrassment.

But somehow he knew instinctively that, as far as Maitland was concerned, she would not be sympathetic to him. He had come up against a hard, well-formed element in her character whose existence he had long suspected but never seen expressed, and nothing he said, no jokes that he made, no sympathy that he attempted to engender would move or alter it.

He shifted on to safer ground.

'How's it going with Golden Boy, then?'

'Old Crinkle Jaw? Hopeless.'

'But I thought you said he was Chinese Gordon and your local GP and goodness knows who else, all rolled into one.'

'With all their complexes and hang-ups and phobias – yes, he is. How right I was.'

'Oh Lord,' said Roger who was immensely cheered by this news. 'What will you do now?'

'Spend the rest of the weekend eating my heart out over Harold Maitland, I daresay. You know me. Pity about the Harold bit. It's not exactly the sort of name you can whisper in the velvety darkness with any large measure of conviction.'

Roger's spirits rose briefly. 'I believe some of his friends call him Hal,' he said. 'I call him Maitland myself.'

'Hal Maitland. Yes, that sounds better. Well, that's one obstacle o'er-leapt. The next is the fact that he obviously regards me as something lower than an ant's knees – that is if he has ever given me a moment's thought. I suppose you couldn't put in a word for me, could you?'

Roger pulled a face.

'Oh, please, Roger, say you will. Just as a favour to me.'

'Well, I don't really see how . . .' began Roger.

'If you don't,' said Jean sternly, 'you'll never write another article for me as long as you live.'

'I could certainly see how the land lies,' said Roger, who was not quite sure whether she was being serious.

'Good, that's settled then. When?'

'This evening?'

'Or better still, how about now?'

'You haven't even asked me about Fiona yet,' Roger complained sulkily.

'I know about you and Fiona,' she said, not unkindly. 'All talk and no do, as usual.'

'Normally I would be forced to agree with you,' said Roger. 'However, on this occasion, I rather think you're going to have to eat your words.'

And so the afternoon wore on in a haze of dappled sunlight, alcohol and idle conversation.

Brian and Keith, looking strangely undressed without their equipment, sat side by side in a pair of upright canvas chairs, watching some of the most fantastic shots in cinema history going down the drain in front of their very eyes.

'It's got a sort of "Elvira Madigan" feel about it, don't you think?' said Brian.

'I was going to say "Le Bonheur",' said Keith.

'Never saw that.'

'Agnes Varda at her best.'

'Great director, Agnes Varda.'

'One of the best. For a woman.'

'There's more than a slight hint of "The Go-Between" with the river and the reeds and everything.'

'Now there's a good director.'

'Works you hard.'

'A perfectionist.'

'Bloody good, though.'

'Ever worked with him?'

'No. You?'

'No.'

Roger lay on the grass with his eyes closed, letting the distant sounds drift vaguely over him like thistledown on the summer breeze.

'Rog.'

He opened his eyes to find Jackie kneeling beside him, her hair almost white against the blue sky.

'Can I have a word with you?'

'Yes, of course. What is it?'

Roger propped himself up on one elbow.

'It's about Reg.'

'What about Reg?'

'It's just that . . . well, the thing is . . . I don't rightly know . . .'

Her lower lip quivered and a large tear began to roll down her right cheek, taking with it a deposit of mascara. Roger offered her his handkerchief and hoped that mascara didn't stain.

'But I thought everything was fine between you and Reg. I mean, this morning in the car, when he said . . .'

'I heard what he said in the car, and I knew what you must have been thinking, but it isn't true. At least, it isn't true the way you think it is.'

'You mean he didn't get his leg over, I mean, you know, last night?'

'Oh yes, he got his leg over all right,' she blubbed, 'but not over me.'

'Good God. Over who then?'

'Over Mrs Venables.'

It was nearly four by the time they finally made their way to the landing stage and into the punts, armed with an assortment of bottles of wine, glasses, bowls of fruit and parasols that had been distributed for the occasion.

'Lost the sun now all right,' groaned Brian.

'Knew we would,' said Keith.

'Miss Black and the camera crew, if you would take that

one there. Miss Hollingsworth and Mr Powell-Brett, this one here. And . . .'

'Er. I wonder if it would be possible . . .?' said Dick anxiously.

'Actually I'd rather . . .' said Jean.

'If you don't mind . . .' said Jackie.

'Oh well, sort it out amongst yourselves,' said Fiona sharply. 'Roger, if you'd like to come with me and lead the way . . . Does everyone know how to punt?'

'I punted for my college at Oxford, as a matter of fact,' volunteered Powell-Brett.

'Good. Anyone else? Mr Dick? No? Never mind. Those who don't know how can paddle. I suggest we keep fairly close together to begin with until you get the hang of it, then we can go our separate ways. Don't go too far. It's four o'clock already and we have guests at six-thirty.'

Fiona crammed a large white floppy hat with trailing ribbons on top of her tumbling locks, stepped efficiently into the first punt, and collapsed on to the squashy striped cushion at the far end.

'Okay,' she said to Roger. 'Let's go.'

Roger's punting was rustier than he had anticipated and for a couple of panic-filled minutes there seemed every chance that they would not succeed in getting under way at all. Matters were not helped by Powell-Brett who insisted on giving instructions on a maddeningly superior voice.

'Push sideways. Sideways. No, the other side. The other side. Move the pole further forward. That's it. Now push. You've got to get your prow out in the middle, otherwise you'll never get under way.'

'I'll get your bloody prow out in the middle in a minute,' muttered Roger under his breath.

Finally the old craft, black and lumpy and blistered with a dozen coats of varnish, glided out into the stream. Powell-Brett followed with Brian and Keith and the camera gear. He punted rather well, Roger was annoyed to see, throwing the pole expertly upwards after each stroke before letting it slip easily through his fingers ready for the

111

next assault on the mud and weed and unsuspecting minnows.

They were followed in turn by Reg Henshawe, who was sprawled across the cushions with a bottle of wine in one hand and a glass in the other, looking for all the world like Mr Toad in one of his more unbearable moods, singing the Eton Boating Song at the top of his voice at Jean and Jackie, who sat on the locker dabbing unenthusiastically at the water with a pair of paddles.

'Good news, bad news joke,' he bellowed. 'Stop me if you've heard it. Mate on slave galley, right? Shouts out to sweating oarsmen, "Right lads. I've got some good news for you and some bad news. First the good news: this evening we shall be putting in to Alexandria where you will be provided with food, wine and women. Now the bad news: this afternoon, the captain wants to go water-skiing."'

Reg laughed so much that he dropped his glass over the side.

'Never mind,' he said. 'Fish might want a drink.' And throwing back his head, he lowered the neck of the bottle into his gaping mouth.

Bringing up the rear of the convoy were Barbara Black and Cyril Dick who, by way of making up for his weakness in other directions, was perched precariously on the locker, wobbling wildly and wielding his pole with all the skill and grace of Aaron when he discovered that there was more to his rod than met the eye.

'Cambridge man, I perceive,' Powell-Brett called out facetiously. 'Standing at the locker end.'

'Bugger off,' Dick's voice came winging its way across the shimmering surface of the water.

13

Despite a short sharp bout of freestyle wrestling with an otherwise charming weeping willow, Roger soon succeeded in putting a good two hundred yards between him and the rest of the convoy. After a while they came to a tight right-hand bend which was followed almost at once by a fork in the river.

'Take the smaller channel on the right,' Fiona told him urgently. 'Quick, do as I say, while we are still out of sight of the others. They are bound to follow the main stream to the left. Those who don't still won't find us.'

Hallo, Roger thought. He pictured the conversation he would be having later with Jean and permitted himself the faintest smile of satisfaction.

'Take that silly look off your face and get punting,' Fiona snapped at him.

Roger decided, as he strained against the slippery pole from which river water and the occasional piece of weed was now cascading non-stop on to his white flannels, that Fiona Fox-Bronzing was quite the most delicious girl he had ever met. Having administered the verbal lash with moderately satisfactory results, she was now leaning back in the cushions, trailing her fingers through the water and smiling gently at some secret joke, like a girl in a scent advertisement.

The tough, bossy side of her nature which revealed itself from time to time and which seemed at odds with her gentle, placid appearance had rather thrown him off-balance at first. On the other hand, determination was a characteristic that he found by no means unattractive in a woman. On the contrary. He liked a bit of edge, a hint of fire.

'Now, it should be along here somewhere,' Fiona was saying, peering closely at the bank of her left. 'I nearly always manage to miss it. Oh no. Here it is. Take a sharp right here.'

'Here?' said Roger, staring in amazement at the impenetrable tangle of bushes and low-hanging trees that lined the river bank.

'Hang on a sec,' said Fiona. She walked to the far end of the punt, seized a particularly densely leaved branch and raised it high above her head. 'Go now.'

Roger eased the punt forward, crouched down as the branch passed over him, then stood up again to discover that they were now in some tiny tributary of the main channel, completely hidden from view by the branch. On either side of them the banks were overladen with tall grasses and Ladies' Lace, white daisies and purple columbine.

'How absolutely amazing,' said Roger.

'Do you like it?' said Fiona.

'It's lovely.'

'I often come here when I want to get away from that stuffy old house and George's stuffy old friends.'

'I don't think the house is stuffy,' Roger said eagerly.

'You don't have to live there.'

'No, I suppose not.'

'Nor are you married to someone who is forty-five years older than yourself.'

'No.' said Roger.

A ring dove purred in a nearby tree. A bumble bee, bored with sucking on wild flowers, broke off to circle the punt in a gentlemanly sort of way for a while before returning to his duties on a large cornflower. Away in the distance, the bellringers were hard at work in the grey coolness of Toughingham St Peter parish church.

Fiona sat there for a while looking at him solemnly, as though he were someone who had applied for a job and she were assessing his worth. Suddenly she seemed to come to an important decision, for she shifted her position in the cushions, took off her hat, ran her fingers through her hair, gave a toss of her head, and said,

'When I married George last year, I did so knowing very well that our sex life would almost certainly be fairly thinly spread, and very possibly non-existent. I didn't mind. I was very fond of him. He had been very kind to me after I had been through a rough patch, and I had rather gone off all that sort of thing anyway. As it turned out, there had never been the slightest question of our being man and wife in the physical sense. George had been blown up by a shell in North Africa in 1942 and that was the end of that. We had a long talk about it the night before the wedding. George said that if I wanted to go off and have things on the side he wouldn't mind, as long as he did not know about them. He was very sweet about it. Then earlier this year Fergus, his son from his first marriage, was killed in a car accident. He's more or less got over it now. The only trouble is, he has got it into his head that he must produce another heir before he dies.'

'But I thought you said . . .'

'I know I did. But he went to see some quack in London who charged him an absolute fortune and told him that if he put his mind to it, it might be on.'

'And is it?'

'Of course it isn't. I tell you, when I saw how excited and happy he was when he came back from London that day, I could cheerfully have killed that bloody man. What he could have hoped to gain by telling George such a thing, I cannot imagine.'

'More money?'

'I suppose so. Anyway, he's been putting his mind to it every night since. I go along with it, pretend everything's going to be all right, tell him not to worry and so on. What else can I do? It's the only serious bit of acting I've done since leaving drama school.'

'But surely he must know?'

'Deep down I suppose he must. But he's so obsessed by the idea of producing another son that he has actually persuaded himself that the doctor was right. If I told him tomorrow I was pregnant, I am sure he would believe it was he who had done it.'

'What a tragic story,' said Roger, genuinely moved in a detached sort of way. 'I don't see how I can help though.'

'I think you can,' said Fiona.

'How?' said Roger.

'I should have thought it was obvious.'

The full significance of what Fiona was suggesting suddenly struck Roger.

'You're surely not suggesting that I . . . that we . . . I mean, it's not possible. That's to say, it *is* possible, I suppose. But all the same . . .'

'Mmm,' said Fiona. 'Are the rest of your family as indecisive as you?'

'I don't know what you mean,' said Roger. 'My father was a doctor and my mother was a staff nurse – when she met my father, that is. Though I don't quite see . . .'

'Oh well,' said Fiona with a sigh. 'I suppose one can't expect everything. With a bit of luck he may take after them.'

'Now look here . . .'

'I realise you're not getting on very well at the moment. That's because you haven't quite sorted out what it is you want in life. On the other hand, you have talent. I looked up some of your pieces when I heard you were coming. In fact I looked up everyone's work. My God, that Powell-Brett's an affected writer, isn't he? Basically queer, of course. Dick is just a boring hack. Reg is fundamentally illiterate. No, I was quite impressed with your stuff. If you'd only put your mind to it and find some definite line of your own, you could do very well indeed. I'd rather like him to have a father who was a writer. Who knows, he might take after you. Actually, though, the real reason I have picked on you is that you look very like George did at your age. He was very handsome.'

116

There was genuine affection in the smile she gave him, but Roger was not in the mood to notice such fine details. How often he had dreamed of such a situation. Of being on a travel writers' trip in some wildly romantic spot, and suddenly realising that the prettiest girl in the party had all the time been fancying him every bit as much as he had been fancying her. And suddenly here it was – the fickle finger of fate was pointing unequivocally in his direction, demanding instant action.

'Well?' said Fiona. 'What do you say?'

'Well,' said Roger, 'now this is something that needs thinking about. I mean, it's not the sort of thing one goes rushing into just like that. When would you need to know exactly?'

'In about a minute and a half?' said Fiona.

'I see. And when exactly would you like the thing itself . . . you know . . . to . . . thing?'

'Now's as good a time as any.'

'You mean right here and now? Out in the open?' Roger's heart was beating so hard and so fast that he wondered for a moment if for the first time in his life he was going to faint.

'Can you suggest a better place?' Fiona asked him.

Roger admitted that he couldn't.

'What nicer place for a child to be conceived than out in the fresh air, on a warm summer's evening, surrounded by birds and bees and wild flowers, with the sound of church bells in the distance across the meadows? So Christian and healthy and natural.'

Roger said, 'I agree, it's a very nice part of the world. But what if someone comes?'

'That's the object of the exercise,' said Fiona.

'I beg your pardon?' said Roger. She sighed.

'No one ever has before.'

'What do you mean before?'

'Whenever I've been here with Teddy.'

'Teddy?'

'Teddy Holt. You know. The valet.'

117

'You mean he . . . and you . . .?'

'Yes,' she said simply. 'We knew each other years ago at drama school and had a bit of a thing then – nothing very serious. It was only after I married that I discovered he was George's godson. He came to stay one weekend and told us he was out of work, and George suggested he might like to earn a little pin money as a valet until another job came along. We found we still liked each other and, well, we just sort of carried on where we had left off. It's very nice. We're more like brother and sister really than lovers.'

'Why don't you ask him to be the father of George's son?'

'What, and have him grow up and want to go on the stage? No fear. No, I think you're definitely the one. Now come on. Let's get on with it. It's turning chilly, and the Dishforths are due in an hour.'

Fiona stood up and began to undo the buttons at the back of her frock. Roger stared at her, unable to move, as if in a dream. His brain was ready for action, but he knew, beyond all doubt, that his body was not, and, more importantly, could not. Psychological shock probably. Sort of thing that could happen to anyone. Thrown at you like that. Put you right off. Problem was, should he say something straightaway, put it off till later, give himself a chance to work up to it? Or press ahead and hope for the best? Trouble was, if it didn't work, what then? Would he be offered a second crack at the title? Either way was bound to be a tester. Got to do something quickly before she gets her dress off. Mustn't humiliate her. He clapped both hands to his forehead and fell to his knees in the duckboards.

'What's the matter?'

'Damn and blast,' he muttered. 'Would you believe it? Bloody migraine. Haven't had one for months, and it has to choose now to come on. Probably the cheese at lunch.'

He peered through his open fingers. Fiona was quickly buttoning her frock.

'What's cheese got to do with it?' she asked, clearly worried.

'Cheese, chocolate, coffee. Anything can set it off. You never know. It just comes over you without any warning.'

'Oh, Poor you,' said Fiona. 'Is there anything I can do?'

'No no, honestly; I'll be all right,' said Roger. 'If I can just lie down for half an hour or so in a darkened room, it'll probably pass off.'

'Will you be able to punt back to the boathouse?'

'I'll try.'

'We'd better go then.'

'I suppose so.'

'Try again another day.'

'I hope so.'

'So do I.'

As they rounded the bend in the river, they quickly became aware that something was going on by the boathouse that shouldn't have been. There were at least two people, possibly three, in the water. Some others were on the landing stage, gesticulating and pointing and holding out a boat hook. One of them threw a lifebelt into the water. There was a great deal of shouting.

'Whatever's going on?' asked Fiona.

'Can't really see properly,' said Roger faintly, his face screwed up as if in pain.

'Don't say someone's managed to sink one of the punts. George will be furious. They take days to get out.'

As they came nearer, two of the people in the water began to swim in a strange jerky fashion towards the landing stage.

'They seem to be dragging something,' said Roger.

'Or someone.'

'My God.'

Now two people were scrambling out of the river, helped by the others, who in turn were hauling out a heavy, awkwardly shaped object which they carried along the landing stage and laid gently on the grass. Roger leaned on the pole with all his strength and the punt shot forward.

As they arrived at the landing stage, half a dozen people

were standing or kneeling in a semi-circle peering at a dark shape that lay on the grass.

'What's going on?' Fiona shouted out. 'What's happened?'

The group turned and stared at them in silence. Roger leapt from the punt and ran along the landing stage and on to the grass. As though at a given signal, the group stepped back to reveal, lying on its back, staring sightlessly at the pale blue sky, the sodden, inert body of Reg Henshawe.

14

The English are unique among the nations of the earth inasmuch as they are the only people who never seem to know when the weather has got the better of them. And at no time are they more indomitable than at the end of a warm day in early summer when, despite the fact that the sun has dropped behind the trees, and a light, cool breeze has got up, and the temperature has dropped to below fifty-five, they still insist on serving drinks outdoors in the garden.

Indeed, had anyone at half-past six on that Saturday in May so much as suggested to Sir George Fox-Bronzing that it was turning a little chilly and perhaps it might be a good thing if they moved indoors, he would almost certainly not have had the faintest idea what they were talking about. Not that anyone present would ever have dreamt of saying anything. Their noses might have been turning blue and their goose-pimples might have started clustering together for warmth, but the fact remained that in the summer in England, wherever possible, and providing of course that it was not actually raining and snow was not lying an inch deep on the ground, drinks took place out of doors.

Roger took a mouthful of whisky and soda from a heavy cut-glass tumbler and congratulated himself on having had the foresight to slip on a vest at the last moment. Maitland, on the other hand, in whose direction he had begun to move, had far too much on his mind to worry about tiny details like the weather.

'Funny this American chap hasn't turned up yet,' said Roger. 'He surely can't still be stuck in the traffic.'

'No, he isn't,' snapped Maitland. 'He's stuck in bloody Copenhagen, that's where he is. Or possibly Amsterdam. His bureau chief wasn't quite sure.'

'But I thought you said he was staying in the Centurion Hotel?'

'He was, and the last time I spoke to him, which was yesterday evening, he was about to get on the phone to hire a car to come down here. However, by nine o'clock he was on his way to London Airport, and by midnight was installed in an equally luxurious suite in a hotel in Copenhagen.'

'Or Amsterdam.'

'Or Amsterdam.'

'Well, is he coming or isn't he?' said Roger, who could see an excellent opportunity for acquiring an entrée into the American magazine market rapidly disappearing down the plughole.

'God knows,' sighed Maitland, irritably scratching his head. 'The bureau chief thinks he might be finished with his assignment by late this afternoon. In which case, he could well be back in London by the middle of this evening. If he got his skates on he could probably just make the eleven o'clock train to Norwich and be here by two, half-past two. Even if he didn't get here till tomorrow morning, it would still be worth it. He could cover matins at Toughingham St Peter, drinks before lunch, lunch itself. We don't expect to be leaving much before four-thirty, so that would give him plenty of time to pick up all the background stuff, interviews, atmosphere and so on he needed. I'm wondering if it's worth having a helicopter laid on at London Airport.'

'That'll cost you a bit,' said Roger.

'Peanuts compared with the amount of money a paragraph in *World* could bring in. You've got to think big if you want to be big. That's why you'll always be essentially a small man.'

'I have my successes,' Roger murmured.

'Oh, by the way, that reminds me,' Maitland said.

'How's it going with . . . you know?' He nudged Roger in the ribs and chuckled suggestively.

He had fully intended, in the event of Maitland raising the subject, to say nothing. However, the prospect of putting his flatmate in his place proved irresistible. He tapped the side of his nose and winked, a gesture that he had never made in his life before, and murmured, 'We're just good friends.'

'You dirty beast,' said Maitland and laughed in a knowing way. But Roger knew that really he was quite angry.

At six-thirty on the dot the Dishforths arrived with a friend named Kitty McArdle, a small, grey, wiry spinster with sharp features and a brisk, rather masculine voice, like a Jack Russell terrier.

Sir Francis and Lady Dishforth were an unexpected couple, who looked as though they might have done some modelling in their time for saucy seaside postcards.

Sir Francis was quite the shortest man Roger had ever seen. He had a round, red face to which a permanent smile was attached, and a little round head to which a toupee was attached – though without a great show of conviction. His wife was a ferociously ugly woman with small piggy eyes, a jaw of palaeolithic proportions, huge, square teeth, set apart like tombstones in a graveyard, and a body like a badly stuffed settee, beneath which her husband sheltered like a man caught unawares by bad weather on Shap Fell. Her name was Betty, or at least it was to Sir George, Fiona and Mrs Venables. To the rest of the party she quickly became known as Grendel's Mother.

Introductions were made, drinks were handed round by the eagle-eyed Hedges (Roger fancied he must have specialised in designing very tall buildings before the axe fell and he was reduced to servitude), hands and arms were rubbed to maintain the circulation, and cocktail chit-chat was entered into.

No, Jean didn't know this part of the world well. In fact this was her first visit. Sir Francis said how interesting that was and wanted to know what part of the country she did come from in that case. His interest upon learning that she came from Surrey was even greater than the interest he had expressed about her not coming from Norfolk. However, it was nothing compared with the fascination he experienced upon learning that Cyril Dick not only lived in Norwich, but actually worked there on the *Norwich Mercury*. In fact, so fascinated was he by this astounding revelation, that he called Grendel's Mother over in order that she should be able to share in the good news.

Five minutes passed. Glasses were re-furbished ('Oh, just a small one for me. I've got to drive. It wouldn't do for a magistrate to fail the breathalyser test, what? Ha, ha'), partners were changed, and identical chit-chat resumed.

No, Lady Dishforth didn't know the Botham-Whettams actually. Where did they live actually? Oh, did they? No, she really didn't know that part of Norfolk at all well. Did Mrs Veal know Norfolk well? Only the area round the Botham-Whettams? How interesting.

Nor were the proceedings made any less surreal by the ubiquitous presence of Brian and Keith who, they explained to Roger when he asked them at one point why they were lying on their backs on the ground filming, were trying to get a Fellini feeling into the picture.

Gradually the light faded. The sky above Toughingham St Peter turned pink, then mauve, then dark brown, then finally dark blue. The figures on the South Terrace, backlit by the lights of the Great Dining Room, began to look increasingly like players in some modern-dress masque as they moved and gestured and conversed against the dark walls and bright windows of the great house.

Anyone coming unexpectedly upon the scene at that moment might have been forgiven for supposing he had stumbled into Wonderland. Certainly that was what the man who now rounded the corner of the house believed.

'What ho, lads,' he shouted at the top of his voice while still a good hundred yards away. 'Don't drink it all before I get there.'

'Oh no!' groaned Mrs Venables.

'I can't bear it,' wailed Fiona.

'Damn the fellow,' muttered Sir George.

'Who on earth's that?' exclaimed Grendel's Mother.

'He's another of our house guests,' said Sir George. 'Mr Henshawe. He's been . . . er . . . resting. He hasn't been very well.'

'So I see,' said Sir Francis.

'He's very pleasant when you get to know him,' Sir George told his old friend. 'Amusing sort of chap. Hallo, Mr Henshawe!'

As Reg approached the lights of the terrace, it could be seen that he was dressed in pyjamas and dressing gown, and had an old-fashioned sleeping cap on his head. It was also clear that somewhere between his bedroom and the terrace he had come into contact with a bottle of something.

'What ho, what ho,' Reg shouted yet again. Then he raised his arms, like a Druid at an eisteddfod and, at the top of his voice, sang the whole of the first verse of 'I Dwelt I Dreamt in Marble Halls'. Very slowly.

'Come along, come along,' said Sir George in a kindly way. 'I'm so glad you're feeling better. I don't believe you've met Francis and Elizabeth Dishforth. And this is a friend of theirs, Miss McArdle.'

Reg bowed low over the ladies' hands and intoned over Kitty McArdle's,

Beg your pardle, Mrs McArdle.

There's a kitting in your gardle;

Eating of a mutting bone.

'How do you do?' said Kitty McArdle politely and rather slowly, as though humouring a lunatic.

If Sir George was angry or embarrassed by this unexpected intrusion into what had hitherto been one of the more successful events of the weekend, he showed no sign of it. Indeed, to the Dishforths, who could have had little idea, even from this bizarre interlude, how sorely their old friend had been tried over the previous twenty-four hours, it must have appeared that Reg Henshawe was some much-loved, somewhat eccentric friend from his youth, to judge from the way Sir George received him and made him welcome.

'A pity you didn't finish the job off properly,' Roger said to Jean under his breath.

'Jackie would have done, too, if I hadn't stopped her. She held him under for well over a minute. He couldn't have held his breath for more than half of that. He was far too drunk.'

'I still don't understand how he came to be in the water in the first place.'

'He was sitting next to Jackie on the cushion at the time. I was paddling. Everything was fine. Then suddenly he said something about getting a leg over, made a grab for Jackie's bosom. Whereupon she threw him out of the boat.'

'Just like that?'

'Just like that. She's very strong, and goes in for judo and so on. That's why I had such difficulty getting her to let go of him once she'd got his head under the water. Anyway, in the end she came to her senses, which is more than he did. And then we both jumped in and started to pull him out. Which was when you arrived on the scene.'

'I thought at first he was dead. So did Fiona.'

'So did we. It must have given him the shock of his life when he came to to find Jeremy Powell-Brett giving him the kiss of life.'

'He probably thought he was dead and that this was his version of hell.'

'He was as merry as a grig when we put him to bed and the doctor said he'd be up and about by the morning. Even so, the last thing I expected was to see him up this evening. He must have a terrific constitution.'

'Alcohol is a great healer,' said Roger.

'So is sex,' said Jean.

'What?'

'You've forgotten, haven't you?'

'Forgotten what? Oh, damn. Yes. I'm afraid I have. I'll do it straightaway.'

126

'It's the least you can do for me.'

'All right, all right. I will. I promise you. Don't go on about it. I'm sorry I forgot. I'll do what I can. Satisfied?'

'Hope to be.'

'I don't know what it is about this place, but it seems to have turned everyone into sex maniacs: you, Fiona, Reg. Reg! My God, I'd almost forgotten. If he gets a few drinks inside him, he's bound to start blabbing to someone. And if Sir George gets to hear about that . . .'

'What *are* you gibbering about?' said Jean. 'What about Reg?'

'Mrs Venables.'

'What's Mrs Venables got to do with Reg?'

'He's been getting his leg over her, according to Jackie.'

'Reg? Over Mrs Venables?'

'According to Jackie. I assume that's why she chucked him out of the punt.'

'I assumed she didn't care to have her bosom handled in that off-hand way and decided he needed cooling off. But why should the fact of Reg getting his leg over Mrs Venables concern Jackie?'

'Because Jackie's deeply in love with Reg. Haven't you been following *anything* that's going on?'

'Apparently not. And anyway, the more I think about it, the more unlikely it seems. He hasn't, as far as I am aware, cast a single look in Mrs V's direction all day.'

'Of course not. Reg is very old-fashioned about these things. Apart from anything else he has this great respect for Sir George. He was telling me about it at lunchtime. On the other hand, of course, if he goes and gets tight there's no knowing what he'll do. We're not exactly in the Fox-Bronzings' best books as it is, you know.'

'It wouldn't surprise me in the least.'

'I feel I have a certain responsibility towards the family, an affection even, and I think they have a certain regard and respect for me, and I'm damned if I'm going to allow Reg Henshawe or anyone else to jeopardise what might one day turn into a real friendship.'

'I say,' said Jean quietly, 'You really have got it badly for her, haven't you?'

'I don't know what you mean,' said Roger.

Nothing, but nothing, is guaranteed to put the kiss of death on a smart drinks party on the terrace of a beautiful country house on an early summer's eve than the presence of one guest who has had too much to drink. True, Reg Henshawe was but mildly merry when he appeared like Marley's Ghost out of the dusk shortly after six forty-five. Half an hour and six large gins and tonic later, however, he was very drunk indeed, and death was definitely beginning to purse its chilly lips.

'I simply must show you my roses before you go,' Sir George called out to his friends in accents of jollity so forced that they seemed to have been squeezed from a tube. 'You may not actually be able to see them, but you will certainly be able to smell them.'

Several people laughed, more out of relief than at the quality of the joke, and gratefully scurried after Sir George as he led the way down the steps of the terrace and across the grass like some aged, cigar-smoking Pied Piper. The few who remained behind – Jean, Jeremy Powell-Brett, Jackie – at once made a beeline for the French windows at the back of the terrace and the reviving warmth of the Long Library.

'There's nothing that captures the essence of the English countryside in summer better than the rose, I always think, don't you?' remarked Grendel's Mother as the party made its way briskly across the dewy grass.

'Hear hear,' Reg's cheerful voice boomed out of the gloom.

By the time they arrived at the rose garden, the twilight had very nearly gone.

'What a pity,' said Francis Dishforth.

'The scent makes up for what the eye cannot see,' said Roger.

'I agree,' barked Kitty McArdle.

'Me too,' said Reg.

'Tell you what I could do,' suggested Sir George. 'I could go and turn on the lights of the summerhouse. It's not the perfect solution, but it's always rather charming anyway.'

'Oh do. What a good idea. I love summerhouses. Oh yes, do,' several voices exclaimed in unison.

The group moved silently across the grass towards the ghostly white shape on the far side of the rose garden.

'Think you might manage to get something here, Bri?' said Keith.

'Should do,' said Brian.

They all stood expectantly in a semi-circle staring at the glass façade of the little building, while Sir George slipped round to the side door, opened it, stuck his hand through and switched on all the lights.

Eight simultaneous gasps greeted this dramatic gesture. The interior of the summerhouse was utterly enchanting. Around the white wooden walls were little baskets containing all manner of hanging plants. Several more, larger baskets of flowers hung from the ceiling. Ranged along the white shelves at the back of the room were books, white china figures of animals and birds and large art deco figures of dancers and skaters. To the right was a white table on wheels with drinks and glasses on it; to the left, another with an old gramophone and a pile of seventy-eight r.p.m. records. Ranged about the room were a number of white wicker armchairs with pale striped cushions, with holes in the arms for resting drinks in.

But it was not the decor that had produced the gasps of wonderment, nor the hanging plants, nor yet the white wicker furniture. It was the sight of Cyril Dick and Barbara Black lying on the floor, their pale, naked bodies locked together as though in mortal combat, their staring agonized faces, white and motionless as death.

'You know,' said Brian, as he pressed the trigger on his camera, 'it's almost got a Bunuel feel to it.'

*

As the Dishforths clambered into their Bentley, watched from the front steps by their host and a handful of guests, a figure hurried out of the darkness, leant through the open window and pressed something into Sir Francis's hand. The figure then walked slowly across the gravel and up the steps. It was Maitland.

'What was that you pushed into Francis's hand just then?' Sir George asked him as they walked together across the hall.

'Oh, you know,' said Maitland. 'Just a little something to show there were no hard feelings and to say thank you for coming.'

'Do you mean to say,' said Sir George, 'that to add insult to injury you actually offered my friends money?'

'Yes.'

'Naturally they did not accept.'

'Of course they did,' said Maitland. 'I know of very few people who'll turn down a hundred quid in cash these days.'

15

'Well?'

She came through the door with all the elegance and grace of a water buffalo and stood there, hands on hips, snorting gently, her head thrust forward as though making up her mind whether or not to charge.

Roger, who had enough on his plate at that moment with a recalcitrant velvet bow tie and an angry little pimple that had decided to put in a last-minute appearance on the side of his nose, spun round from the valuable eighteenth-century gilt mirror into which he had been peering despairingly for the previous ten minutes and stood there swaying slightly like a Scots pine in the face of a brisk nor'easter.

'What?'

'I said, "Well?"'

She marched forward into the room, where she took up a commanding position between the bed and the fireplace.

'You've dressed, I see,' said Roger, gesturing towards her simple black dress with thin shoulder straps that crossed over in the middle of her back.

'It's not an unknown habit prior to going down to dinner,' said Jean, who was clearly in no mood for idle chit-chat.

'And done your hair differently,' continued Roger. 'I like it up like that. Shows off your shoulders. You have very good shoulders. Did you know?'

'Stop gabbling and answer my question,' she snapped. 'Your future as a freelance contributor to my page is already very much in question. I wouldn't like to be the one responsible for snatching the last few meagre crusts from your mouth. Now then, have you or have you not spread the glad tidings of my inordinate affection for the man Maitland?'

Roger was not a stupid man, nor was he entirely lacking in a sense of humour. Had he been so, he would not, he was constantly reassuring himself, be where he was today. However, he suffered, and had always suffered since early childhood, from an inability to tell when someone was pulling his leg and when they were being serious. He looked at Jean who was standing drumming her fingers against the bedpost and decided one can never be too sure of anything once lust has reared its ugly head.

'Have I spoken to Maitland?' he repeated. 'Yes, I have.'

'And?'

'And . . . he . . . well . . . likes you.'

'Worships and adores, I think, are the words you are searching for.'

'It's difficult to tell,' Roger said with a shrug. 'Such words have never been known to cross his lips. Being a strong, silent, masterful type, he'd think all that sort of stuff is rather wet.'

'Rather wet?' Jean screwed her face up in disbelief. 'Rather wet? Anyone would think he was being made to wear pink woolly slippers in the dorm the way you talk. I've said it before and I'll say it again: private education retards people by at least ten years. Rather wet!'

'What I mean is, Maitland is not the sort of man who easily expresses his emotions.'

'I'm not interested in his emotions,' she retorted, 'It's his body I'm after. Does he or does he not see me sexually?'

'He doesn't see you at all at the moment,' Roger told her. 'Mainly because his only real concern at present is whether or not this American fellow from *World* magazine is going to turn up and if so when, but also because you spend most of your time lurking about in darkened rooms, talking about it all, instead of getting out there and finding out for yourself. Whatever else you may say about Barbara Black and Spotty, at least they do get on with it.'

Jean threw herself into an armchair by the fire, took a cigarette from a small mother-of-pearl case and lit up. Her hands, Roger noticed, were shaking.

'I suppose so,' she sighed. 'Oh Roger, why am I so hopeless at organising my own life? I'm forever handing out advice to others, but when it comes to making decisions for myself, I am either reduced to a quivering jellyfish, or else, if I do decide on someone, nine times out of ten he's a complete flop. If only you had kissed me that night after the cinema as I wanted you to, instead of rabbiting on about where we were going to eat, our worries might be over by now, and we'd be sitting in a little cottage in the country, surrounded by sheep and dogs and children, living off the land, reading Jane Austen to each other by the light of a flickering oil lamp. . . .'

'And bored to distraction,' said Roger.

'It's true. I'd hate to be away from London and my friends and the people I work with and the photographers, and the printers who get me out of trouble every week, and waking up on Sunday morning and seeing my page. . . .'

'And cursing and swearing and roughing out your letter of resignation.'

'Yes, all that. And seeing you, and gossiping about everybody and everything, and occasionally going on ridiculous junkets like this, and worrying myself sick over some handsome brute who doesn't give a damn for anyone or anything and hasn't an ounce of humour in him, and would almost certainly bore me to death within minutes of our first outing . . . I hate it and I love it. I want to chuck it all up now and settle down with a perfectly ordinary little man who loves me and makes me laugh and doesn't give a damn about reputation or money or being talked about or being recognised in the street or being asked to go on 'Nationwide'. And at the same time, I am still sufficiently excited after fifteen years by the rush and the talk and the fun and the drama of the newspaper world to want to carry on. It's pitiful really, isn't it?'

'Not really,' said Roger. 'At least you have a job and a

133

title and money every week and expenses. And when people ask you what you do, you can tell them. Just look at me. Thirty-four years old, scratching around on the fringes of Fleet Street, picking up the odd article here and there, and being paid a good deal less for it than a man who goes out every morning cleaning windows. I have no position, no influence, no guarantees, and not much prospect of getting any of them.'

'At least you've got your freedom. You can do what you want when you want.'

'And a fat lot of good it does me, too,' said Roger. 'My love life's in an even more hopeless state than yours.'

'That's true,' Jean nodded glumly. 'I suppose we could always stage a sensational double suicide on the bed. Then in years to come, when whoever lives in the house is showing people round and they come into this room, he will be able to tell them the tragic tale of two great friends who loved life too much to be able to go on living it.'

She stubbed out half her cigarette in a white porcelain ashtray.

'Talking about future generations at Hatching Park,' said Roger returning to the mirror to do battle with his tie, 'reminds me that before we start planning this dramatic gesture, I have a rather unusual duty to perform, and I'd value any views you might have on the subject. Curse this tie to hell. Why will it keep twisting in that maddening way?'

'Try getting the first knot round the other way,' suggested Jean.

'Don't be ridiculous,' Roger said promptly. 'How can I . . . look . . . oh, I see what you mean. How did you know that?'

'I told you, I'm always going out with hopeless men. What is this unusual duty?'

'You're not going to believe this,' began Roger.
She didn't.
'I mean it's positively bestial.'
'Eh?'

134

'I don't mean bestial. What I mean is, she obviously thinks of you in terms of a prize bull. Actually, now I come to look at you, you do have a slightly bovine look about you. Have you ever been called upon to service anyone in this way before?'

'I think there's a little more to it than that,' Roger said stiffly.

'What, for instance?'

'She could have chosen anyone. A girl in her position must know all sorts of suitable men. But no, she has chosen me. That would suggest to me that she harbours some sort of feelings for me to match my own for her. Now, either you have some constructive suggestions to make or we'll drop the subject and never mention it again.'

'Goodness,' said Jean. 'You sounded just like the Galloping Major for a moment. I don't quite understand what the problem is that requires suggestions.'

'I should have thought that was obvious. What exactly should be my next move? The deed, you understand, has not yet been done. Migraine stopped play. However, I was left in no doubt whatever that the fixture was to be resumed at another time and in another place. But where? And when? Fiona has been with her husband constantly ever since, and has given not the slightest indication that she is even aware of my presence, let alone that sometime between now and four o'clock tomorrow afternoon, I'm supposed to be providing them both with a son and heir.'

'Are you sure you didn't fall asleep in the punt and dream the whole thing?'

'At the time I was convinced I was asleep,' Roger admitted. 'And it ended in that maddeningly frustrating way all those sort of dreams end. But it was real enough. I have a pair of sodden canvas shoes to prove it.'

'The problem as I see it,' said Jean, 'is that the ball is to a large extent in her court. And, in the absence of a bold move from your corner, likely to remain so, if you'll pardon the mixed metaphor.'

'My brain has been working more or less along the same lines,' said Roger. 'During the last two hours, I've run through the gamut of classic bold moves, from notes being passed in folded handkerchiefs to the straightforward, "May I have a word with you in private?" Every single one has a built-in drawback. "May I see that handkerchief, my dear? Anything you may wish to say to my wife, Mr Noakes, you may also say to me. There are no secrets between us." Let's face it, any move I make is going to lose me face.'

'In that case, don't do anything. Wait for her to make the first move.'

'I can't bear it,' grumbled Roger. 'I'm all keyed up to the idea now. I must have a definite answer one way or the other. You've no idea what the suspense is doing to me. I mean, look, I've even started coming out in spots.'

'Right,' said Jean, in the tone of voice that mothers adopt towards their children when the grizzling and the fighting get beyond a joke and bed is the only answer. She clapped her hands together and stood up quickly from the chair. 'I'll tell you exactly what you do. You finish getting dressed and patching up your nose, you take me down to dinner and you wait and see if she makes any move. If she doesn't, you wait until everyone has gone to bed and then you hop along to her room which, as you know, is next door to her husband's. If she boots you out, you can probably take it the deal's no longer on. If not, then you can get on with the dirty deed there and then, and be back and tucked up in bed with an apple and a good book in no time at all. Sir George will be none the wiser, Fiona will have her baby – or not, as the case may be – and one way and another everyone will be satisfied.'

'But what happens if . . .'

'I've no idea,' said Jean impatiently. 'Just as I've no idea what would happen if the roof fell in or you were struck by lightning. You'd get your fingers burnt, I daresay. Now have you finished with that piece of minor surgery?'

'Won't be a tick,' said Roger, bringing another tissue into play.

'You already are,' said Jean. 'I'm going on down. See you shortly.'

No sooner had Jean swept out of the room than Edward appeared in the doorway. He smiled in a decidedly sly sort of way and coughed lightly.

'Was there anything you wanted?' he said.

Was it Roger's imagination, or was there more to the question than met the ear?

'What do you mean exactly?' Roger asked him warily.

'I mean,' said Edward, 'is there anything you'd particularly like me to do for you?'

There was no doubt he had placed just that little bit too much emphasis on the word 'me' than was natural. Obviously he knew. Fiona must have told him. It wasn't all that surprising. After all, she had said they were like brother and sister. The thing was, should he, Roger, make it clear to him, Edward, that he knew that he knew?

'What exactly did you have in mind?' He gave him a knowing sort of look, to which Edward reacted with a completely straight face.

'I mean,' he said, looking slightly puzzled, 'would you like me to press your trousers, or clean your shoes, or anything?'

'Make me look my best, in other words?' He smiled and nodded encouragingly.

'I'm sorry?'

'For this evening. You know . . . later.'

'Later?'

'After dinner.'

'I understood you were all playing mah-jong after dinner.'

'But not all night.'

'That's up to you.'

Again, the hint of slyness, a slight emphasis on the word 'you'.

'It's up to both of us,' said Roger with the hint of a wink.

'Now look here,' said Edward angrily. 'I don't know

what you're suggesting, but whatever it is, you can start looking somewhere else for your fun and games.'

He marched across to the bed and started to turn back the sheets. Roger, astonished by this sudden and unexpected outburst, moved towards him.

'But why?' he said, his voice registering deep disappointment.

Edward straightened up smartly and backed away.

'Keep away from me,' he said, his eyes narrowing dangerously.

'I don't understand,' insisted Roger. 'Why this sudden change of heart? I thought it was all more or less understood . . .'

Edward reached behind him and seized the first object that came to hand which happened to be the box of biscuits and brandished it above his head.

'Never mind what you understand or didn't understand,' he shouted, waving the biscuit box in a threatening way. 'Just you stick to your own sort, that's all. Don't start trying to involve other people in something they don't understand.'

'I like that,' said Roger hotly. '*Me* trying to involve people in things *they* don't understand. Look, I'm sorry if you feel so strongly about it. You've every right to be angry. But really, it was never my idea in the first place.'

'I see,' said Edward, 'I suppose it was mine, was it?'

Roger stared at him.

'Yours?'

He stepped forward again, meaning to . . . he wasn't quite sure what. Calm the fellow down? Take the biscuit box away from him? Whatever his motive, the move was a mistake, Edward's arm swung quickly back and by the time it came forward again, the biscuit tin was no longer in it. Roger ducked just in time to see the box fly over his head and smash into the eighteenth-century gilt mirror, scattering fragments of glass and Marie biscuits all over the eighteenth-century carpet.

At that moment, somewhere below, someone began playing a Beethoven sonata.

16

Roger tip-toed out on to the landing and peered over the banisters into the lighted hall. Seated at the grand piano, wearing a dark green velvet smoking-jacket, large black silk bow tie, black trousers and monogrammed slippers, was Sir George Fox-Bronzing, head thrown back, eyes closed, fingers moving lightly over the keyboard, lost in the music. Beside him, on the piano, a recently lit Romeo y Julieta was burning gently in a heavy glass ashtray.

Roger surveyed this pleasant scene of English country house life, cursed softly under his breath, and drew the handkerchief full of broken antique glass further beneath his double-breasted dinner jacket.

It had been his plan to slip out into the garden and bury the incriminating fragments in a convenient flower bed. Now he would have to think again. Or would he?

He began to move swiftly and silently along the landing.

He was between the bottom of the stairs and the front door when Sir George suddenly opened his eyes and, still playing, smiled blissfully at him.

Roger mouthed words to the effect that he was just popping outside for a second, and indicated the door.

'Along the corridor and second on the left,' said Sir George. 'In case you've forgotten.'

Roger made some knowing chuckling noises to indicate that the little joke had been thoroughly appreciated, and a gesture with both hands to show that he did not wish Sir George to stop playing on his account, whereupon the small white bundle, which he had been holding against his side with one elbow, slipped down out of his dinner jacket and fell with a tinkle on to the stone floor. Roger smiled apologetically, snatched the object from the floor and tucked it back inside his jacket. Sir George stopped playing.

'What have you got there?' he asked.

'Oh, it's nothing,' said Roger vaguely.

'It can't be nothing,' insisted Sir George, 'I just saw you pick it up and place it inside your jacket.'

'It's nothing. Really,' Roger maintained. 'Just some old apple cores that needed chucking out. I didn't want to leave them about in my room.'

'Apple cores?' said Sir George, half frowning, half smiling in disbelief.

'Actually, it's not apple cores at all,' said Roger in rather a loud voice as though defying the man to be angry with him. 'It's glass. Broken glass.' He had never been a good liar. 'One of the mirrors in my room got broken by mistake.'

'I didn't imagine you'd do it on purpose,' said Sir George mildly. 'I expect it fell off the wall.'

'As a matter of fact it did,' said Roger, and gave a little laugh.

'I thought it might have done.'

'It seemed to be hanging slightly crookedly, so I went to adjust it slightly . . .'

'And it came away in your hand.'

'Sort of.'

'And so, not unnaturally, you thought to yourself, "Oh no. Not twice in one day. The old man is never going to believe this. I'll nip out and chuck the bits away in the dustbin . . ."'

'I was going to bury them in one of the flower-beds actually,' said Roger, who had decided that he might as well be hung for a lamb as for a goat or whatever the expression was.

'I see,' said Sir George. 'What funny people you journalists are, I must say. Anyone else I know who had met with a similar accident would have come to me and said, "Look here, George" – or "Sir George", depending on how well I knew them – "the thing is, I'm afraid I've made rather a nasty mess of your mirror. I'm so sorry, it was a complete accident. I wonder if you could get your butler to pop upstairs and clear up the broken glass before I go to bed tonight?' I might be mildly irritated for a moment or two. The next day I'd have forgotten all about it. Things have been broken in this house for nearly three hundred years and in the next three hundred I expect a great many more will suffer the same fate. Why, good heavens, if I worried about every mirror and cup and plate and ornament that got broken in this house. I'd be a gibbering idiot by now. The thing is, I suppose you Fleet Street people get so used to dealing in half truths over the years, that in the end it becomes second nature to you. Sad, sad.' He shook his head mournfully and turned once more to the keyboard. He was about to start playing again when he stopped and said:

'That particular mirror is only a cheap imitation anyway. I'm surprised you didn't spot that immediately.'

And he turned back to the keyboard and resumed the Second Movement.

Roger headed glumly for the Long Library where drinks were being served. On the way, he slipped into the lavatory, dropped the contents of the handkerchief into a waste paper basket and adjusted his bow tie in front of the mirror. It was a large room, as lavatories go, with a grey stone floor, a heavy, square wash-basin with big, old-fashioned taps, and an equally heavy lavatory basin with a wooden seat and an overhead cistern from which hung an elegant china handle on a chain. Just inside the door was an ornate, cast-iron stand full of umbrellas and walking sticks. One whole wall was covered with coats and mackintoshes, beneath which were ranged all manner of boots, Wellingtons, heavy walking shoes, tennis shoes and rackets, and golf shoes. There were also two bags of clubs.

Roger had finished brushing his hair and re-arranging his tie, and was just performing some last minute cosmetic surgery on the spot beside his nose, when the door was pushed open. He spun round.

'What the . . .?'

The room was suddenly filled with a brilliant light.

'Don't take any notice of us,' said a flat, south London voice. 'You just carry on as though we weren't here.'

And into the room walked Brian, very slowly, his camera glued to his right eye, followed by Keith holding in one hand a small, powerful arc lamp and in the other a long, tubular microphone which he pointed at Roger over Brian's head.

Roger stood, his back to the mirror, his face frozen in shocked disbelief.

'Cut,' said Brian, taking his eye away from the camera. 'If you could just be combing your hair, or doing something with your tie.'

Roger stared at him.

Keith said: 'Get him to undo his tie and then do it up again.'

'Good idea,' said Brian, stepping forward, his fingers aimed at Roger's throat. Roger recoiled and put his hand over his tie. Brian stopped.

'Well, you do it then,' he said.

'Are you quite sure,' said Roger, 'you wouldn't rather film me going to the lavatory? Sitting down perhaps, with my trousers round my ankles, reading the *Shooting Times*?'

'I think tying your bow tie would be better,' said Brian.

'Or brushing your hair,' said Keith.

'This is unbelievable,' said Roger, pronouncing every syllable of the word very slowly. 'Have you film people no sense of privacy? Is nowhere safe from your prying eyes?'

Brian was clearly hurt.

'There's no need to get shirty with us, mate,' he said in an aggrieved voice. 'We're only doing our job. Mr Maitland asked us to build up a picture of the day in the life of a house party, so what could be more natural than

142

showing someone doing up their bow tie before dinner?'

'In the lavatory?'

'Why not? It's a very nice lavatory. Very homely, with all these boots and coats and what not.'

'Oh really,' said Roger wearily, 'it's hopeless talking to people like you. Where's Maitland?'

Brian looked at Keith, and they both shrugged.

'Right,' said Roger firmly, and pushing his way past them, he strode back along the corridor towards the hall. Sir George was still deep in communion with Beethoven. Ignoring him, Roger headed for the dining room. He was on the point of opening one of the big double doors when the other one swung open and Hahned issued forth. He had changed into an astonishing costume consisting of a red silk jacket with gold braiding, white silk baggy pants, gold lamé shoes with curled-up toes and a dark blue turban topped by a magnificent peacock feather.

'Where's Maitland?' Roger snapped at him.

'Just because I'm dressed like a servant, it doesn't mean you have to address me like one,' he replied. 'I'm only doing this to help out with the filming, you know. I happen to come from a very good family in Abu Dhabi. My father is extremely well-known in banking circles there and—'

'Yes yes,' said Roger impatiently. 'I'm quite sure he is, but we haven't got time to go into all that now. I just wondered if you happened to know—'

'Why haven't you got time to go into it now?' said Hahned, his voice rising slightly. Roger looked round at Sir George, but he was still deep in his music.

'Because we haven't, that's why,' Roger hissed back at him.

'You seem to think that you are in some way better than I am and I should like to know why.'

'Oh for goodness sake.'

'No,' persisted Hahned. 'Go on. I'd like to know. What does your father do, for example?'

'He's dead, since you ask.'

'I'm sorry. What did he do, then?'

'He was a doctor.'

Hahned smiled and nodded. 'My uncle is a doctor,' he announced triumphantly.

'Bully for him,' said Roger. 'Now then, do you know where—?'

'His father was a judge.'

'Fancy.'

'And I am a public relations manager.'

'I am aware of that.'

'Not some bloody black servant, to be kicked about and shouted at and treated all to hell.'

'I quite agree,' said Roger, nodding emphatically.

'Just so long as you remember that. All of you.'

'I'm sure we do.'

'If my parents could see me now, dressed up in these ridiculous clothes, they would die of shame.'

Roger patted him on the shoulder, and looked him straight in his soft brown eye.

'We must all learn to sacrifice our standards on the altar of commerce,' he said quietly.

Hahned nodded sadly.

'Now then,' said Roger. 'Where's Maitland?'

'He's in the kitchen,' said Hahned.

'Right,' said Roger and headed for the door under the stairs.

Halfway along the stone passageway on the left there was a door covered in green baize. Behind it were some stone stairs that led to the kitchens. Roger was on his way down when he encountered Maitland coming up. He was holding a clip-board in one hand and a pencil in the other.

'Hello, laddie,' he said cheerfully. 'Come to see how the other half lives?'

'Look, Maitland,' said Roger, 'I want to talk to you.'

'Sorry, old lad. No time now. We're behind schedule as it is.'

'That is your concern, not mine.'

'Yes,' said Maitland in a distracted way, 'well, I haven't got time to go into all that now. Look, why don't you pop along to the Long Library and wait there patiently like a good boy with the others?'

He started to push past Roger.

'Now look here, Maitland, you may think you can push other people about, but you're not going to try that stuff with me. I've known you for fifteen years, and lived with you for ten. During that time you have behaved pretty bloody badly one way and another. But I would never have believed that anyone could be capable of quite such a bad show of behaviour and manners as you have been since you arrived this morning. On top of which—'

'A bad show?' said Maitland, as though he could not quite trust his ears. 'A bad show? This is the 1980s, laddie, not the 1930s. Despite what I said to you this morning, you still seem to think that all this is some sort of jolly jape that has been specially laid on for your personal entertainment and pleasure. You're still convinced that you are taking part in a novel by Dornford Yates. Noakesy and Co. The fact of the matter is – and I'm not going to say this again – the reason we are all here this weekend – you, me, the Fox-Bronzings, Jean, Hahned, the staff – is to make money. We are here on business, do you understand? Not to lie about and enjoy ourselves and make so-called witty conversation and complain every time some little thing crops up that irritates us or offends our sense of propriety.'

'I'd hardly call being filmed in the lavatory a little thing,' snapped Roger.

'Well, all I can say,' said Maitland, his voice cold and hard, 'is that if you think that's going too far, I hate to think what you'll be saying by the time this evening's over.'

Roger suddenly realized that Maitland, as well as being determined and ruthless, could actually be very frightening when he put his mind to it. He had always suspected there might be a side to his character that was even worse than that to which he had become accustomed. He was only sorry that it was in these surroundings and amongst these people that it had to be revealed.

'What do you mean by that?' said Roger.

'You'll find out soon enough, laddie.'

Maitland continued on up the stairs and out into the passage. Roger pursued him and caught up with him at the door into the hall.

'One more thing, Maitland,' he said, fighting to keep his temper under control.

'Yes?' Maitland turned, still looking as his clip-board.

'As soon as we get back to London, you had better start looking for new accommodation.'

'Don't be silly,' said Maitland with a pitying smile.

'Right,' shouted Roger. 'You've asked for it. First thing Monday morning I shall be on the phone to your managing director. I think he'll be very interested in what I have to tell him.'

'I doubt it.' Maitland was still smiling.

'Oh, I think he will,' said Roger menacingly. 'When I tell him which paper I'm representing.'

'I think not.'

'Really?' said Roger. 'And what exactly makes you think that?'

'As from five o'clock this afternoon,' said Maitland, 'I am the managing director.'

17

Shortly after nine o'clock, the doors of the Long Library opened, and Hedges announced that dinner would now be served.

'About time too,' muttered Jean.

'I'm not so sure about that,' said Roger.

Sir George in gay mood bustled about arranging who should take whose arm. His own he offered to Jean for whom he appeared to have suddenly acquired a particular fondness.

'I do so hope the food hasn't become spoiled as a result of the delay,' he confided in her. 'Mrs Eames and I spent hours over the menu.'

'I'm sure it hasn't,' Jean reassured him.

Roger waited in line behind them, harnessed to the stout figure of Audrey Veal who was not at all pleased at this arbitrary relegation to the second division and was glaring at Jean with undisguised hatred.

Fiona who, to Roger's dismay, had so far that evening failed even to acknowledge his presence, was next in the line with Reg Henshawe.

The remainder of the party were sorting themselves out into pairs when Maitland walked in with Buster Legge and Eddie Fowler, both looking exceedingly uncomfortable in ill-fitting dinner suits.

'These two gentlemen have kindly agreed to swell the numbers at table,' Maitland explained to Sir George.

'Decent of them,' said Sir George, frowning.

'Yes, well, I thought the table needed dressing up a bit. The film people agreed with me that it might have looked a bit on the empty side. We don't want to give our potential clients the impression that our parties are undersubscribed.'

'Nor, I should have thought, that the staff are in the habit of joining us for dinner,' countered Sir George.

'Mr Legge and Mr Fowler are hardly what I'd term staff,' said Maitland in tones of one speaking to a difficult child. 'Mr Legge, after all, is our Transport Director and Mr Fowler is his assistant.'

'How funny,' chipped in Audrey, 'I'd always thought of them as chauffeurs myself.'

'Of course,' Maitland continued, 'this does mean that we now have more men than women. What I suggest is that when we come to the filming, we get a couple of the waitresses to slip off their white aprons and sit in between the men. No one will know the difference.'

'While you're about it,' said Audrey, 'why not get them to take all their clothes off and do a dance on the table?'

'This filming you mention,' said Sir George. 'I hope there's not going to be too much of it.'

'No, no,' Maitland reassured him. 'A couple of shots here and there, you know. Just enough to give an idea of the flavour of the proceedings. You probably won't even know it's happening.'

'I hope you're right,' said Sir George.

The party began to move forward into the Music Salon. From there they proceeded in double slow time into the Robert Adam Saloon, turned sharp left by a Louis XV *escritoire*, exited through the huge double doors into the hall and headed for the matching doors of the Great Dining Room, beyond which stretched a breathtaking vista of highly polished wood, dozens of glasses and vast arrays of silver gleaming and winking in the light of a myriad candles.

'How lovely,' said Roger appreciatively.

'Charming,' said Mrs Venables.

At that moment, as if her words had been a signal, the room was illuminated by a light so bright and so intense that it was as though someone had put a match to several large Roman Candles.

The procession shuffled to a halt.

'Oh, no,' groaned Sir George. 'Not like that.'

He turned to Jean. 'It looks so lovely by candlelight, and now they've gone and ruined the whole thing.'

'It's for the filming, I expect,' she told him.

'Oh damn the filming,' he said. 'There's no point in filming it anyway if it's going to look like that. Mr Maitland, couldn't you tell them to turn those wretched lights off?'

'Sorry, Sir George,' said Maitland, appearing suddenly through the door under the stairs. 'There's nothing we can do about it. You've got to have strong lights for filming, otherwise you won't see a thing.'

'But it's completely ruined the whole effect,' Sir George told him.

'Better that it should look slightly less than perfect than that we shouldn't have it in the film at all,' Maitland argued. 'By the time it gets on to the TV screen, no one will be able to tell the difference. Anyway, I think it looks smashing.'

A general buzz of agreement rose from the ranks.

'Well, what do you want us to do now? Do we go on in, or wait here, or what?' asked Fiona crossly.

'Hang on a tick,' said Maitland, 'I'll just go and check.'

He hurried forward to the doorway and peered in.

'All right, lads?' he called out. 'Ready whenever you are.'

'When I say action,' came Brian's voice from inside the room.

'Roger!' called out Maitland.

'Yes?' said Roger.

'Not you. I was speaking technically.'

'Well, do we go ahead or not?' asked Sir George.

'When you get the signal.'

'You mean, we just walk in as we would do normally and just sit down?'

'That's the idea.'

Maitland stepped back and took up a position against

the wall just to the right of the doorway, out of view of the camera.

'Right,' he said.

The procession began to move forward.

'Hold it, hold it,' yelled Maitland, rushing forward waving his arms. 'I never told you to move.'

'I distinctly heard you say "Right",' Sir George told him.

'The word is "Action",' shouted Maitland, then called out apologetically in the direction of the room, 'Sorry about that, lads.'

'You should have made that clear,' said Sir George.

'I assumed that was something every schoolboy knew,' Maitland said rudely.

'I'm not a schoolboy,' said Sir George.

'All right. Let's try it again,' said Maitland.

After a pause lasting several minutes, Brian called out, 'Sorry, boys and girls. Slight technical hitch at this end. Nothing to worry about.'

'Let's go back to the library,' said Fiona. 'I don't know about anyone else but I wouldn't mind sitting down.'

'I agree,' said her husband.

The party began to move back towards the Robert Adam Saloon.

'Stay where you are,' yelled Maitland. The party froze in its tracks.

'How much longer is all this going to go on?' asked Audrey Veal. 'I'm getting hungry.'

'At this rate,' said Fiona, 'the food won't be worth eating anyway.'

'Any second now,' said Maitland. 'all right, lads?'

'Ready,' said Brian.

'Okay,' said Maitland. 'Back into your places everybody. Now then, on the word "Action".'

'That's looking really nice,' said Brian. 'If you could just close up together a bit . . . that's fine. Okay for sound?'

'Sound running,' said Keith.

'Right,' said Brian. 'And . . . action!'

The procession led by Sir George and Jean Hollings-worth began to advance slowly and suspiciously towards the brilliant light, as though expecting at any moment to be confronted by some extra-terrestrial monster. No one spoke. Someone gave a light cough which was quickly suppressed. The only sound came from the rhythmic tread of feet, as they moved from the soft stone of the hall floor on to the more resonant wooden boards of the dining room. Solemn and unsmiling, they circled the table, shielding their eyes against the almost painfully bright light from the half-dozen film lamps that were ranged around the room.

'Hold it there!'

'Cut!'

'Stop!'

'Hold it!'

They stood there, frozen in the glare, like unwilling guests at a New Year's Eve party who have been talked into playing 'Statues', watched impassively by Hedges, Hahned, Edward and the three girls from the village who had waited at the picnic.

'Sorry,' said Brian, who, it could now be seen, was standing at the far end of the room, one foot firmly planted in the middle of one of Mr Chippendale's better efforts, the other resting lightly on the top of the fireplace which Robert Adam once privately admitted to a friend was as nice a job as he had ever pulled off. 'Sorry, everybody. My fault. Hair at the gate.'

'What does that mean?' asked Sir George.

'Something's got stuck across the place where the film goes through,' Roger told him.

'Oh well. Never mind,' said Sir George. 'I'm sure it's not all that important. Now come along, everybody, let's all sit down and eat. Miss Hollingsworth, I think that's you there, next to me. Mrs Veal, if you'd care to . . .'

'We'll have to go again,' said Brian flatly, shaking his head.

'Go where?'

'He means we'll have to do the scene again,' said

151

Maitland, striding forward from the back of the room. 'Come along now, the quicker we get on with it the sooner we'll be able to eat.'

'But the soup will get cold,' said Audrey looking longingly at the large tureen on the sideboard.

'It's cold soup anyway,' said Maitland crisply. 'Now come along everyone. If you wouldn't mind. Same place, Bri?'

'Might as well take it from the top,' muttered Bri.

'How about if we began the shot as they came into sight in that room on the other side of the hall?' suggested Keith with all the enthusiasm of a cross-channel swimmer about to pitch into the water at Cap Gris-Nez for the return crossing.

'Good idea,' said Bri.

'Okay then. Everyone back into the Adam room,' shouted Maitland, leading the way like an officious tourist guide.

'Oh really!' said Fiona. 'This is too idiotic for words.'

'Don't blame me, love,' Maitland said to her. 'Blame your old man, if you must blame somebody, but don't blame me.'

'Sod off,' said Fiona.

'You always had such a sweet voice, Fiona,' said Maitland in a clipped voice. 'Oh, and that reminds me. Do chat away to each other a bit as you come in. Make it a bit lively. You're supposed to be enjoying yourselves. This is a dinner party, remember? Not a ruddy wake.'

They went through it again, talking gibberish to each other at the tops of their voices, laughing uproariously at nothing, gesturing wildly with their hands and grimacing like mental defectives on a day trip to Bognor, and walking with short, quick, movements, like guests at a Buckingham Palace Garden Party in 1908. In fact the whole effect was that of a very old piece of archive film. Lively it unquestionably was. Unfortunately, Brian was not really striving for a Mack Sennett feel at that stage. It was more 'Nicholas and Alexandra' that he was after.

So of course they had to go back and do it again.

The next time, Brian discovered that he was getting a nasty flare off the magnificent table centrepiece – a statue of St George letting the old dragon have his come-uppance in best quality silver. However, he soon put that to rights by spraying it with something out of an aerosol can.

'That piece happens to be worth several thousand pounds,' Sir George pointed out.

'If this thing gets off the ground,' Maitland reassured him, 'I'll buy you five of them. Now, if we could just try that take once again.'

'That's not the point—' began Sir George, but his protest was drowned by the sound of Maitland clapping his hands together and shouting, 'One more time, everybody. Then I promise you we'll eat.'

If Jean could even bring herself to mention Maitland's name after this little display, thought Roger, I wouldn't write another piece for her silly page if she begged me on bended knee.

They did not eat after the next take, nor after the next, nor after the one after that.

'I'm buggered if I will,' announced Reg Henshawe when they were asked to try it just this one more time, for the sixth time.

'I agree,' said Mrs Venables.

'So do I,' said Mrs Veal.

So did everyone.

'Hard cheese, Maitland,' said Roger gleefully as he took his place between Barbara Black and Audrey at Sir George's end of the table.

'Bloody amateurs,' muttered Maitland, and marched off in the direction of the kitchen.

In front of each place was a small menu in a silver holder. Sir George picked his up, and peered at it over a pair of half moon spectacles.

'I hope you like all these things, my dear,' he said to

Jean. 'Smoked salmon, watercress soup, yes. What's this? *Loup de mer farci?*'

'I'm very partial to a touch of the old stuffed mother's wolf myself,' said Reg, earning himself a laugh from everyone, except his host.

'But I specially ordered sole,' he said. 'Hedges!'

The butler glided across.

'What is this thing here supposed to be?' He pointed a disdainful finger at the offending words.

'I understand it is some variety of Mediterranean fish, sir. Mr Maitland had it specially flown over from Nice this morning.'

'Mr Maitland did? What on earth for?'

'I have no idea, sir. All I know is that it is a very large fish.'

'And what about this lamb *provençal?* I understood we were having duck.'

'So did I, sir, until late this afternoon when this van arrived, and out stepped a man with a small lamb on a piece of string.'

'You mean he was carrying it by the string?'

'No, sir. Leading it.'

'Good God.'

'Oh, the poor little thing,' exclaimed Jean. 'I shan't be able to face a single mouthful now.'

'I'm not sure that I will either,' said Sir George. 'What is going on, Hedges? I turn my back for one moment and suddenly anarchy breaks loose in the kitchen. What with huge fish being flown over from the Riviera, lamb being brought in on the hoof, whatever can we expect next? Purple soup perhaps?'

A shifty look passed across Hedges' face and seemed about to find expression in some sort of dramatic confession. However, the *moment critique* passed, and instead he simply said:

'Shall I serve the wine now, sir?'

'I suppose no one's been tampering with that, have they, Hedges?'

'No sir,' said Hedges.

It was probably his most confident statement of the day so far.

Sir George peered suspiciously at his plate of smoked salmon, but to his relief could find no fault with it. The cold Gewürtztraminer was equally irreproachable. Brian and Keith switched off their lights and stood impassively at the side of the room, watching the proceedings. Servants moved hither and thither, plates were emptied and refilled, glasses drained and refurbished, and before very long the room resounded to the reassuring clatter of family silver against good Staffordshire china and the din of conversation.

Audrey told Sir George about a fish dinner she had eaten recently in La Rochelle. Buster Legge told Fiona about a car journey he had once made from London to Norwich in less than two hours. Barbara Black told Roger that if he'd only shown a fraction of the enthusiasm towards her that Cyril Dick had done, things might have turned out very differently for both of them. And Jean told Jeremy Powell-Brett to take his hand off her leg.

Plates and cutlery were removed and replaced with soup bowls; last mouthfuls of Alsatian wine were swallowed, pale fino sherry appeared as if by magic in people's glasses and cold soup was ladled out.

For a moment it seemed that Brian and Keith might be about to capture the dark curious-tasting liquid on film, but at the last moment Maitland appeared through the door that led to the kitchens and shook his head at them.

Everyone was beginning to enjoy himself at last. The drink flowed, the din of conversation grew ever louder and the shrieks of laughter more frequent.

Audrey Veal told Sir George about the time she had had to demonstrate how to cook a soufflé on 'Nationwide' and someone at the last moment had forgotten to switch on the oven. Jean told Audrey about the time she had had to report on the Paris fashions on 'News at Ten', and at the last moment had forgotten to switch on her microphone.

Jeremy Powell-Brett told Jackie Ericson about the time he had been invited to drinks with Mrs Oscar Hammerstein in Montego Bay. And Jackie told Jeremy about the time she had once done something very uncomfortable to someone who kept feeling her thigh like that.

Roger smiled at Fiona and she smiled back and raised her glass in salute. Reg and Mrs Venables pursed their lips at each other across the table. Audrey told Sir George that he was one of the most attractive men she had ever come across. And Buster told Eddy that he really wasn't such a bad driver after all.

The soup bowls were removed, glasses were filled with a simply delicious Sancerre which Mrs Veal pronounced 'delicately frosty' and Mrs Venables could hardly pronounce at all, and Jackie said that if Jeremy really wanted to put his hand there, she didn't mind really.

Yes, it was, after all, a very amusing and successful evening.

And then the arc lights came on again.

18

It was as though an enormous bowl of ice-cold water had been thrown over the entire company. Conversation came to an abrupt halt. The two most photogenic waitresses hurried to empty seats. Glasses were lowered gently on to the table. Jeremy Powell-Brett removed his hand.

'Oh hell,' muttered Sir George beneath his breath. 'Now what?'

The huge double doors at the far end of the room were flung open and into the room stepped four footmen in velvet knee breeches and powdered wigs holding what looked like a large wooden stretcher upon which lay the largest dead fish Roger had ever laid eyes on outside the Natural History Museum.

It lay there, steaming gently, covered in what looked like burnt grass and twigs, staring balefully with its one opaque eye at the assembled company who stared back at it in utter astonishment as it was carried twice around the table, pursued by Brian with his camera and Keith who held his microphone over the creature as it passed, as if hoping for a last-minute statement before it was consumed for ever. At last the poor thing was laid to rest on a trestle that Hedges had placed in a position which allowed Brian to film the last rites to their best advantage.

Sir George goggled down the table at his wife who goggled back and shrugged her shoulders helplessly.

'I understand,' Sir George announced at last, 'that this fish was flown over from the South of France this morning.'

'Why?' said Reg. 'Couldn't it swim?'

Roars of laughter were followed by a general buzz of conversation; hands were put back round glasses (or in the case of Jeremy Powell-Brett, Jackie's thigh), and an atmosphere of keen anticipation hung over the proceedings as Hedges took a large knife, neatly sliced the fish along its backbone and began to serve up the white flesh in healthy-looking chunks.

Brian recorded the fish's last moments with loving care, then, as though disgusted at his own morbidity, quickly switched off the lights and allowed the sad creature to pass into gastronomic legend by the flickering light of the candles. The two waitresses returned unobtrusively to their more normal duties.

As they ate, Audrey described to Sir George how to make real *bouillabaisse*. Barbara described to Roger how to do a very unusual and sexy thing with a fur coat. Jeremy described to Jackie what he was planning to do to her later that night. And Reg Henshawe described a perfect arc as he toppled slowly off his chair.

A Vosne-Romanée was the next wine to hit their already confused and, to a large extent, anaesthetized palates. Mrs Veal proclaimed the portiness of its nose, while Roger, ever cautious, restricted himself to the description, 'Superb'.

Yes, he decided, this was definitely the life for him. Fine surroundings, good furniture and pictures, a few close friends, first-class food and wine, good conversation.

He pondered briefly on the child he was about to beget that evening – the scion of a noble line that stretched back to the Conquest, and possibly even further than that. What would become of him? Would he, thirty years hence, be sitting where Sir George was now sitting? Or would he be in Roger's place, being entertained handsomely and for nothing by an ex-trades union official, or an ageing Arab sheik with a controlling interest in North Sea Oil. . . .

He sipped at his wine. It really was quite superb.

Then the lights came on again.

The two waitresses scurried to their places and sat there staring straight ahead at each other, pink with embarrassment.

'Oh really,' said Sir George, letting his hands drop onto

the table in a gesture of tired exasperation. 'Are we to have no peace? What possible percentage can there be in photographing a plate of roast lamb?'

He did not have long to wait for his answer.

Once again the big double doors swung back on their massive hinges, and once again through them appeared the four footmen, their arms straining, their knees buckling beneath the weight of an even larger wooden stretcher upon which lay a whole roast lamb. Beside it walked the splendid, dignified figure of Hahned. In one hand he held a ladle which which he basted the creature as he went, with the meat juices in which it lay.

In an atmosphere of stunned silence, the glistening carcass was paraded round the table three times, while Brian recorded every inch of its progress. He filmed it in long shot, in medium shot, in close-up and in extreme close-up. He filmed it from above, from the same level and from below. At one point he became so absorbed in his efforts to find yet more breath-taking angles that he actually leapt on to the dining table and smashed two glasses and a side plate before he felt entirely satisfied that he had got the shot he had in mind.

Sir George beckoned Hedges over. 'Who *are* these men?' he asked him quietly, indicating the footmen.

'I have no idea, sir,' replied Hedges. 'I have never seen them before.'

'But this is the most extraordinary state of affairs I have ever come across in all my life. First, the menu which I agreed three days ago with Mrs Eames has been completely altered without so much as a by-your-leave. Next, we are joined at the table by the two drivers and two of the waitresses. Now I discover that my domestic staff has been enlarged to the tune of four footmen. Where is Mr Maitland?'

'I believe he is in the kitchen, sir.'

'In the kitchen? What on earth is he doing in the kitchen?'

'I understand he is supervising the dessert, sir.'

159

'But that is Mrs Eames' job.'

'So I should have thought, sir.'

'And what does she have to say about all this?'

'Owing to the fact that I have been refused admission to the kitchen since six o'clock this evening, sir, I'm afraid I cannot answer that.'

'Who refused you admission, Hedges?'

'Mr Maitland, sir.'

'But this is an outrage,' exclaimed Sir George. 'Why did you not tell me about this before?'

'I understood you were already *au courant* with tonight's arrangements, sir. I knew you already had a lot on your mind, and I did not wish to make a song and dance about it. I was planning to say something to you about it in the morning.'

'You were quite right so to plan, Hedges,' said Sir George. 'I'm extremely sorry that this should have happened. As you must realise by now, I have not been *au courant* with this evening's arrangements or indeed any other arrangements as I would have liked, ever since Mr Maitland's arrival early this morning. Under normal circumstances, of course, such outrages would never be allowed to occur. Unfortunately, these are not normal circumstances, Hedges. We have been unwise enough to place ourselves in the hands of others, and until tomorrow afternoon, we shall all just have to muddle through as best we can.'

'I quite understand, sir,' said Hedges. 'I once experienced a similar situation over a large building I was helping to design in Newcastle. Will that be all, sir?'

'Yes, thank you, Hedges.'

'Thank you, sir.'

Sir George turned to Jean on his left.

'I say,' he said. 'I hope all this isn't going to come out in your article?'

'You mustn't judge us all by Harold Maitland,' said Roger.

Sir George turned to Audrey.

'And I'm really only interested in the food and wine angle,' she said giving his arm a reassuring pat.

'Tonight's menu is not quite what I had planned, as you will have gathered. However, I trust that what you have eaten so far meets with your approval?'

'I thought the soup was perhaps a little on the bitter side,' she told him. 'The colour was a little unusual, too. I couldn't really see very well in the candlelight but it looked almost purple to me. A strange colour for watercress. However, the fish was superb, and as for that whole baby lamb . . . if it tastes half as good as it looks. Did I ever tell you about the time I was in St Paul-de-Vence . . .?'

But that particular gastronomic adventure was to remain for ever unsung, for at that moment, through the double doors, appeared a man the size and build of a Turkish wrestler, wearing blue check trousers, a white coat, a magnificent pair of moustaches and a chef's bonnet perched at a jaunty angle on the side of his head. Once inside the room he paused briefly, gave a little bow to the room in general and stalked slowly and with enormous dignity towards the motley group of servants who stood respectfully around the lamb like medical students awaiting the arrival of a great surgeon.

'Who the dickens are you?' Sir George asked him as he swept by.

'Ah em der shiff, m'sieur,' he replied, in a deep, resonant voice.

'Der what?'

'Der shiff, m'sieur. What have cookered der meal.'

'But Mrs Eames is my cook,' protested Sir George.

'Not tonight, m'sieur. Tonight, ah em der cook.'

'Oh are you indeed? Hedges?'

'Sir?'

'Ask Mr Maitland if he wouldn't mind abandoning the dessert for a few moments. I should like to have a word with him.'

'As I explained earlier, sir, I have been refused admission to the kitchen.'

'In case you've forgotten, Hedges, they are *my* kitchens.'

'Yes, sir. Of course, sir.'

Hedges floated away and a moment later Maitland came marching into the room.

'What is it now? he asked crossly.

Sir George gave him the sort of look most people reserve for Bombay Duck.

'This man claims responsibility for having cooked tonight's meal. Is this true?'

'Perfectly true.'

'But I don't understand . . .'

'There's nothing *to* understand,' said Maitland. 'Having decided to change the menu, I suddenly realised that your woman probably wouldn't have the foggiest idea how to do a *loup de mer*, and as for the whole roast baby lamb, she would have gone shrieking out of the kitchen the moment it walked in through the door . . .'

'Oh, don't,' shrieked Jean, covering her mouth with her hands. 'How can you be so beastly?'

Maitland stared at her coldly for a second or two and returned to the business in hand.

'So there was only one thing for it. I got on the blower to our Paris office, and got them to send their chap over toot sweet, and here he is. Monsieur Poincaré. He arrived late this afternoon.'

'And will be leaving early tonight, if I have anything to do with it. What about Mrs Eames?'

'What about Mrs Eames?'

'How has she reacted to someone being brought in over her head, and a foreigner at that?'

'Oh, she put her hat and coat on at once and went home. I knew she would. Still, don't worry. I'll have a quiet word in her ear tomorrow and slip a little something behind the clock on the mantelpiece and she'll be back first thing on Monday morning, you'll see. Anyway, if the worst comes to the worst, I don't suppose you'll have a lot of difficulty finding a replacement.'

'Mrs Eames is irreplaceable,' said Sir George. 'She has

been in service in this house since she was fourteen. That's over forty-five years.'

'Ah well, she's due for retirement in a year's time anyway.'

'We'll discuss this later,' Sir George told Maitland grimly. 'Oh, and while we're on the subject of staff, who exactly are those four?'

He indicated the footmen.

'Oh them. They're out-of-work actors. I got my secretary to find them through Spotlight. I think they're rather fun, don't you? We needed four chaps anyway to carry in the food, and rather than dress them up in the usual soup and fish, I thought, why not give them something that'll add a little extra colour and zest to the film?'

'But don't you see?' protested Sir George. 'You're totally misrepresenting the way we live here. I mean, just look at them.'

He gestured towards the bizarre assortment of men and women who were standing in a row beside the trestle table, waiting for Monsieur Poincaré to make the first incision: Hedges in his black jacket and pin-stripe trousers, Edward in a white jacket and black trousers, four footmen in eighteenth-century powder-blue velvet, three waitresses in black frocks, Poincaré himself looking like the poor man's Escoffier, and last but by no means least, the public relations manager of Blue Blood Tours, looking like a left-over from the Greek Durbar of 1911.

'What's wrong with them?' said Maitland.

'Individually, nothing, I suppose. But together . . . I mean, it gives completely the wrong impression of how things are done in a house like this.'

'What *does* it matter?' said Maitland in a weary tone of voice. 'Do you really imagine that the sort of people who are going to watch this film in Houston, or Qatar, or Adelaide, or Frankfurt, have the faintest idea how things are done in this or any other house? As far as they're concerned, all English country houses are staffed by dozens of servants dressed in all sorts of weird and wonderful

163

costumes, and our film will merely confirm their beliefs. The kind of people who are prepared to cough up a thousand quid to spend a week here are going to be the worst snobs in the world, so the more servants in fancy outfits we can show them in the film, the more likely they are to rush out and book up. Now do stop fussing, for goodness sake, and enjoy yourself.'

Maitland patted the old man on one of his drooping shoulders and walked quickly away towards the door to the kitchen. Sir George shook his head sadly.

'I don't understand anything any more,' he said.

Roger looked at him for a while in silence, then he frowned across at Jean. To his astonishment, she smiled and gave a little shrug of her shoulders. That decided it.

'Will you excuse me for a moment?' he murmured. He scraped his chair back, stood up and walked slowly and deliberately towards the door through which Maitland had recently disappeared.

He found him in the passageway just outside the kitchen stairs.

'You bastard, Maitland,' he shouted at him. 'You bloody bastard.'

Maitland looked at him as if at a yapping poodle. He let his clip-board and pencil drop to his side and sighed.

'Oh for heavens' sake,' he said in a tired voice. 'What is it now?'

'By God, you've gone just a little bit too far this time,' Roger shouted at him. 'Being businesslike is one thing, but when it comes to upsetting people like Mrs Eames so much that she actually gives in her notice, well, I think the time has come to draw a line. That woman has worked in this house since she was a child. Have you any idea what that means to someone like her?'

'You're the expert on English country house life,' said Maitland. 'You tell me.'

'Only that you've ruined her whole bloody life, that's all,' Roger screamed at him. 'As for Sir George, he's a broken man because of you. Do you realise that? A broken man. Perhaps now you're satisfied. Well, all I can say is that if that's what big business is all about, then I am glad I have nothing to do with it.'

Maitland frowned. 'I don't know what you're talking about,' he said. 'You've been involved in big business one way and another ever since you came down from Oxford. I mean, what do you think the travel industry is? Or newspapers?'

'Don't try and change the subject,' snapped Roger. 'You know bloody well what I'm talking about. Now, you go back in there and apologise to Sir George. Do you hear? This instant. Well, go on!'

Maitland stood there, smiling at him and shaking his head in mocking disbelief.

'In that case,' shouted Roger, completely losing his temper at last, 'I'll bloody well make you.'

He rushed forward, meaning to seize him and drag him bodily into the dining room. He might have succeeded, too, had Hahned not chosen that particular moment to hurry out from the kitchen with an extra supply of gravy, and throw the door back straight into Roger's face as he lurched forward. Roger staggered back, eyes blinded with tears, his entire face numb with pain. Hahned stood there motionless, his eyes wide with astonishment, as Maitland shook with helpless laughter and gravy splashed gently on to the stone floor.

'Are you all right?' said Jean anxiously when he returned some ten minutes later to his place at the table.

'Fine, thank you,' said Roger vaguely. Despite several minutes of intense ministration with a cold sponge, his nose still felt about the size and colour of a large tomato. It was also intensely painful. He touched it gently. 'It's nothing,' he added casually.

'What happened?' Audrey asked him. 'What have you been up to?'

Roger looked around the table.

'Just settling an old score,' he said modestly.

'I think I understand,' she said, nodding understandingly.

'Well done,' said Jean, and clearly meant it.

Even Fiona, he noticed, was smiling approvingly.

Sir George looked puzzled. It was difficult to tell whether he had understood what had been going on or not. Obviously Roger could hardly spell it out for him. He just had to hope that all would be revealed to him by someone else after dinner. In the meantime, the best he could hope to do would be to demonstrate his sympathy towards the old man in a different, rather more oblique way.

'I don't think I could somehow,' he said to Hedges when he brought him a plateful of the most delicious-looking roast leg of lamb he had seen in a long time. He looked towards Sir George for some sort of reaction, but the old man was by then deep in conversation with Jean Hollingsworth, and it was not until the food had been removed that he finally looked up and said:

'Oh, aren't you having any of the lamb? What a pity. It's simply delicious.'

He speared a choice morsel and turned it over reflectively between his teeth.

At that moment a voice by his left elbow was heard to say:

'That's great. And again.'

Sir George looked down to find Brian crouching beside his chair pointing the camera straight at his masticating jaws. Wearily, he cut another piece of meat as Brian moved in for a close-up.

At last, the poor lamb (the meat, not Sir George) was carried away by the four footmen, intact except for one leg which looked as though it had been savaged by wolves.

'I wonder what this dessert can be that Mr Maitland was supervising?' said Audrey Veal brightly, as conversation at that end of the table began to show distinct signs of sagging.

To Sir George who, in the interests of art and commerce, had consumed three helpings of meat and two and a half of vegetables, it was not a question to which he particularly wished to know the answer. Manners, however, triumphed once again over indigestion. He lowered his glass of Perrier water and said quietly,

'I daresay it's meant to be a surprise.'

It was.

Borne on an even larger wooden stretcher by the four out-of-work actors, who certainly would never have taken the job on if they'd had any idea of the physical hard work involved, was a vast silver salver at either end of which sat two vast swans, carved out of ice, their heads magnificently erect, their beaks dripping. On either side of the salver, ice dolphins leapt and glistened in the candlelight, and in the middle, towering above fish and birds alike, was a mountainous white *bombe*, entirely covered with pink spun sugar. Sticking out on all sides, like the spines on the back of a gigantic albino hedgehog, were dozens of lighted sparklers that hissed and twinkled, while perched on the top was a Roman Candle, also alight, that threw out spray after spray of silver and golden rain that illuminated the solemn faces of footmen and guests alike in a wondrous, eerie glow.

It was Reg Henshawe who succeeded in finding the two words that best summed up the feelings of all present.

'Bugger me,' he said.

'Blimey,' added Jeremy Powell-Brett.

'Too amusing,' opined Audrey Veal.

As one, the entire table turned towards Sir George. For a moment or two, his face registered no emotion whatever. And then, very slowly, there passed across it an expression of ineffable contempt, mixed with real physical pain. He picked up his glass and sipped some Perrier. He opened his mouth as if about to speak, but in the end thought better of it. He placed the glass carefully on the table and quietly closed his eyes.

The procession had covered half the distance between the door and the trestle table when there was a short, sharp explosion, and from the top of the Roman Candle a small ball of fire flew high over the table, narrowly missed the chain that supported the central chandelier and exploded in a breathtaking shower of gold and silver lights against Goya's *Head of a Young Girl.*

19

'Of course,' Audrey Veal was saying, 'they can do wonders with damaged paintings nowadays.'

'Exactly,' said Jeremy Powell-Brett. 'Look at *The Night Watch* in the Rijksmuseum in Amsterdam. They even allowed the public to stand behind a glass screen and watch repair work actually going on.'

'Except that *The Night Watch* was cut with a knife, not set on fire by a Roman Candle,' Roger pointed out.

The others glared at him and grimaced in the direction of Fiona Fox-Bronzing who was standing at the table behind the sofa pouring out coffee.

It was a sober and somewhat depleted party that now sat around the fireplace in the Long Library, trying to pick up the broken fragments of the evening and jolly them back together into life. Sir George had not been seen since the moment he had leapt to his feet from the dinner table, doused the smouldering masterpiece in the remains of his Perrier and hurried out of the room with it clutched in both hands. Eddy and Buster had peeled away from the main party in the hall and disappeared into the night, and the film people were presumably still in the dining room dismantling their lamps, rolling up their cables and knocking yet more lumps off the Chippendale.

'I know a man in Whitechapel who could touch it up for you so you'd never know the difference,' Reg suggested helpfully.

'Really, Reg!' said Audrey.

'Only trying to help,' he said, with a shrug of his shoulders.

'Of course, it's probably insured,' Jean said after a pause.

'Must be,' said Powell-Brett.

'Wonder how much it's worth?' pondered Reg. 'Twenty thousand? Thirty?'

'Quarter of a million actually,' said Fiona as she walked round from behind the sofa with her coffee and sat in a hard, upright armchair.

Reg whistled.

'If I were your old man, I'd take the money and run,' he said.

'The value in money terms of the painting is neither here nor there,' said Fiona. 'The point is, that picture has been in my husband's family now for over a hundred and sixty years. It was a present to Sir Geoffrey Fox-Bronzing, George's great-great-great uncle, from the Duke of Wellington by way of saying thank you for saving his life in the lines of Torres Vedras.'

'That was during the Peninsular War, wasn't it?' said Roger, plunging his hand into the mud of his subconscious and coming up with a long-forgotten historical oyster. Fiona gave a little shrug.

'I've no idea,' she said.

'Wasn't it?' he repeated, looking eagerly round at the rest of them.

'I always thought it was the Napoleonic Wars myself,' said Jackie.

'Same thing,' said Roger.

'Oh,' said Jackie.

'Does it matter?' asked Jeremy, rushing to Jackie's defence. 'Please go on, Lady Fox-Bronzing.'

'That's all really. I just know that it had great sentimental associations for my husband. He cares about things like that, you know.'

'I quite understand,' piped Audrey.

'So you say,' Fiona said, not unkindly. 'But I doubt if you do really. I doubt if you can. I don't really understand it myself. Hatching is not just a house, as far as my husband is concerned; it's his whole life. Of course he could ring up Christie's tomorrow and sell off a couple of pictures, or a

170

piece of Sèvres, or a half-a-dozen rare books, and live extremely well for several years on the proceeds. Do you honestly think that if we had sold that Goya when I suggested it last year, you would be sitting where you are now? But no, he wouldn't sell, not just because he is extremely fond of the painting, but because it has always hung there in that same place in the Great Dining Room ever since he can remember and to get rid of it would be to get rid of part of his childhood and part of his life. Perhaps you think he is dotty. I mean, if it were up to me, I'd be round to the insurance people first thing in the morning collecting the money. But he won't. He'd rather have a patched-up, valueless piece of junk sitting there on the wall than all the money in the world.' She shrugged her shoulders in resignation. 'Now then, who's for a game of cards?'

Relieved of the uncomfortable burden of guilt and embarrassment under which they had been struggling for the last half hour, the journalists fell upon their hostess's invitation with delight and an enthusiasm that was quite disproportionate to the quality of the entertainment offered.

'What a simply wonderful idea,' exclaimed Audrey, her nasal tones scaling new heights of affectation.

'I'm on,' said Powell-Brett, crinkling his face up with unwonted glee.

'Count me in every time,' bellowed Reg. 'How about it, Mrs V?'

Mrs Venables said that she wouldn't mind.

'What would you like to play?' Fiona asked them. 'Bridge? Whist? According to the programme it should be mah-jong, but . . .'

Despite several attempts by his aunt to introduce him to bridge, Roger had never succeeded in grasping even the most fundamental principles of the game. He was not a mah-jong player either. In fact, he could not swear that he had ever actually set eyes on a mah-jong set. However, it always had been one of his great ambitions to be able to claim that just once in his life, after dinner in a country house, he had played mah-jong and danced to a wind-up gramophone.

'Oh, mah-jong every time,' he declared grandly. 'No country house party is ever complete without a game of mah-jong after dinner.'

'Really?' said Fiona. 'We never play it ourselves. Still, if that's what you'd all like to do, then of course . . . Hedges, would you be very kind and slip up into the attic and see if you can find that mah-jong set of ours? It should be with the Monopoly and Snakes and Ladders and so on. I had no idea we were going to have a real player amongst us. I've always wanted to learn how to play. Does anyone else know it?'

They all shook their heads. Roger goggled at them in disbelief.

'Audrey,' he said in an encouraging tone of voice, 'surely you must have played mah-jong at some time during your grand and varied life?'

'I was a generation too late, I'm afraid,' she said.

Roger looked round quickly at the others, realised that none of them was going to come to his rescue and then, like the cartoon cat that discovers too late that, although it is still running, it is in fact several yards beyond the top of the cliff, he began to scrabble at the thin air in a desperate effort to gain a foothold.

'Well, if no one else wants to play. I don't at all mind *not* playing. I mean, I *love* playing. But of course it is pretty complicated, and since no one else actually knows the game . . . I mean, I'm not suggesting that you wouldn't all pick it up straightaway. It's not as difficult as all that, but it is *quite* difficult; in fact it can be quite boring until you have begun to get the hang of it, and since it is rather late . . .'

Fiona stared at him.

'We don't have to play,' she said softly. 'It was your idea. I simply said I'd always wanted to play, and thought you might be able to teach us, but if you don't want to . . .?

'It's not that I don't *want* to,' said Roger hurriedly. 'But it is rather complicated, and . . .'

'Fine, fine. Let's play something else then.'

'I just didn't want you to think . . .'

'It's all right. We don't. Don't worry. How about bridge then?'

'I'm hopeless at bridge,' said Jean promptly.

'Me too,' said Fiona. 'It's such a boring game.'

'I'd be very happy to give someone a game of backgammon,' said Jeremy.

You would, thought Roger. You're just the backgammon type.

'I'll give you a game,' said Fiona.

'Have you got a board?'

'No.'

'I have. Upstairs. I'll run up and fetch it.'

'Anyone for gin rummy?' said Reg Henshawe.

'Too difficult,' said Jackie. 'Why can't we play something easy?'

'Suggest something.'

'Beat-your-neighbour-out-of-doors?'

'How about cribbage?' suggested Cyril Dick. 'That's easy enough. My father and I used to play when I was ill in bed with glandular fever once.'

'How about Dumb Crambo?' said Roger.

'No racialist games round here, if you don't mind,' said Reg in a pantomime negro accent.

'What is Dumb Crambo exactly?' said Fiona. 'I've always wanted to know.'

'Sounds like some sort of jam,' said Cyril Dick.

'Surely you must have played it here dozens of times,' said Roger, 'At Christmas and so on?'

'No. Why? Should we have?'

Roger launched into an explanation that turned out to be a good deal longer and more complicated that he had anticipated, largely owing to the fact that he had rather forgotten how to play it himself.

'Oh, I couldn't do that,' said Barbara. 'I'm no good at doing things in front of a lot of people.'

'Oh, I wouldn't say that,' said Audrey with a sly grin.

'I must say it sounds jolly hard work to me,' said Dick.

'Especially at this late stage,' chipped in Mrs Venables.

'Well, how about "The Game" then?' Roger suggested brightly.

'What do you mean, "The Game"?'

'You know, someone brings in a whole lot of things on a tray, you have two minutes to look at them, then they are taken away and you have to write down as many of the things as you can remember. The Royal Family play it a lot. I was taught how to play by a friend of Princess Margaret's as a matter of fact.'

'Obviously not a very close friend,' said Dick. 'That's called Kim's Game.'

In the end it was agreed that everyone should play pontoon.

'Cheer up,' said Jean, throwing herself onto a sofa in one of the end alcoves.

'Well, honestly,' said Roger in disgust, dropping into a small armchair beside her.

In the main body of the room more brandies and liqueurs were being dispensed, packs of cards were being unwrapped and facetious remarks were being tossed hither and thither.

'Just because no one wanted to play any of your games. Do you really know how to play mah-jong, as a matter of interest?'

'Of course,' said Roger without hesitation.

Jean sipped at her kümmel. At last she said:

'You didn't say anything to your friend Maitland about . . . you know . . .'

'Certainly not.'

'Good. I shouldn't bother if I were you.'

'I wasn't planning to.'

'I'm glad to hear it. How *can* you have lived with him all these years?'

'I should have chucked him out years ago. I will now.'

'If I'd been Sir George, I'd have strangled him with my bare hands, manners or no manners.'

'Where is the old chap, by the way?'

'Gone to bed, Fiona says. He's not feeling very well. Mark you, none of us would be exactly on tip-top form if we'd just watched a painting worth a quarter of a million pounds going up in smoke.'

'In the circumstances,' said Roger. 'I'm wondering if your idea of my sneaking into Fiona's room at dead of night is such a good one after all.'

Jean gave an impatient tut.

'Well, don't go then. You asked me what I thought you should do and I told you. There's no percentage in it for me one way or the other. As far as I'm concerned, the whole idea of her asking you to perpetuate the Fox-Bronzing line is as improbable as your believing it. However, if you feel you must live out your fantasy, then why not do it properly in traditional Edwardian fashion by sneaking along to her room while her husband dozes fitfully in the next room? It will make such good copy, apart from anything else.'

'Oh, I wasn't planning to write about it,' said Roger earnestly.

'But only the other day,' said Jean, 'you were holding us all enthralled with your theories about honesty in journalism and the importance of describing all the little incidents that occur during a trip.'

'Yes, but I don't think it's quite the same sort of thing at all.'

'I see,' said Jean solemnly.

'You don't think I should perhaps mention something about it to Fiona before we all go up? Prepare her for it to a certain extent? I mean, it might come as a bit of a shock to wake up and find a man in her room. She might scream or shout for help or something. Then what would happen?'

'Good thinking,' said Jean seriously. 'I've got a better idea. Why don't you pop upstairs now and buttonhole Sir George before he has a chance to get his head down. Explain what you have in mind, and warn him that if by chance he should be woken in the middle of the night by his wife screaming for help in the next room, there's absolutely no cause for alarm: it'll just be you popping in for a moment to impregnate his wife. I'm sure he'd understand.'

Roger looked at her sharply.

'I do think you might be a bit helpful over this,' he said.

After they had been playing pontoon for about half an hour, it was decided to have a short break for refreshments.

'We have a problem,' murmured Jean taking Roger's arm and drawing him away to an empty part of the room.

'Fiona?'

'Do you never stop thinking about yourself?' she said. 'No, it's Reg.'

Roger groaned. 'Oh Lord. What's he done now?'

'It's not what he's done, it's what he's planning to do.'

'Don't tell me,' said Roger, 'he's going to elope with Mrs Venables.'

Jean stared at him.

'Has he been talking to you too?' she said.

'No,' said Roger, taken aback by her serious manner. 'Why?'

'Because that's exactly what he is planning to do.'

Roger laughed. 'You're not serious?'

'I am serious,' she said. 'And what's more, so is he.'

Roger frowned.

'Reg eloping with Mrs Venables?' he chuckled. 'It's really too ludicrous for words. You mean, out of the window, knotted sheets, fast car, Gretna Green and so on?'

'More or less, yes. Although I believe he is thinking more in terms of an extendable ladder than knotted sheets, but the principle is the same.'

'But why?'

'I imagine because he wants to run away with her.'

'No no. What I mean is, why should he bother to go to all that trouble when he could perfectly well ring for a taxi and walk out of the front door with her? Or better still, take her with us tomorrow?'

'Firstly because he's nervous of what Jackie might do if

176

she found out, and secondly, he is worried that Sir George might talk her out of it before he's even got her halfway across the hall.'

'But she's a woman of mature years. She must know her own mind.'

'Not on this occasion.'

'Why not?'

'Because he hasn't told her yet, that's why not. Apparently he thinks she will be more likely to fall in with his plan if he springs it on her out of the blue. His theory is that beneath that sober, forbidding exterior there beats the heart of a romantic, impulsive, deeply passionate woman, who has been sitting about for all these years in a stuffy Victorian flat in Hans Crescent like some dreary chrysalis, just waiting for the moment when some equally passionate soul mate will burst in, break open the dull shell and release the colourful butterfly.'

'Did Reg tell you all this?'

'No, Barbara did, just now. Apparently Reg decided that, as a result of the summerhouse incident, Cyril Dick was a man after his own heart, and revealed the plan to him earlier this evening. Cyril obviously told Barbara who in turn told me just a few moments ago. Goodness knows why. She seemed genuinely concerned.'

'Guilty conscience, I daresay,' said Roger. 'And you mean to say you believe all this?'

'I certainly wouldn't put it past Reg to make a complete ass of himself one way or another tonight.'

'And of us,' said Roger grimly.

'Trust you to think of that.'

'Well . . .'

'I know, I know.'

'The thing is, what, if anything, are we going to do to prevent it? The game is about to re-start, and by the look of things Mrs Venables is already on her way to bed.'

'I've thought of one possibility,' said Jean. 'But I'll need your help.'

'You can always count on me,' said Roger.

Fifteen minutes later, Reg Henshawe put his last two matches on a king, was dealt a seven by Jean, twisted and was handed a five for his pains. A look of enormous bliss transfused his hitherto tortoise-like features. He squinted at his watch.

'Past my bedtime anyway,' he remarked with great satisfaction and some difficulty.

'Oh, surely not?' said Jean. 'You can't leave us now that we've reached such an exciting stage.'

'What's exciting about it?' said Reg. 'I've just lost all my matches.'

'You could buy some more.' She reached for the matchbox. 'Look, how many more would you like? Twenty? Four bob's worth? Ten? Take ten. See how you get on.'

She counted out ten matches and pushed them across the table.

'I don't want ten,' he said belligerently, his eyes floating, his head lolling like a dog in the back window of a Morris Marina.

'Come along now, Reg, don't be a spoil sport. Just one more hand. If you go now, all the life will go out of the party.'

The others, for whom Reg's increasing input of brandy and correspondingly decreasing output of coherent thought was beginning to prove a source of considerable embarrassment, goggled at Jean like characters in a Bateman cartoon.

'At least have another drink. I'm going to have another one. Anyone else? Roger?'

'Not for me thanks.'

'There you are. Roger's having another one,' she said picking up his glass. 'I'm having another one. Jeremy, I'm sure you're going to. Yes? You don't mind, do you, Fiona? Good. So that's another large brandy for Mr Henshawe, Bridges, and a small one for me and Mr Noakes . . .'

A grin edged its way cautiously on to one side of Reg's face, giving him the look of a lop-sided potato.

'Oh well,' he said, his head wobbling badly, 'since you intwist on sisting my arm.'

'We do, don't we, Roger?'

If looks could have killed, Roger would at that moment have been a shapeless bloody pulp on the floor. A well-aimed kick helped to get the point home.

'Oh yes,' he said. 'Rather.'

The others smiled weakly.

On the next hand, Reg earned himself a royal pontoon, fifty matches and the bank.

Jean pushed the pack of cards firmly across the table towards him.

The moment Reg Henshawe gained control of the bank, his fortunes took a dramatic upward turn. Soon his modest pile of sixty matches had increased to a little mound of a hundred and thence to a positive massif of twice that number. Five times in a row he served himself a ten or a face card followed by another ten or another face card. He then had a lucky run of eighteens and nineteens, followed by a mixed bag including one thirteen, two fifteens and a five-card trick. The fact that both Jean and Roger threw away every chance they were given, even to the extent of twisting on twenty, although greeted with astonished stares by every other player, apparently failed to register with the banker. But then, of course, Jean and Roger did not insist on refilling their glasses after every hand.

Half an hour later, Reg was still firmly in possession of the bank, though barely of his faculties. His luck, however, could not by the law of averages last for ever, and the end came shortly after twelve-thirty, when Jeremy Powell-Brett turned an ace face up on his other card to indicate the presence of a royal pontoon, whereupon Reg, in a fit of drunken disbelief, threw the entire pack of cards up into the air where they hung for a moment against the fluted columns before fluttering onto the wooden floor like the leaves of Vallombrosa. He then fell head first into his mountain of matchsticks.

'Time for your beddy-byes, Reggie, old thing,' said Jean and nodded at Roger.

'Don't move anyone,' Roger told the others. 'We can manage. Go on playing. We'll be back in a couple of minutes. We've got some winning to do.'

They all sat there, their faces registering a mixture of amazement and suspicion, as Roger and Jean half-helped, half-carried the pathetic, crumpled figure of the assistant sports editor of one of the largest-circulation newspapers in Fleet Street across the Long Library and out through the door.

Five minutes later, they were laying him on his bed in his room. They stood back, breathing heavily from their exertions, and looked down at the inert, snoring figure.

'Do you think we ought to lie him on his side?' whispered Roger anxiously. 'They say you should never leave a drunken person asleep on his back in case he is sick and chokes on his own vomit.'

'It might solve a lot of problems for everyone if he did,' said Jean.

'Jean!' Roger was genuinely shocked.

'Well,' she said. 'You know what I mean. Oh, all right then.' They turned him on to his side. His face fell across the pillow like a badly set blancmange.

'Shouldn't we undress him?' asked Roger.

'What,' said Jean, 'and give him naughty ideas?'

As they tip-toed across the room, the snoring suddenly stopped and a voice, very like Reg's but much younger, said quite distinctly:

'Dirty sod, that Casablancas.'

And then the snoring started again.

Roger closed the door carefully behind him, locked it, put the key into his dinner jacket pocket and hurried down the stairs after Jean.

They arrived back in the Long Library to find that the pontoon game had been abandoned, Brian and Keith were

180

busy setting up their lights, and Powell-Brett, Fiona, and Audrey Veal were settling to a game of bridge.

'Jean,' Fiona called out as they came into the room, 'You're just in time. You wouldn't be an angel, would you, and make up a four? It's not a real game. Just something for Brian to photograph.'

Jean said she would be happy to.

'What happened to the pontoon then?' asked Roger.

'Oh, we got bored with that,' said Jeremy, shuffling a pack of cards.

'Well, really,' said Roger in aggrieved tones. 'I call that a bit much. We did tell you we were coming back.'

'We heard you,' said Jeremy – rather nastily, Roger thought. 'But we really couldn't be bothered to wait.'

'But I lost a lot of money on that game,' said Roger, irritated and slightly nonplussed by Powell-Brett's offhand manner.

'One pound thirty-five p, to be precise,' said Jeremy. 'If you wouldn't mind.' He held out a hand, palm up. Roger laughed lightly.

'I think under the circumstances we might call it quits, don't you?'

'Circumstances? What circumstances?' Powell-Brett's face was hard and pinched. He reminded Roger of a prefect at school who had once caught him cheating on a run. 'You'll get a bit of stick for that,' he had said in just that hard, pinched way. Roger was suddenly rather nervous of Powell-Brett.

'Well,' said Roger with a brave stab at a smile, 'it was all in a good cause, after all.'

'What was?'

'Well, you know. Losing like that. To Reg.'

'I don't quite understand.'

Now they were all looking at him with blank expressions, waiting for some sort of explanation. He turned to Jean for help. She frowned and moved her head very slightly from side to side.

Roger laughed again, and reached into his pocket.

'Oh, it doesn't matter,' he said, waving his other hand in a small dismissive gesture. 'It was meant to be a joke. Not a very good one. Forget it. I always was a terrible loser. How much do I owe you?'

Roger stood behind Audrey, watching the play, as he was asked to do by Brian. Cyril Dick and Barbara Black sat on a nearby sofa, drinking and chatting, like a couple at a charity ball in an over-inked Tatler photograph.

After the filming was over, Roger was standing by one of the book cases at the far end of the room when Cyril Dick came sliding up beside him.

'I just wanted to tell you,' he said, 'that you're an even worse swine than I took you for.'

'And I want to tell you,' said Roger, 'that if you don't do something about that spot on your chin before very long, it stands a very good chance of being arrested under the Obscenity Act.'

'Only a real swine like you would draw attention to it,' he said. 'And only a real swine like you would treat a man like Reg Henshawe the way you treated him this evening.'

Roger felt himself flushing furiously.

'I don't know what you mean,' he said angrily.

'You know perfectly well what I mean,' said Dick. 'And so does everyone else in this room. You obviously enjoy humiliating people.'

'I don't . . .'

'But then perhaps that's your way of making up for failures in other directions. Good night, Noakes.'

Dick turned and walked across to where Barbara was standing waiting for him. She gave him a knowing smile and the two of them turned and left the room.

'Where's Maitland?'

Roger did not particularly care where Maitland was. Any more than he particularly cared whether or not the journalist from *World* magazine would turn up the next day. They were just a couple of desultory thoughts to throw

182

out at Jean as they sat alone together on the sofa in front of the non-existent fire, drinking Bournvita. He didn't particularly want to drink Bournvita. It was just that Hedges, in the course of clearing up the glasses, had happened to suggest it and he had thought, Well, why not?

Jean's answer to the question about the journalist had been: 'Not if I know anything about American journalists.' The answer to his second question, about Maitland, was: 'The last time I saw him he was hurrying out of the front door with his brief-case in his hand, jumping into his sports car and tearing off down the drive.'

'Perhaps he's gone to fetch the American journalist.'

'Who knows?' she said. She sipped at her Bournvita and made a face. 'Who cares?'

'Just so long as you don't.'

'In my view,' she said some minutes later, 'the sooner you give up this sort of thing the better.'

'What do you mean, this sort of thing?'

'Well,' she gestured vaguely at the room, 'this kind of life.'

'I don't see why,' said Roger. 'It all seems very agreeable to me. Pleasant surroundings, good food, amusing company: what more could one ask?'

'I don't mean that. I mean these press junkets. All these terrible people. This pointless way of life. I'm sure it must be very bad for your character. It makes you believe you are far better than you are and behave far worse than you should.'

Words of protest began to form themselves automatically on Roger's lips, just as they always did whenever Maitland started making fun of him over the Corn Flakes; as they did every time his aunt asked him when he was planning to get down to a real job of work. What do you mean, freeloading? What's pointless about it? Travel writers are no better and no worse than anyone else. This is not a junket: it's work. And so on, and so on.

But tonight he did not protest. Perhaps he was too tired. Or too full of brandy. Or perhaps he knew better than to try and pull the wool over Jean's eyes. Instead he said: 'I think perhaps you're right.'

He swallowed the last dregs of his Bournvita, placed the cup carefully on the eighteenth-century sofa table and, with a great groan, stood up.

'But first,' he said, buttoning his jacket, 'I have one very important duty to carry out.'

'Ah, yes,' said Jean. 'I'd almost forgotten.'

'There's one thing that puzzles me,' Roger said as they walked towards the door. 'Why were you so anxious to discourage Reg Henshawe from doing something which, if discovered, would very possibly upset Sir George, and yet you actually encouraged me to go ahead and do something which, if he found out about it, might destroy him for ever?'

Jean paused by the door with her hand on the light switch.

'When you've been in Fleet Street as long as I have,' she said, 'you get to recognise a real story when you see one.'

And with that she turned off the lights.

20

Roger had never realised before that Cyril Dick had been made house captain. It must have happened while he was away on the Algarve trip.

'You're an even worse swine than I took you for,' Dick was saying to Roger as he leaned back in his chair with his feet up on his desk. 'Well, since you're so fond of humiliating people, I'm going to humiliate you.'

He gave the side of his shoe an ominous little whack with the long bamboo cane which he was holding in his right hand.

'It wasn't my idea to take Reg on the run in the first place; it was Jean's,' Roger explained desperately. 'How did I know he was going to collapse? That's why we had to turn back – to get him home to bed. We didn't really cheat at all, Dick. Honestly we didn't.'

Now Powell-Brett came into the study, wearing his prefect's tie and a hard, pinched expression on his face.

'Yes, you did,' said Powell-Brett. 'You cheated at cards. I saw you. We all saw you.'

'You'll get a bit of stick for that,' said Cyril Dick, and stood up, swishing his cane through the air.

'And you owe me £1.35p,' said Powell-Brett.

He seized Roger by the shoulder and began to shake him violently from side to side.

'£1.35p,' he repeated. '£1.35p.'

'Get it from Maitland,' Roger said. 'Maitland's dealing with expenses. Put in a chit to him. Cashiers will be open till four. Get it from Maitland.'

'Maitland's gone,' said Powell-Brett, shaking Roger even harder. 'He's gone, he's gone. . . .'

185

Roger opened his eyes to find that it wasn't Powell-Brett who was shaking him at all, but Jean.

'He's gone,' she said anxiously. 'He's gone.'

Roger looked up at her.

'Maitland?' he said dopily.

'No, Reg. He's escaped from his room. I don't know where he is.'

Roger propped himself up on one elbow. He was on top of the eiderdown, still fully dressed. The bedside light was on.

'Whatever time is it?'

'Just gone two.'

A great yawning hole formed itself in Roger's stomach. He swung his legs off the bed and stood upright.

'But I've missed the whole thing,' he said, his voice filled with real panic. 'I mean, she'll be asleep by now. I meant to go soon after we came up. I must have fallen asleep. Oh hell and damnation. It's too late now. What am I going to do?'

'First, come and help me look for Reg.'

Roger looked at her, as the meaning of her words began to sink in properly for the first time.

'What do you mean he's gone? Gone where?'

'If I knew that, I wouldn't be here,' she said sharply. 'I don't know where he's gone. All I do know is that I woke up in rather a sweat about ten minutes ago, and remembering what you said about people choking to death in their sleep, decided just to pop along and see if the old chap was all right. Well, the door was still locked, but somehow or other Reg had still managed to escape. I hunted everywhere. In all the cupboards and wardrobes, in the bathroom, in the bed, but he definitely wasn't there.'

'Did you check the windows?'

Jean nodded.

'All firmly closed.'

'How extraordinary,' said Roger. 'I'd better come and take a look.'

They tip-toed along the landing which was illuminated by just one table-lamp downstairs in the hall. No cracks of

186

light showed under any of the doors. They slipped into Reg's room and switched on the light.

There was a dent in the eiderdown and pillow where Reg had been lying when they last saw him, but apart from that, the bedclothes were undisturbed. Roger walked quickly across and felt the place. There was still a hint of warmth against the back of his hand.

'He can't have gone far,' said Roger, looking wildly around the room as though hoping that Reg might suddenly materialise, ghost-like, through the wood-panelled walls.

Then he suddenly remembered. Through the walls. Like Jean. Perhaps that was it. He moved quickly along one wall, feeling the panelling for some kind of handle or knob or finger-hole.

'What are you doing?' hissed Jean.

'Looking for the way out.'

He found it at last, by chance, in the shape of a carved wooden rose that formed the corner-piece to one of the panels and seemed to protrude that much further than its corresponding fellows. Roger pulled it and pushed it. Nothing happened. Then he twisted it. As he did so, he felt the panel give slightly beneath his hand. He pushed harder, and the whole panel swung inwards to reveal a narrow staircase that disappeared into the mysterious vitals of the old house.

'Reg?' Roger called out softly into the darkness. 'Are you there, Reg?'

No answer.

'There should be a torch on the bedside table,' said Jean.

But there wasn't.

'He must have taken it with him,' she said.

'Well,' announced Roger firmly, 'I can tell you, I have no intention of negotiating that staircase without some form of light. If I have to stumble across Reg's lifeless body, or anyone else's for that matter, I'd rather do so having had some sort of warning first.'

'There might be some matches somewhere. On the mantelpiece perhaps.'

'I'll go,' said Roger.

Not only were there matches, but also a candle in a holder.

'I thought there might be,' said Roger.

On the return journey, his eye was caught by something he had not hitherto noticed. In a far, dark corner of the room was an antique clothes-horse over which some clothes had been carelessly thrown. Closer investigation revealed these to consist of a dinner suit, an evening dress shirt and a black bow tie.

Roger looked across at the bed, and at the pyjamas which had been carefully laid out across the turned-back sheets. Then he looked at Jean and pulled a face.

'Still,' she said, 'at least he's still wearing his underpants.'

'Not in fact,' said Roger and pointed to the other corner of the room where, mounted upon a marble plinth, was the bust of some eighteenth-century figure – an ancestor of Sir George's no doubt – dressed in the Roman style. Or rather, partly in the Roman style. Draped across his chest and gathered on one shoulder by an ornamental clasp were the loose folds of a toga. His face wore an expression of enormous superiority. But on this occasion his head was crowned, not with the traditional laurel wreath, but with a pair of white, combed cotton, Y-front underpants.

Jean groaned.

'I suppose you're expecting me to investigate the staircase?' Roger said.

'Why? Who else did you have in mind?'

Roger raised his eyes in the direction of the ceiling and sighed. Then, clutching the lighted candle, he stepped gingerly through the open panel and disappeared from sight.

He was back a good deal sooner than either of them had anticipated.

'Well?'

'Nothing very exciting, I'm afraid,' Roger told her. 'Just a short flight of stairs leading to an open door.'

'And . . .?'

'I have no idea. At that point the candle blew out, and all the matches turned out to be dead.'

'Ugh,' said Jean. 'I can't bear people who put used matches back in the box. Did you get any idea of where the door leads to?'

'Not really. However, the fact that there was enough of a draught to blow the candle out rather suggests that it might be a passage or a corridor. I don't think it's a room. Don't ask me why; it's just a feeling I got.'

'I bet it's the passage that leads from the hall through to the Breakfast Room.'

'Something like that,' said Roger.

'Then the chances are that he's still somewhere in the house.'

'He might be a repressed naturist.'

'Like the lady I once heard on "Have a Go" who was asked by Wilfrid Pickles to name her secret ambition . . .?'

'"I'd like to run naked through the dewy grass," I know. I heard that one too.'

'Perhaps he's just gone for a midnight swim?'

She walked across to the window, cupped her hand against the glass and squinted down into the garden.

'I don't like to worry you,' she said.

'But . . .'

'In Reg's case, it's something a good deal more recherché than dewy grass that he likes running through.'

At that moment from outside on the lawn came sounds of ornithological outrage the like of which Roger had not heard since the day at London Zoo when, as a small child, he had watched a crowd of drunken tars trying to feed an ostrich with Guinness.

He leapt across the room and peered down through the darkness towards the Long Walk. At first he could see very little, but then the moon came out from behind a cloud, illuminating the scene below in such a way that Roger had the impression he was watching a badly under-exposed amateur effort at pornographic film-making entitled 'Reg and the Peacocks,' in which a fat little man, naked except for a pair of black silk evening socks, pursues a flock of peacocks across the lawn of a country house, though to what strange purpose, nobody quite knows. . . .

'We've got to stop him,' said Roger. 'He'll wake the whole neighbourhood at this rate. Look, you run down and switch off the light in the dining room or wherever it is. Apart from anything else, it might bring him to his senses a bit. I'll nip along to my room and fetch a torch and meet you downstairs, and between us with a bit of luck we might be able to lure him back into his room before he manages to do too much damage.'

'Right,' said Jean, and disappeared in the direction of the main staircase.

Roger hurried along to his room, found the torch and was on his way out again, when he suddenly realised that the peacocks were no longer squawking. Presumably Jean had managed to find the appropriate light switch and the outraged birds had sneaked away under the cover of darkness, thus escaping the clutches of the bird-crazed house guest.

He padded cautiously along the landing carpet. To his surprise, no lights had come on under doors, no furious, tousled figures stood in their dressing gowns in doorways demanding to know what was going on. The crisis had been averted; the great house slept on.

Including, presumably, Fiona.

He could picture her now, her little face tucked into her pillow, her eyes tight shut like a dormouse, her hair tumbling across her pale features like a Victorian child after a heavy day with the hoop and top. A child, yet not a child, with the body of a fifteen-year-old and at the same time all the strength and determination and sense of responsibility of a woman twice that age. A mature woman who knew exactly which man she wanted to be the father of her child, and an innocent girl, keen to learn how to play mah-jong. The combination was irresistible.

And yet Roger had refused her twice: the first time, consciously, in the punt; and now again, sub-consciously, by falling asleep on his bed, when any other man in his position would have been lying naked with her between the sheets, kissing her eyes, and stroking her childish breasts, and . . .

Which was her room anyway?

Jean had said that she slept in the room next to her husband. And Sir George's room was the one that occupied the north and east corner of the first floor, beyond Jean's. In which case, Fiona's had to be the one on the far side of the landing beyond that.

Roger retraced his steps towards his own room, turned right along the landing, past Jean's room, past Sir George's room, until he was standing outside Fiona's door – only feet away from her sleeping form.

He took a deep breath, seized the crusty antique door knob in both hands and very, very slowly turned it to the right.

The door swung open without a sound. Roger, barely breathing, placed one foot gingerly over the threshold, then the other. The figure in the bed slept on.

'Fiona,' Roger whispered into the dark. 'Fiona.'

The figure did not move. He turned and began to close the door. Then he began to move further towards the bed.

'Are you asleep?' he hissed. 'It's me. Roger.'

Still no response. The bedclothes were pulled right up over her head.

He was by the bedside table now and was on the point of leaning forward and shaking her by the shoulder when his eye was caught by something that gleamed dully on the table. He bent down and peered at the object more closely.

It was a pair of spectacles.

Roger frowned.

And then he saw the teeth. They were sitting grinning at him from the watery depths of a cut-glass Waterford goblet.

Roger goggled back at them. Glasses? Teeth? Now,

191

suddenly, like some high-speed camera, his eyes began to take in other objects. The jewellery, the dress on the hanger, the travelling alarm clock. the open suit-case. . . . He wasn't in Fiona's room at all. He was in Mrs Venables'.

At that moment, he became aware that someone was tapping very gently on the bedroom door. He stepped back and knocked over a small bedroom chair. The knocking stopped. Roger began to tiptoe towards a large wardrobe in the corner of the room. He was halfway there when the knocking started again. This time it was accompanied by a strange, low voice saying, 'It's only me, my little chickadee. It's only me, your big brave Chanticleer.'

The sleeping figure, disturbed more no doubt by the sound of the overturned chair than by the bizarre knockings and cooings coming from outside on the landing, now began to turn and groan and re-arrange the bedclothes around the sleeping ears and would no doubt have slid happily back into the Land of Nod, had not the door at that moment been edged open and the light from an electric torch been flashed around the bed area, like a drunken searchlight operator during the blitz trying to pick out a Heinkel.

Roger, faced with the alternative of throwing himself into the wardrobe or hurling himself under the bed and incapable of deciding which, stood frozen to the spot, his mouth half-open in a warning that never found expression. The sleeping figure, woken by the torch light, sat up in bed and switched on the bedside light. At the very same moment, through the open door, like a circus performer propelled from a gun, shot a small man, naked except for a pair of black silk evening socks and a peacock feather protruding from his bottom. With a shriek of delight he headed for the bed. He was a good yard away when his little legs gave one mighty push, his fat white body flew through the air, and with a triumphant shout of 'Cock-a-doodle doo,' Reg Henshawe finally came to rest in the toothless, bewildered arms of the Right Reverend Claud Fox-Bronzing, Bishop of Kananga.

21

Whether it was the peacocks that woke him or the headache, he could not tell. All he knew was that, as consciousness returned, both were going full blast. He lay there for a while, his stomach sinking, his eyes tightly closed in a pathetic attempt to shut out the reality of the events of a few hours previously. The pain which began somewhere above his eyes and finished up in the nape of his neck bit into his brain like the merciless claw of some giant bird of prey, and he gave a long, high-pitched moan. It didn't help. With a superhuman effort he raised his head, turned the pillow over and sank gently into the cool, clean linen. For a short while he fancied that the pain had subsided, but the recovery was to be short-lived. All too soon the bird had begun to tighten its grip again, so that he squeaked with the agony of it.

There was only one thing to do, and he knew that until he did it, the situation would not and could not improve, namely to take a couple of restorative Disprin. But that involved getting out of bed, stumbling to the bathroom, fishing the box out of the sponge-bag, dropping the life-saving tablets into an inch of water in the bottom of a tooth-mug, waiting for them to dissolve, drinking them down, tottering back to bed and lying there feeling even worse, until finally, twenty minutes later, with luck, the magic potion would begin to work, the heavy black clouds would begin to disperse inside his head and warm sunshine and gentle laughter and the song of the bluebird would once more be over the land.

Ten minutes later he was still lying there, convinced that

this was Providence paying him back for the invented migraine with which he had tempted her the previous afternoon in the punt.

Meanwhile the peacocks, as though to extract revenge for the indignities suffered earlier that night at the hands of the demented Reg Henshawe, continued to scream harsh abuse from the lawn immediately beneath his window.

At last, mind triumphed over matter. He stretched a cautious arm in the direction of the bedside light and promptly knocked over the glass of water he had left there the night before. The water pattered gently on to the carpet.

'Your tea, sir.'

'Hah?'

He squinted upwards through half-open lids at the figure who stood beside the bed, watching his attempts to struggle back to life with an expression of contempt tinged with pity.

Edward placed the tea tray on the floor and marched across to the far side of the room, ripped back the curtains and threw open the window.

'It's a beautiful morning, sir,' he said, with special emphasis on the word 'sir'.

Brilliant sunshine flooded into the room. Roger threw a protective arm over his eyes.

'Meteorologically speaking perhaps,' he mumbled.

'I like it. I like it.' The voice came from beside the bed at about face level. Edward was still over by the window. Roger opened his eyes again and turned his head sideways to find himself staring straight into a camera lens.

'Oh, no,' he groaned.

'Fantastic,' said Brian. 'That's great. That's just the way everyone feels when they first wake up in the morning. It'll make a great contrast with the lively, animated church stuff.'

'A great cutting point,' agreed Keith.

'Okay,' said Brian. 'Now change that expression to a smile, as you suddenly realise where you are, and think of all the good things that you are going to enjoy later in the day.'

Roger glowered at him as the giant claw began to make new and even more effective inroads into his skull.

'Sod off,' he said quietly.

'Great,' said Brian enthusiastically, 'that's really beautiful. Okay, now for the smile.'

Roger turned over and pulled the bedclothes up over his head.

'Bloody rude, I call that,' said Keith.

'Never mind,' said Brian. 'Let's try someone else.'

Roger heard them clump across the room, then he heard Brian saying,

'They're all the same these Fleet Street types. No sense of professionalism.'

The door closed, and Roger sighed. Given half a chance, no doubt they'd have suggested filming him cleaning his teeth or cutting his toe nails.

'This table's all wet.'

'What?'

'There's water everywhere. Did you tip something over?'

Roger drew back the bedclothes and sat up.

Edward was standing by the bedside table, holding a sodden lace tablecloth distastefully by one corner as though it were a drowned rat. He looked accusingly at Roger.

'I might have done,' said Roger.

'But everything's completely soaked.' Edward's tone was marginally more aggressive than it had been the day before.

'Well, it doesn't matter, does it? It's surely not the end of the world, just because a glass of water gets knocked over by accident in the night?'

'When the thing it gets knocked over on to is an antique and the glass of water is actually a glass of whisky and the veneer is completely ruined, it may not be the end of the world, but it is certainly the end of an important piece of eighteenth-century furniture worth anything between two and five thousand pounds.'

Roger looked at him coldly.

'I'm very sorry if the table is damaged, and I'm sorry if it was worth a lot of money,' he said loudly. 'However, I am not in the habit of deliberately taking glasses of whisky and pouring them over pieces of antique furniture just for the hell of it. It was an accident, and if Sir George or Lady Fox-Bronzing wish to make an issue out of it, then that is up to them, not you. You are a valet. Perhaps not a full-time valet, but certainly not in a position to complain to guests about what they may or may not have done to the furniture. And if I hear another word on the subject, I shall certainly have something to say when I see Sir George at breakfast. That will be all.'

'Have it your own way,' said Edward, giving the table a wipe with the sodden tablecloth. He turned and walked towards the door. 'But if what I hear is true, Sir George is going to have a few things to say to you one way and another.'

'What do you mean?'

'Sir George has never been averse to the odd fun and games, but not the sort you people get up to and certainly not at the expense of his own family.'

'How dare you . . .'

'Just warning you,' said Edward.

'Get out.' Roger hauled himself further up the bed.

'I wasn't planning on staying,' said Edward backing away nervously. 'I have enough trouble with people like you in my business as it is.'

Roger dropped the two white pills into the water and watched them as they dissolved in a little head of white foam. He swizzled the opaque liquid around in the glass, threw back his head and swallowed the mixture in one gulp. He followed it up with a chaser of cold Norfolk tap water and decided he felt better already.

He peered at himself in the mirror and pulled several faces. Then he returned to the bedroom where he drank two cups of very sweet tea.

After that he sat on the bed, staring across at the open window through which the sun was now beginning to stream, along with a large number of flies and insects, and the sounds of small birds tuning up for the long, hot day ahead.

It was the sort of morning that, under normal circumstances, would have had him jumping out of bed, throwing on his clothes, bounding down to breakfast, and one way and another skipping and leaping like a young ram. But then, under normal circumstances, he would not have been caught by his host, crouching on the floor of his brother's bedroom at half-past two in the morning, watching Reg Henshawe attempting to disentangle himself from the unexpected embrace of the Anglican Church.

What Sir George thought he was doing padding round the house in dressing gown and slippers, when he should have been tucked up in bed, sleeping off the twin effects of mental strain and indigestion had yet to be explained. Last night had been more a time for brisk retreat than for detailed analysis of everyone's movement. No doubt all would shortly be revealed, as the cheeky valet had suggested, over the eggs and the kedgeree.

There was certainly nothing in his own behaviour for which he had any reason to feel guilty or ashamed, but what about poor old Reg? How was he going to look Sir George in the eye over the toast and coffee? What far-fetched tale was he even now fabricating in the silence of his lonely room? And, more importantly, to what extent had his depravity rubbed off, in Sir George's mind, on to the rest of them?

Apparently not at all, was the answer.

'Good morning, good morning,' Sir George called out cheerily, looking up from his papers as Roger came cautiously into the Breakfast Room. 'Help yourself. You know where everything is by now, I think. I can recommend the kidneys. They're simply delicious. Mrs Eames has quite surpassed herself. She's back, by the way. I went round to her cottage first thing this morning. It took quite a bit of persistence and clever boxing on my part, mind you, not to mention the promise of a rise in salary that makes a complete nonsense of the Government's pay guide lines. I told her how important it was that everybody should start this last day with a really good, nourishing breakfast, and the long and the short of it was that she put on her hat and coat, and *voilà!* The most delicious kidneys you have eaten or are ever likely to eat.'

He gestured towards the sideboard.

'Newspapers?' he went on as Roger, his plate modestly filled, took a seat across the table from his elegant, pinstriped host. He pointed to a nearby chair that was piled high with several copies of all the Sunday newspapers. 'I know just how impossible it is for you journalist people to get through a Sunday without first consulting the papers. Perhaps you even have an article in one of them today? The *Sunday People* perhaps? No, of course not. Quite the wrong market for you. The *Sunday Times* perhaps?'

'As a matter of fact I haven't . . .' Roger began.

'Good morning, good morning.'

Now it was Cyril Dick and Jeremy Powell-Brett's turn to sample some of the genial host treatment.

'I say,' said Powell-Brett jovially, stabbing at a kidney, 'whatever was all that kerfuffle I heard going on in the small hours?'

'Kerfuffle?' said Sir George. 'What kerfuffle would that be?'

'Well, I don't know. . . . First I was woken up by the peacocks making a most frightful din out on the lawn. Then I must have fallen asleep again. But then I was woken up again, only a short time later, by - well, I know this sounds ridiculous - but by what sounded like someone being attacked by a cockerel.'

Sir George put down his paper and reached for his coffee cup.

'Oh, yes, I remember now,' he said, casually. 'Something rather odd did occur at one point during the night. Nothing to worry about. One of the peacocks managed to get into the house and found its way up the stairs. Goodness knows how. Or indeed why. It's never happened before. Most peculiar.'

Roger buried his face even deeper into the *Sunday Times* Colour Magazine's survey of greenhouses.

'Aha, here he is! The man himself!'

Roger looked up, as into the room walked Reg Henshawe, dressed in a dark blue suit, white shirt and dark blue tie, his black shoes shining and his normal straggle of nondescript-coloured hair plastered down flat across his head, like an undertaker on an outing. He paused in the doorway, grinned at everyone round the table, and with a couple of cheery 'What ho's' made a hand-rubbing bee-line for the sideboard.

'You slept well, I hope?' said Sir George.

'Like a baby, my dear old fellow. Just like a ruddy baby.'

'Good, good.'

Roger goggled at both of them in turn, but in neither could he detect the slightest hint that this banal snatch of polite early-morning dialogue was anything other than what it seemed. Surely, now that the social niceties had been suitably disposed of, one or the other of them would start getting down to the real business in hand: Sir George to demanding an explanation and an apology, and Henshawe to supplying both – possibly on bended knee?

To his amazement, Reg worked his way through a glass of orange juice, a bowl of porridge, a pair of kippers, a plateful of kidneys, mushrooms and bacon, a boiled egg, two croissants, three slices of toast and several large cups of coffee, without the slightest reference to the previous night's events. Nor, for his part, did Sir George seem at all anxious to bring the subject out into the open. He talked amusingly and enthusiastically about the rights and wrongs of fox hunting, England's chances of retaining the Ashes in the forthcoming series against Australia, women's fashions, the increasing expense of maintaining a garden and the decline of the French Riviera since the last war. But at no stage did he touch on the exotic sexual habits of assistant sports editors, nor after a while did there seem the slightest likelihood that he was going to.

Indeed, his reluctance to touch upon the subject that was in the forefront of at least three out of the five minds seated around the breakfast table on that May morning became even more evident when, shortly after nine-thirty, the door opened and into the room, his purple cassock thrust forward like a well-set spinnaker, sailed the tall, portly frame of the Bishop of Kananga. He beamed round the room through round spectacles that seemed several sizes too small for his face.

'Good morning, George. Good morning, everybody,' he boomed. 'No, please don't get up. I'm sorry I'm so late, but I was inveigled into assisting with Holy Communion. Quite a good turn-out this morning, I'm glad to say. If they all come to the second house at eleven, it may be a question of standing room only. No, no. I'm only joking. Who on earth wants to sit and listen to the views of an unknown bishop who is out of place, out of date and generally out of breath?' He turned his owlish attentions to the now sadly depleted sideboard.

'Mrs Eames has done us proud again, I'm glad to see,' he said, helping himself to the last of the kidneys. 'I must say, what with one thing and another, I have quite an appetite this morning.'

'Had I had the faintest clue that it was you doing the honours at the early sitting this morning,' Reg told the bishop, 'I'd have been there in the front row along with the best of them, instead of snoozing away in bed.'

'I was rather surprised myself,' said the bishop, pouring himself some coffee. 'You certainly seem the sort of chap who likes to throw himself wholeheartedly into the hurly-burly of modern life. By the way, I never did catch your name. . .?'

'Henshawe,' said Reg, 'Reginald Henshawe. Haven't we met somewhere before?'

'I believe so,' said the Bishop.

'Thought so,' said Reg with satisfaction. 'I never forget a face.'

'Henshawe, Henshawe,' murmured the bishop, gazing, as if for inspiration, at the ceiling. 'That name sounds familiar. . . .'

'Used to be,' said Reg quietly. 'Once upon a time.'

'No relation of Henshawe, who was once Bishop of Salisbury – or was it Worcester?'

'Doesn't sound like our family,' said Reg, for whom conversations along those lines had a habit of running rather quickly out of steam.

'Ah well,' said the bishop after a hopeful pause, clearly disappointed at his assailant's failure to place himself either socially or ecclesiastically.

However, bishops are not as easily put off the scent as that. Within the next five minutes he had succeeded in harvesting more background detail about the male members of the party than Roger had done, or for that matter bothered to try and do, since three o'clock on Friday afternoon. But then of course there was one great difference between Bishop Fox-Bronzing and Roger Noakes – which was that the bishop quite clearly had not yet grasped the basic fact that these people round the breakfast table were not close personal friends of his brother.

'It's so reassuring,' the bishop told his brother, as he folded his napkin, 'to learn that the weekend country house party, as we knew it in the old days, is still so very much a part of English life. Of course, certain things have changed. The rigid social barriers of our youth have, I am glad to see, been broken down. Indeed, one might almost say they hardly seem to exist at all any more. And a very good thing too. The day when people from radically differing backgrounds cannot meet together at the weekend in pleasant surroundings to talk together and exchange views will be a black one indeed in the history of our country.'

'Hear, hear,' said Henshawe. 'In the words of that great French philosopher and expert on life, Brigitte Bardot, '*Vive la différence*'. Did I ever tell you, Sir George – now this will interest you, Bishop, seeing as how you're a travelling man yourself – I was on a yacht once with the lady in question . . .'

'Excuse me, sir.'

'Yes, Hedges, what is it?'

'There's someone asking to see you, sir.'

'Who is it?'

'Mr Hahned, sir.' The astonishment in his voice was unconcealed.

'Yes, well, could you ask him to wait in my study? I'll see him in a few minutes. A domestic matter,' he added for the bishop's benefit.

'He says it's very urgent, sir.'

Sir George frowned.

'Well, he'll just have to wait, won't he? Well, go on Hedges. What are you waiting for? Show him to my study.'

Hedges was obviously suffering from an attack of acute embarrassment.

'The thing is, sir, it isn't quite as simple as that. I'm not sure that I know quite how to explain . . .'

'Don't bother, Hedges,' a voice called out from the passage outside. 'I'll explain myself.' And through the open door, dressed in a snappy three-piece, pin-stripe suit and carrying a black brief-case, walked the public relations manager of Blue Blood Tours.

'What is the meaning of this?' said Sir George.

'The meaning of this, Sir George,' said Hahned politely, his voice as smooth and milk and honey, 'is quite simply that, as from eight o'clock this morning, I am the new Managing Director of Blue Blood Tours.'

22

For the first time that weekend, Sir George's manners were somewhat less than impeccable. Throwing his napkin on to the table, and pushing his chair back noisily, he rose to his feet, looked Hahned straight in the soft brown eyes and said:

'Will you excuse me?'

Then turning to his brother he said:

'Claud, isn't it time you were getting ready for Matins?'

The bishop stared at him.

'But I haven't finished my breakfast yet,' he protested through a mouthful of toast and kidneys.

'Never mind that now,' insisted the baronet, practically pulling the chair from beneath his brother's bottom in his anxiety to remove him from a situation which could only result in unhappiness for them both.

'George, have you taken leave of your senses? Matins is not until eleven. It is now only nine forty-five. It cannot take me an hour and a quarter to get to Toughingham Church, even if I go via Norwich.'

'The traffic can be very bad at this time of year,' Sir George pointed out. 'Besides, I've got something very important I want to talk to you about first. Family business. You know.'

'Well, if you really insist . . .'

The bishop stood up, politely asked his fellow breakfasters if they would be so good as to excuse him, then turned to Hahned and said:

'See you in church later, Mr Arnold.'

'I think not,' said Hahned quietly.

'Good, good,' said the bishop, and sailed out of the room

after his brother like a galleon in the morning wind.

Roger was as surprised at Sir George's rapid departure as at his apparent total lack of interest in this latest dramatic twist in the Blue Blood Tours story. It seemed that an Arab consortium, headed by Hahned's father, had been negotiating for weeks to buy Da Silva Kleinman, and that late on Friday afternoon, unknown to Maitland, the deal had been closed. Roger could perfectly well understand just how tiresome such news would be to a man like Sir George. On the other hand, the very fact that he would no longer be compelled to have any dealings with Maitland must surely be reason enough for rejoicing? Perhaps, though, he had reached a stage at which even the crude, blundering devil he knew seemed preferable to the smooth, polite type who, until a few hours ago, he had known only as a waiter.

He was preparing to leave the breakfast table when the door opened and Sir George reappeared. In one hand he held a type-written sheet of paper, in the other, a smouldering Corona.

'Aha,' he said. 'I'm glad I've caught you all together still.' He gave his right ear a slight tweak with his cigar hand. 'Now look here, I don't know what you think about this. I know you must all be pretty tired after yesterday. We all had rather a late night, some indeed rather later than others. But I was just wondering – I mean, if the idea doesn't appeal to you, you only have to say so – I was wondering, since we have some free time at our disposal between now and setting off for church, whether you might like to do something that is not actually on the programme but which I think you'd all find most interesting. A sort of surprise item, as it were.'

He gave a funny little gesture of embarrassment with his hands, went across to the table, tapped some ash into an ashtray, cleared his throat and looked enquiringly at them.

'Rather,' said Roger, ever anxious to please.

'Sounds intriguing,' said Powell-Brett.

'I'm all for surprise items,' said Dick.

'What exactly did you have in mind?' asked Reg Henshawe warily.

'Well,' said Sir George, 'the thing is this. As you know, there have been Fox-Bronzings living here at Hatching since the sixteenth century. This house is actually the third, and some say even the fourth, to have been built in these grounds. A couple of years ago, I was rung up by a local amateur archaeological society who said that they were doing a survey in the neighbourhood and that according to some old documents they had come across in the Norwich Museum, the first two houses had stood about a quarter of a mile away beyond what is now the kitchen garden.'

'How fascinating,' said Roger.

'But the really interesting thing they had found out was that the first house, according to Hawkesworth, boasted the greatest cellars in the whole of the east of England, and that these cellars were filled from floor to ceiling with "a mighty abundance of French wine and sherries as might befit the palace of the king himself".'

'How extraordinary,' said Roger.

'Now apparently when the first house was destroyed by fire in 1545, the owner, Sir Humphrey de Fox, ordered that the doors of the cellars be bolted and barred so that the wine at least should be saved from the holocaust. Unfortunately, very soon after that, the family suffered a further setback when Sir Humphrey quarrelled violently with the king, with the result that he, his wife, his infant son and all his servants were banished to France. He died there three years later, and within the year his wife was also dead. Over the next few years, all the original servants either died or married French girls and decided to settle there, so that by the time Sir Humphrey's son, William, was finally allowed to return to Hatching, there was no one left who knew anything of the fabled cellars. The charred ruins of the house had long since been razed to the ground, and all that remained was rubble and weeds.'

'How riveting,' said Roger.

'Anyway, the archaeological society asked if they could

come here and dig around on the old site and see if they could locate the old cellars and even perhaps a few of the old casks. Blow me down, if they didn't go and find them.'

'The cellars or the casks?' asked Reg.

'Both,' said Sir George. 'Of course, the cellars were hardly in pristine condition after more than four hundred years. One or two of the original walls were still standing, but most of them had collapsed many years ago. Unfortunately, the wine too – at least, such as had survived – had not exactly improved with age. However, traces of some of the original casks were still to be seen.'

'Fascinating,' said Roger.

'Yes. Well, anyway, they were here on and off for nearly a year, digging and scraping and so on. For all their efforts and enthusiasm, they were not able to uncover a quarter of what must have been there at one time. However, the amount they did uncover gives some indication of just how enormous the original cellars must have been.'

'And you're suggesting we might like to have a look for ourselves?' said Jeremy.

'Only if it would amuse you,' said Sir George, with a casual wave of one hand. 'Some of the ladies might like to come along too. It's all perfectly safe. We've made sure of that. We've even had a little stone entrance built for easy access.'

'I'd love to have a look,' said Roger enthusiastically. Here was an opportunity for all of them to re-establish themselves as the keen, polite, enquiring journalists Sir George had obviously believed them to be when they first arrived – before Maitland took his first blundering, insensitive, mannerless step inside the first door. 'In fact we'd all be fascinated to see it,' he added, looking round at the others. 'Wouldn't we? And I'm sure the ladies would too. Would you like me to go and tell them perhaps?'

'That would be very kind,' said Sir George. 'Perhaps if we were all to meet in the hall in, say, fifteen minutes? Would that give everyone time to do whatever it is they have to do?'

'Plenty,' said Roger at once.

'Good,' said Sir George.

'Hell,' said Jean, 'I was hoping to wash my hair.'

'All the others are coming,' said Roger as persuasively as he knew how.

'In that case, one less won't make any difference.'

'It most certainly will. We've all got to go. Don't you see? The old fellow's been so nice and understanding about last night. In fact he hasn't even mentioned it. Doesn't want to embarrass any of us, you see? And now, on top of that, he is offering us a chance not only to see something that he normally reserves for his friends and family, but also to prove to him that we're not the selfish, grabbing, free-loading yobs that he obviously believes us to be. You've got to come. Your hair will have to wait till you get home tonight. It looks fine to me as it is, anyway.'

'It's funny that he should suddenly have taken it into his head to suggest going and looking at these cellars now, isn't it? I mean, they're obviously an important feature of the place, and clearly he's very proud of them. Why were we not taken there soon after we arrived? Why now, at this late stage, as though it were an after-thought almost?'

Roger frowned at her.

'I don't understand what you mean,' he said. 'Why should it make any difference whether he asked us twelve hours ago or fifteen minutes ago? Perhaps he didn't think we'd be interested before. Perhaps he felt the programme was full enough already. Perhaps he forgot. I don't know, nor does it seem to me to matter in the slightest. The fact is, he's asked us and I think it's up to all of us, purely out of politeness if nothing else, to show a bit of interest, and think about pleasing someone else for a change instead of pleasing ourselves. After all, he need not even have mentioned the cellars' existence.'

'Precisely,' said Jean.

'Well, come on, let's get a move on then,' urged Roger.

'The only reason you're so keen to go and look,' said Jean, 'is because you are angling for another invitation up here, and you think that your chances will be drastically improved if you prove that you and Sir George have common interests.'

'What *are* you talking about?' exclaimed Roger, furious at the accuracy once again of Jean's aim.

'You know very well what I am talking about,' she told him. 'One of the pleasures and advantages of being a journalist is that it gives you the opportunity to mix with people you would never otherwise have met and to be allowed through doors that normally would be closed to you. But it is a fatal mistake to think that meeting such people and being allowed through such doors makes you in any way a better person than you really are.'

'I see,' said Roger stiffly. 'Anyway, we're all meeting in the hall in four minutes. Don't be late.'

He descended the main staircase just in time to see Brian and Keith disappearing through the front door, knees bent beneath the weight of their equipment.

'Just off then?' he asked them.

They grunted and nodded their heads.

'I thought you'd be sure to want to film the old cellars,' he said as he helped them load their car.

'Don't know anything about that,' said Brian.

'Sounds interesting,' said Keith.

'Got a sort of Roger Corman feel to it,' said Brian.

'But you don't fancy it?'

'Not up to us,' said Brian.

'Out of our hands,' said Keith.

'What with this shake-up.'

'New chap doesn't seem as keen on a film as the other one.'

'Still,' said Brian. 'We got our money.'

'That's the main thing,' said Keith.

*

As the party crossed the lawn towards the red brick wall of the kitchen garden, Cyril Dick took Roger by the arm and drew him aside.

'I suppose you don't happen to have seen Fiona Fox-Bronzing this morning?' he said in a low voice, looking about him suspiciously.

Roger scowled at him.

'What?' he said.

'Fiona,' muttered Dick, 'Fox-Bronzing. I was just wondering if you knew whether she was likely to be coming along on this thing?'

'How on earth should I know?' said Roger irritably.

'I just wondered,' said Dick.

'Why the sudden concern for Lady Fox-Bronzing?' Roger asked him. 'Barbara been giving you a hard time? I'm told she never knows quite where to draw the line.'

Dick ignored the calculated insult. His forehead wrinkled in puzzlement.

'The fact is, Noakes,' he hissed, 'the most extraordinary thing happened to me last night. I was going along the landing on my way to the toilet at about one fifteen, when suddenly Fiona Fox-Bronzing popped her head out and said that if I had nothing better to do, perhaps I wouldn't mind stepping into her room for a second. Well, naturally I didn't think anything of it. But then, no sooner had she closed the door behind me than she had started in on some long garbled story about wanting to have a baby and her husband not being able to because of a hunting accident and . . .'

Roger's heart began to pump very fast and he suddenly felt rather sick.

'I know,' he said sharply before Dick had a chance to elaborate further. 'She told me.'

'Oh, she did?' he said with obvious relief. 'Oh, that's all right then. Then you won't mind my mentioning the incident.'

209

'Not at all,' said Roger.

'Good. Well, anyway, she went on and on about how much she wanted to have this baby—'

'Hang on a bit,' said Roger. 'This bit about an accident. Are you sure she said it was a hunting accident, not something to do with the war?'

'Yes, why?'

'Oh nothing. Anyway, she went on and on about it, you said . . .'

'Yes, well,' said Dick. 'As I say, she kept going on and on about this baby, and then she . . . well . . . she came out with it.'

'Came out with what?'

'Well, that she wanted me to . . . you know . . .'

If Spotty Dick had at that moment taken a length of lead piping from his inside pocket and casually bent it over Roger's head, he could not at that moment have been more surprised or suffered more pain. He stopped dead in his tracks, turned towards Dick and said to him in measured tones of disbelief:

'She said she wanted you to *what?*'

Dick grinned at him foolishly.

'What do you think?' he said with a giggle.

Had Roger's limbs not suddenly become paralysed, he would have punched Dick very hard on the nose.

'You refused, of course?' he said at last.

'Good heavens no,' said Dick cheerfully. 'Why on earth should I refuse? Opportunities like that don't occur twice.'

And so the party continued on its merry way, through the kitchen garden, past the neat rows of potatoes and peas and beans, past the shallots and beetroots and spring onions, past the tiny marrows basking in the warm sunshine in their cold frames and the tomatoes, like giant drops of blood inside the greenhouse, until at last they came to the far wall where pear trees stood with their arms pinned back against the bricks like prisoners in front of a firing squad, and figs ripened coyly beneath their green leaves.

A green wooden door led out of the garden, and then they were in a long cool walk of cypresses. Jackie and Jeremy were holding hands loosely and giggling happily over some childish joke. Audrey Veal would have been holding hands with Sir George, given half a chance, but she was content enough just to talk to him, and chide him facetiously about the quantities of food he had given them that weekend, and complain coyly that she was fat enough already as it was. He looked down at her dumpy frame and gave a little cough. 'I like you very well as you are, Mrs Veal,' he said, and she gave a squeak of girlish joy.

Further away, Reg Henshawe was telling Jean that, as far as he knew, Mrs Venables had returned to London unexpectedly, which was probably just as well. Only one person seemed out of place in this otherwise pleasant English scene, and that was the new Managing Director of Blue Blood Tours. In his sombre suit, with his brief-case swinging loosely at his side, his dark features set in an expression of earnest solemnity, he looked like an under-taker at a wedding. The church bells started to ring out across the fields.

At the end of the walk, they turned right into a little square, also of cypresses. Set into one side, down half a dozen stone steps, was what at first sight appeared to be a superior air-raid shelter, enclosed in a long, low, brick-covered mound behind a stout wooden door.

Sir George stepped quickly forward and descended the steps. He took a large key from his jacket pocket, turned it a couple of times in the lock, and pushed against the door. It swung back heavily. Sir George reached inside to turn on the light, revealing a dozen more stone steps and beyond, a brick-lined room about sixty feet long and twenty feet wide. The original sixteenth-century barrel-vaulted ceiling illuminated by several hidden spotlights that had been carefully positioned at intervals the whole length of the room, had been superbly restored. So, too, had the brickwork of the walls, which on either side were divided into a series of recesses in which had once rested countless casks of claret and sherry. High on one wall was a small window, heavily barred.

Standing in the centre of the cellar and running practically the whole length of it was a rough table, or more precisely, a number of tables, placed end to end, and piled high with what looked like old newspapers.

'Hallo,' said Reg. 'Somebody down here likes us.'

A few people laughed, but without much conviction. There was something contrived, almost theatrical, about the way the newspapers had been placed there. It was as though they had been put there specially for the occasion. Roger was not the only one who was beginning to feel uneasy.

But any anxiety any of them might have been feeling, any feelings of apprehension, were quickly evaporated in the humour and warmth of Sir George's voice as he recounted, mainly for the benefit of the ladies who had missed it earlier, the story of the cellars and how they came to be rediscovered.

Really, thought Roger, he had had the great good fortune to meet a lot of amusing, charming, well-known, civilized men during the five years or so he had been in journalism – writers, producers, actors, business men, lawyers and academics – but never had he met a man more after his own heart and one that he would like to know better than Sir George Fox-Bronzing.

'That then, in a nutshell, is the story of the Hatching Park cellars. Now then, I daresay some of you are wondering why I decided to bring you here this morning. After all, this is something you don't come across every day of the week. Why then did I not show it to you yesterday? Why leave it until the eleventh hour, so to speak? Well, I'll tell you.'

Sir George took his lighter from his pocket and, taking great care not to singe the end of his nose, lit the dead stub of his cigar.

'As I explained in my welcoming speech on Friday night, it was with the very greatest reluctance that I ever agreed to enter upon this money-making venture. I am not, as you will probably have gathered by now, familiar with the world of commerce, nor that of newspapers, and when Mr Casablanca suggested the idea of inviting a small group of journalists down to sample one of these weekends I immediately expressed the strongest possible doubts. Here at Hatching we have never before become involved in publicity stunts of any sort, and the idea that my home should be publicised and my private life written about in the press for anyone to pore over was quite abhorrent to me.'

'Hear, hear,' mumbled Audrey Veal.

'However,' Sir George continued, 'this man Casablanca was far more understanding than I had hitherto believed him to be. He told me that both he and his associates had had a great deal of experience in these matters, and that I could rest assured that the journalists whom he was planning to invite for this weekend would be both sympathetic and familiar with the kind of life which we lead up here, and which we hoped would commend itself to our guests when they came. A list of names was forwarded for my approval. I must confess that there was not one that I either recognised or had heard of. However, once again, Mr Casablanca insisted that every one of them was of the very highest quality and integrity; that they were, as he put it, "My kind of people," and that the weekend would prove to be an enjoyable, entertaining and profitable experience for all of us.'

'He had better taste than I thought, that Casablancas,' said Reg and earned himself a big laugh.

Sir George smiled and drew carefully on his cigar.

'The evening you all arrived, I began to wonder whether I had not been right all along. However, I decided to give you the benefit of the doubt, particularly in the light of your long and tiring journey. And besides, I really thought that one or two of you seemed to be fundamentally decent types.'

213

'Yes,' said Reg expansively, 'well, we're not really too bad a bunch, taken all in all. We've got our failings, but then who hasn't?'

'However,' Sir George continued, 'the following day, my worst fears soon began to be realised.' He looked round at them with a pleasant smile. 'Not only was it perfectly clear to me, even before the arrival of Mr Maitland, that, despite the efforts of some of you to persuade me otherwise, you neither understood nor cared two hoots about Hatching. Not only was it quite obvious that not one of you, with the possible exception of Miss Hollingsworth – and how she came to be mixed up in this sorry little set-up, I cannot imagine – not one of you had the slightest idea of how to behave in civilized company. Not only did you consider it highly amusing to consume my best wine as though it were so much tap water, to misbehave in front of my friends, to abuse my brother, to make suggestions of an improper nature to members of my staff and even to attempt to dishonour my wife—?'

'I think I can explain,' Dick interrupted hastily. The others stared at him, their faces a mixture of fear, horror and loathing, as though implying that he alone was the cause of all their shortcomings.

'You?' said Sir George. 'Why should you be in any position to explain? What has it to do with you? Mr Noakes is the one to whom we should be turning for explanations.'

The company transferred their hostility at once from Dick to Roger who, as if to confirm his guilt, flushed furiously.

'But I never—' he began.

'Silence,' snapped Sir George.

'But it was nothing to do with me,' gabbled Roger, appealing to the others as much as to Sir George. 'It was her idea, not mine. I mean, I'm just not like that.' He gestured in despair towards his stony-faced colleagues. 'Ask them, they'll tell you.' Sir George looked at him coldly.

'Look, the thing is,' Roger said, pursuing a let's-bereasonable-after-all-we-are-both-men-of-the-world tack, 'we were in this punt, and Fiona, your wife, said . . .'

The words dried in his throat. However great the need to clear his own name, however unreasonable the old man's behaviour, he knew he could not go on. Fortunately, Sir George did not press him further. Instead he said quietly:

'My wife is given to saying a lot of things she does not mean. She is very young and often rather fanciful. I daresay it has something to do with her drama school training.'

Roger stared at him. He wanted to say something, anything that would help to restore his reputation and dissociate him from the others. But as far as Sir George was concerned, the episode was closed, for he gave Roger a dismissive nod and addressed his next remarks to the party in general.

'As I was saying, not only was I compelled to suffer these insults and indignities, but to cap it all, not one of you is a top-notch journalist of the sort that I had been led to expect. Apart from anything else, I cannot recall seeing one of you with a notebook and pencil in his hand.'

'Well, I must say, I think that's going a bit far,' said Powell-Brett, flexing his jaws purposefully. 'I mean, dammit, we're all in our own way pretty highly thought of in and around Fleet Street. Jean Hollingsworth, for example, is the Women's Editor of one of the most important national newspapers in the country, Reg Henshawe was once . . .'

'I have already said that I think Miss Hollingsworth made a grave error in judgement by associating herself with the rest of you. Mr Henshawe may once have been the Editor of *The Times* for all I know or care, but he quite clearly is not anything like that now. Mrs Veal, as far as one can make out, writes about food and wine for some pretentious little publication or other, though I should have thought that what she actually knows about either food or wine could be written down on the back of a very small envelope. It's no good you giving me those reproachful looks, my dear. You are utterly bogus and well you know it.'

Audrey, to everyone's amazement, now burst into floods of tears that poured down her chubby features, coursing their way through her many folds and creases, taking with them heavy deposits of mascara and make-up.

'And to think,' she sobbed, her waterlogged features screwed up with hatred and fury, 'that I took you for a gentleman.'

'I would never have believed,' said Sir George calmly, 'that a journalist of your age and experience could have been so easily taken in by appearances.'

'I hate you,' she screamed.

'I sometimes do not care very much for myself either,' he said.

'As for the rest of you: Mr Dick, Dickensian by name, but not alas by nature, is employed as nothing more than a junior reporter by a local newspaper in Norwich. Miss Black, Mr Noakes and Mr Powell-Brett are not, as far as I can make out, employed by any newspaper at all, but earn their livings by getting themselves free invitations here, there and everywhere, and afterwards selling such information as they have been able to garner to anyone who is prepared to pay for it.'

'I call that going a bit far,' said Powell-Brett angrily. 'You make us sound like mercenaries or something.'

'That's precisely how I think of you,' retorted Sir George.

'I mean to say, I do happen to be a regular contributor to *Home and Beauty*. I'd hardly call that second league stuff, would you?'

'Yes,' said Sir George. He went on: 'Miss Ericson, like Miss Hollingsworth, has been unwise enough to allow herself to be caught up in this sorry little venture. She is not so much out of her depth as six feet under water. Well, that's just too bad. Maybe next time she'll know better. As for you, Mr Hahned, I know very little about you, except that you would have been wiser to have stuck to serving at table, a job to which you are almost certainly a great deal better suited than trying to run a travel business.'

Hahned looked impassively at Sir George through eyes which had turned from deep liquid pools into holes of dried-up mud. He opened his mouth to say something, thought better of the idea and closed it again. It was not turning out to be the most perfect start to his first day in a new job.

Sir George drew on the last remains of his cigar, found it had gone out again and dropped it into an ashtray on the table. He looked round at his house guests, who were by now wearing a variety of expressions that ranged from real shame and humility to undisguised fury. He took a deep breath and sighed.

'Who you all are, and what you all do, and how you choose to style yourselves, I do not know, nor do I very much care. As I understand it, you have all come here posing as travel writers. Well, I'm sorry to have to tell you that I hate travel writers and travel writing of the sort that is practised by people like you. I hate your smug little thousand-word pieces and your facile language. I hate your neat descriptions and your clever jokes. I hate your knowing little references to obscure restaurants that you have discovered and colourful local characters whom you have met. Above all I hate the fact that after spending only a few days in a place, you try to give the impression you have been going there for years. I have no doubt that after only forty-eight hours in this house, you were all planning to write about it as though you have known it for a lifetime.'

'Now look here . . .' Powell-Brett began feebly, but he was no match for Sir George Fox-Bronzing in full flow.

'I cannot imagine who reads what you write, or cares. As far as I can make out, travel writers write only to impress other travel writers. Well, now is your chance to impress each other to your hearts' content. On the table before you you will find all the quality Sundays and most of the dailies from the last five years. My butler has always been a great one for hoarding, and for once his squirrel-like passion has paid off. Somewhere amongst that useless load of old ink and paper you may, if you are what you say you are, find many examples of your own and your colleagues' brilliance, which should afford all of you hours of undiluted pleasure as you read them out to each other, congratulating and being congratulated on your wit and your perception, your clever turns of phrase and the humour of your anecdotes.'

Roger stared at Sir George. Had he gone mad? He certainly didn't look mad. Perhaps it was some elaborate joke. But to what purpose? Not to make them laugh, clearly. To frighten them perhaps. If so, he was certainly succeeding as far as Roger was concerned.

Sir George began to move slowly backwards in the direction of the open door.

'I wish you well on your second-hand travels,' he said, with a polite little gesture of the head. 'My brother will be sorry you missed his sermon. He is leaving immediately after lunch for Harrogate. At the same time my wife and I are also about to embark on a real journey. To Provence, a part of France of which we are both particularly fond. But no doubt you have all been there several times yourselves, so I won't bore you with my impressions. As for the rest of the company, my sister, Mrs Venables, is at this moment being driven back to the comparative safety of her flat in Hans Crescent by the redoubtable Mr Legge, with Mr Fowler in close attendance. As far as they are concerned, there has been a sudden, last-minute change of plan, and their services will not be required until further notice. As for the staff, they have all been sent away on a well-deserved holiday, but not before first making sure that you are well provided with food and drink, which you will find in one of the recesses at the far end of the cellar. I fear the food may not be quite up to the standard you have come to expect over the last couple of days and the wine, though perfectly drinkable, is not quite like yesterday's tap water.

On the other hand, it is all free, and that's what really counts, isn't it?

'Those of you who are wondering about the future of Blue Blood Tours in relation to Hatching Park will be interested to learn that I shall not be going ahead with the proposed programme after all. Instead I have decided to sell *The Head of a Young Girl* by Goya. It was scarcely damaged at all by the firework last night, and I've never much cared for it.

'One of these days your newspapers may begin to wonder what has happened to you. Some may remember where it was you said you were going. One or two may go so far as to send someone up here to look for you, and who knows, they may even find you. In the meantime, *bon voyage* and pip pip.'

To a horrified outburst of disbelief, anger, tears and supplication, Sir George turned and walked quickly to the open door. When he got there, he paused. Everyone fell silent, hoping perhaps for a last-minute reprieve. But all he said was:

'Funny about that American journalist never turning up, wasn't it?'

Then he closed the door gently, turned the key twice in the lock, and walked silently away across the grass.

For several seconds there was absolute silence, and then, far, far away, almost as though it were in another world, a peacock began to cry.

23

The sun was making its final curtain call behind the willows on the far side of the river when the hired Mercedes crunched to a halt on the gravel. The shadows were long on the lawns. The old house glowed like someone who has rather overdone the sunbathing. Small clouds of gnats hovered aimlessly. A handful of bees worked overtime on the herbaceous border. The peacocks stood, limp and undecorative, beneath the big copper beech, too tired to raise a screech between them. It had been an unusually hot day for mid-May.

The man in the bright blue pullover, open-necked white shirt and white slip-on shoes who stepped from the front seat of the car congratulated himself on having insisted on the convertible model. It had been quite a bit more expensive than the others, but who in the accounts office in New York was going to worry about a tiny detail like that? The bill from the Centurion Hotel was a different matter. . . .

He ran his fingers through his crinkly grey hair and scratched the top of his crown as he looked up at the front of the house. He was surprised to find all the shutters drawn, but supposed that was how they did things in English country houses in the summer. He started to unload his luggage. The tag on his fold-over suitcase revealed that he had recently travelled on Concorde. Also that he was E. G. Branigan of *World* magazine.

Branigan stared up at the house again, uncertain of his next move. He had imagined that by now his arrival would have been noted and some sort of greeting party dispatched in his direction. But the place was showing little sign of life.

He marched up the front steps and attacked the bell several times and at increasing length, but to no visible effect.

He made his way round the side of the house to the terrace and thence to the tradesmen's entrance. He banged, he called, he peered through every conceivable crack, but no-one came.

He began to wonder if the office might have made an error over the dates, and he was halfway to the car with a view to finding a telephone when he remembered it was Sunday. Instead, he set off on a tour of the gardens – though precisely to what purpose he could not say.

First he walked down to the river and then he walked back again. He visited the rose garden. He cupped his hands round the sides of his face and peered through the glass of the summerhouse door.

He strolled through the kitchen garden and thought how much the pear trees resembled prisoners before a firing squad, with their arms pinned back against the warm bricks on the far wall.

He went through the green wooden door and along the cypress walk. The office must have made a mistake he told himself. There was a slight chill now in the air between the dark green trees and he shivered. He would have turned back had he not suddenly heard, coming from somewhere ahead and slightly to the right, the sound of voices.

They sounded at first like those of people enjoying themselves – playing croquet perhaps, or 'He'. But then, as he quickened his pace, he realised that they were raised not in pleasure but in desperation.

Branigan broke into a run.

It took him a moment or two to find the little window, set as it was a little above ankle level in the brickwork that protruded above the long grass.

'Oh, thank God,' sobbed a woman's voice. 'Thank God.'

Branigan knelt down and squinted through the bars and the broken window-pane. For a moment or two it was difficult to make out anything at all in the dim light of the single candle, but then gradually the scene came into focus – the long table, the open tins of food, the piles of newspapers, the semi-circle of pale, frightened faces.

'Tell me, my dear old fellow,' one of them asked, almost in a whisper, 'are you one of them or one of us?'

'I don't know what you mean,' said Branigan. 'I was led to understand there was some kind of a junket going on around here. You wouldn't know anything about that, would you?'

DIARY OF A SOMEBODY
Christopher Matthew

'Quite definitely the funniest book I've had the pleasure of reading.' *Tribune*

At weekend houseparties and the elegant gatherings of the London season, at trendy Workers' Workshops and in the expectant crowds at the new National, Simon Crisp is always noticed. He's the one with the coffee stains on his trousers, the air of punctured dignity and educated worry. Humiliated by hurled apple cores and exploding plastic pants, by practical jokes in the office and in his West London flat, he's a fall-guy for our times.

This is his diary. It curiously resembles that classic of ninety years ago, *The Diary of a Nobody*. Especially in one respect: Simon never sees the joke.

But we do. And deliciously so.

'A genuinely funny book.' *Benny Green, Spectator*

'Spellbinding. I read the diary in one sitting.' *The Times*

LOOSELY ENGAGED

Christopher Matthew

'The hilarious follow-up to *Diary of a Somebody*' *Punch*

Newly promoted and loosely engaged to the boss's daughter, Simon Crisp finally seems all set for success. But whether he is dancing pink-haired in New York's Studio 54 with a model called (he is sure) Ernest Hemingway, or wrecking the central heating system in a Moscow hotel, or attempting to join the Freemasons and winding up with a lifetime membership of the National Trust, Simon is never quite the man he would like to believe he is. Surely even Simon should know by now that nothing succeeds like failure – and that, though he never knows at whose expense it is, there is always a joke going on.

'Addictive' *Evening News*